# TRIPPING
## From Cleveland
## to Paris & Beyond

A novel by

# HERMINE FUERST

# CHAPTERS

# I

# GOODBYE
# CLEVELAND

By the time the Cleveland Riots occurred, the Wade Park Manor had become completely seedy, having given way to the slum that encroached on the whole University area. But at the time I'm talking about, in 1956 when I left home, it still retained some of the stately elegance I had associated with it as a child.

Strange that my life in Cleveland should have begun and ended there. My very first memory was of the apartment we lived in on 107th Street, just a few blocks from the Wade Park Manor. I must have been two or three, and in the bathroom my parents were having a fight. I remember sitting on the bed, hanging onto the bedstead, and listening to the combined sounds of running bathwater and their shouts. Some eighteen years later, my life in Cleveland ended amid shouts (but no bathwater) at the Wade Park Manor itself.

I liked that apartment on 107th Street. In front of the building were two brick pedestals on which stood two iron street lamps. The base of each lamp consisted of four iron feet a few inches high, leaving an open space between lamp and pedestal which I used as an imaginary oven to bake mud pies. It would have been even more fun if I'd had some matches to really bake the mud pies. But I was a good child, an only child, and never disobeyed my mother.

Opposite the apartment was a Catholic high school where, at night, Daddy took Italian lessons. The teacher was a real Italian lady. She gave Daddy special care and said he was her "besta pupe". Before mother had put an end to the lessons for reasons I could not understand, Daddy had had time to teach me how to count to ten in Italian and I also learned the first sentence of his book, "Roberto e Paolo sono due ragazzi."

When I had been good, which was most of the time, mother would reward me with a walk through Wade Park to the Art Museum, Cleveland's rectangle of culture. Downtown, a round place called the Stadium contained our winning teams, the Indians and the Browns. Between them, those two geometric shapes held the best of Cleveland. Of the huge amounts of money earned by the sweating, smoky steel mills and oil refineries, a tithe has always been contributed to Cultural Institutions. Most of these are huddled together around Wade Park, as if to draw reassurance from the reflecting pool of the mall that leads to the neo-Grecian Art Museum. Everything is in white marble – the balustrades, the long flight of steps on which stands Rodin's "The Thinker", and the Museum itself, home of one of the richest and best art collections in the United States.

Almost every day, mother would walk me through Wade Park, where I would hug and kiss the statue of a nymph who sits next to the pool. I would trundle up the marble steps and raise my head respectfully to the impressive bronze Thinker. I knew all the guards of the Museum, and they were always happy to see me. "Here's Miss Barbara Glass," they would announce as if I was someone special. They would let me play in the cloakroom, on their side of the counter, and I would pretend I was going to jump on the lever that set off an alarm that would rally the entire police force, and the guards pretended to be afraid I would. I had no playmates my age (mother was afraid I'd catch germs from other children) and Degas, Rodin, Picasso, Toulouse-Lautrec, Renoir became my daily companions.

When the explosion occurred, during the riots that tore through the area, mother didn't dare write me about it. But the next time I was in Cleveland, she knew I would go to Wade Park so she told me. One night, someone deposited a plastic bomb at the base of "The Thinker". The pedestal was blown to bits and the statue lost its legs up to the knee (yes, it is one of the original five

4

molded by Rodin). I wondered how much anger, frustration and despair had caused that bombing, and why the Museum people had seen fit to display the remains of "The Thinker" in such a way as to create more anger, frustration and despair. Because they didn't restore the statue, or simply remove it. They built a metal armature and hung him over it by the arms, so he tilts at a funny angle and looks for all the world like the truncated Statue of Liberty in "PLANET OF THE APES" that announces the end of our civilization.

Just about the time World War II broke out, we moved away from 107th Street. Even then mother was complaining that the neighborhood was going to the dogs. Imagine how justified she felt a few years later when the bus tragedy occurred right under the windows of our former apartment. For weeks at dinner we spoke of nothing else, which was a pleasant change from mother's unending descriptions of her latest real estate dealings. What happened was that a man was annoying a woman on a bus – not just talking to her but sitting behind her and lighting a cigarette lighter and pretending to burn her hair. Everyone could see what he was doing but no one moved or did anything. The man was a Negro so naturally they were all afraid of him. Finally, at the corner of 107th and Euclid, the driver called in a policeman who walked the length of the bus to where the Negro was bothering the lady. After talking to him a few minutes, the policeman told him he was under arrest, and started to take him by the arm. Now the thing is, it was a mounted policeman, meaning he was supposed to be sitting on a horse, not standing in a bus, and the holsters of his guns were low-slung for easy reach from a seated position, as the Negro was quick to see.

In the ensuing bloodbath, twelve innocent passengers were killed as well as the policeman and the Negro. When it was finally established that the Cleveland Transit System could in no way be held liable for the murders, Daddy was pretty relieved. He worked in the Claims Department of the C.T.S. and as mother said, you'd think the company belonged to him the way he took it to heart. So you can imagine how often the bus tragedy was mentioned in our house. The Negro, incidentally, turned out to have been a veteran who'd been on drugs ever since he was wounded in the war. Drugs! I didn't know exactly what they were, but I knew they made people do crazy things. I also knew that nice people didn't take them.

"It's terrible," said mother, "the way so many Negroes are drug addicts. When I think, if we were still living on 107th Street, one of us might have been on that bus."

"Damned schwartzers," said Daddy.

Daddy's prejudices were monumental to the point of seeming unreal. His most frequent target was the schwartzers, whose main activity it seemed was making life difficult for him at the C.T.S. He told me stories of men pulling out switchblades and cutting off other men's fingers, right there in the streetcar, just because they'd had an argument. Of women who lied and tried to cheat the C.T.S. out of money on phony claims. Our fat, affectionate maid Freddy – short for Frederika – certainly didn't seem like that, but Daddy said they were all alike. He also disdained Polacks, and had been taught that Russians were lower than dogs. As a child, his gang of Hungarian kids had fought the Irish kids. He mistrusted the Germans, and said the only good thing about the French was their music. But Daddy's most deep-seated and most amazing prejudice was his anti-Semitism. At least to me it seemed amazing that a Jew should be anti-Semitic.

Mother explained to me about Daddy's prejudices. Europe, and especially Central Europe, was divided into a myriad of little countries which were fraught with hate for one another, and therefore the people who came from such countries, like my father's Hungarian parents, were automatically prejudiced. As a second generation American, mother laughed at Daddy's dislike of Polacks and Russians, and her racial bias was tempered with chauvinism.

"It's all a question of education," she would say. "With our wonderful American system of free enterprise, anyone who wants to improve himself can do so. It's no different for the Negroes than it was for the Jews. Just a question of wanting to."

Mother also had an explanation for Daddy's anti-Semitism. She gave two reasons, both of which I accepted. The first was that Daddy's father died when he was three. Apparently he was a very religious little boy for whom bearded, venerable Rabbi Goldman became a father figure. Eventually the good rabbi died and was replaced by Rabbi Silber. By the time I was old enough to know what a rabbi was, Rabbi Silber had in turn become bearded and venerable. But when he took over from his predecessor he was a young whippersnapper, unsuitable as a father figure. So there went Daddy's faith in religion.

The other reason was Grace Ellen. She was a fire-and-brimstone Baptist, and Daddy fell madly in love with her when he was eighteen. She loved him too, but said she couldn't marry him unless he converted and was baptized. He couldn't make her understand how much trouble he'd be in if his mother even found out he was dating a shicksa. Eventually Grandma did find out, and she cried, and Grace Ellen cried because Daddy would go to hell and she couldn't save his soul. It became too much for Daddy, who decided religion was to blame for the whole mess.

After quite some time, during which he wrote melancholy poetry, Daddy brought mother home for Grandma's approval. She approved, of course, because mother was a nice Jewish girl despite the fact that she'd been raised in a convent. (If you must know, mother was raised in a convent because her widowed mother had to work and was too poor to send her to private school.) So they got married, and when I came on the scene Daddy refused to let me have a religious education.

"Why teach a small child that we're right and everyone else is wrong?" he would argue. "She'll only have a hard time learning differently when she's older – or worse yet, she won't learn differently."

How he managed to reconcile his commendable religious broadmindedness with his ethnic hatreds I'll never know. I suspect that the incongruity didn't occur to him.

Mother was horrified at the thought of her only daughter growing up with no religion whatsoever. Whenever she made an issue of it, Daddy would stop the argument by promising to read me the Bible. He never did, though. Mother, with her upbringing, had gotten Judaism and Catholicism all mixed up. She loved the sound of Hebrew, but the only prayers she knew were the ones the nuns had taught her. As a compromise solution, she had me say The Lord's Prayer every night. I thought it was a Jewish prayer.

It didn't pay to be unclear about religion where I lived. The Christians and Jews in Cleveland Heights never spoke to each other if they could help it. Each group had its own social life, carefully constructed on a separate-but-almost-equal basis. The Christians, knowing I was Jewish, wouldn't let me anywhere near them. The Jews, appalled that I didn't go to schul, made it clear they wanted no part of me. My father's principles had put me in a no-man's-land.

Finally, when I was about fifteen and Daddy was getting tired, mother managed to get us into a very reformed temple in time for me to be confirmed. My teacher, an enlightened man named Mr. Schwartz, explained to me something that had always puzzled me – why Jews should want to build their own ghetto. Mr. Schwartz said that during the war, the fact that Jews were forced to wear a yellow star was an infamy, dramatically pointed up by the King of Denmark who pinned one on himself. But after the war, what happened? The Jews continued to wear stars – not yellow but blue and white, not pinned to lapels but on armbands or yarmulkas. Basically it was the same thing, and they chose to have it that way. So with the ghetto. After being forced to live in one for centuries, that was the form of life they chose of their own free will – the gilded ghetto, as Mr. Schwartz put it. But it meant a grim life for someone like me.

I realize now that as a child I was subjected to two distinct forms of prejudice. One, the Jews' intolerance of a non-conforming Jew, made me as bitterly anti-Semitic as my father. The other, the great American intolerance of anyone who is "different", was subtle enough to convince me I was the one who was wrong. But what could I do? Was it my fault my mother worked and instead of my being alone after school God forbid, she had me taking piano and violin lessons, going to art school and dramatics classes? Was it my fault I loved it? The sight of my violin as I schlepped it around drew taunts, and every right answer I gave in class made them hate me more.

I answered meanness with sarcasm, spite with indifference. I was alone. I was to remain alone until years later, when Mary Jean Perkins changed my life by standing up and speaking out in Quad Hall.

By the time I was completely alienated from my classmates I had also managed to become alienated from my parents. The main reason was Joanie, a girl in my high school theatrical group. She was Jewish, and her parents were religious, but she spoke to me because I wrote poetry and she wanted to become an actress. Joanie tried to make me accepted, or at least acceptable, but it wasn't easy. All the girls at Heights High wore bobby sox and loafers, collected cashmere sweaters, and spent all their free time at the corner drugstore sipping lime cokes, gossiping and exchanging film magazines. Mother wouldn't let me wear loafers because she said they were bad for a growing girl's feet – she made me wear those awful Girl Scout type shoes that lace up. I was too fat to look good in a cashmere sweater, even if my parents could have been persuaded it wasn't a ridiculous expense. And suppose, by some miracle, after orchestra rehearsal and my violin lesson and art school and dramatics class, I'd found the free time to go to the corner drugstore to gossip with the rest of the girls (about whom? What? I didn't know anybody). I didn't have a single film magazine to exchange. Are you kidding? My mother wouldn't let me read comic books when I was a kid. Said they were an insult to the intelligence.

The worst part was that I didn't even have the price of a lime coke on me. My parents didn't believe in pocket money or allowances. Naturally I wanted to earn money on my own by babysitting like the other girls did, but mother wouldn't hear of it.

"You, babysitting? Don't be ridiculous. What would you do if the baby got sick or the house was on fire? You can't even take your nose out of a book long enough to turn on the heat in winter, or open a window in summer, if Daddy or I aren't there to tell you to do it. And you want to babysit?"

"But Mom, I want to have some pocket money."

"So you can spend it on ice cream and candy that'll ruin your teeth as well as your figure?"

She was right, too, because by that time I was a compulsive eater. Not being able to buy anything, I had to rely on what I could find at home. I sneaked ice cream out of the unopened end of the container if there was any in the freezer. I could eat a quart of ice cream at one sitting. My other passion was chocolate, in which I took after my mother. Daddy used to say she and I should belong to Chocolates Anonymous. Any candy in the house would disappear in no time – mother would eat a bite out of each candy to see what the filling was, and I'd clean up after. Failing that, anything else containing chocolate would do. Chocolate chip cookies, or chocolate chips without cookies, or chocolate syrup from the bottle. If there was no milk to make hot chocolate, I'd eat the cocoa powder mixed with sugar and water.

I knew a girl like me who used to eat flour. Raw flour. I thought both of us were crazy. The stuff everyone knows today about sugar addictions and candida albicans infections hadn't been heard of then by anyone, including my doctor.

But to get back to Joanie, she was really the one who alienated me from my parents, because she got me to say "no". Any time she wanted to go somewhere, to a movie or a pajama party or a hayride and her mother didn't want her to, Joanie would have a fit and end up getting her own way. So before long, when my mother would tell me to do this or that, I began saying I wouldn't. Mother didn't like that, naturally, but Daddy didn't either because it upset his fragile status quo between mother and what mother called Shangri La.

I must have been about seven when mother first told me, with great bitterness, that Daddy wouldn't be home for dinner because he was with Shangri La. Her real name – improbable for a Viennese which mother claimed she was – was Gladys, and she was the nurse of our family dentist, a job Daddy had apparently gotten for her. Poor Gladys was very stupid, said mother, and

Daddy had no intellectual rapport with her, but because she was European she was a slave at Daddy's feet and men love that kind of treatment. Mother called her Shangri La because she said she was Daddy's impossible dream.

I would have been interested to know if Gladys was really Viennese or not, but although over the years mother spoke to me unceasingly of her, the subject was never broached with Daddy. Dinnertime conversation was limited to descriptions of the day's business between my parents, and puns and word play between Daddy and me. Dorothy Parker's wonderful "You can lead a horticulture but you can't make her think" was the kind of thing he'd regale us with. But when, during my last year of high school, I started saying no to my mother, she started taking it out on Daddy and saying it was his fault because he didn't bring me up properly. And that led to fights and shouts and things that would have been better left unsaid. So Daddy got mad at me too for saying no to my mother.

After attending kindergarten, elementary school, junior high school and high school in Cleveland, I expressed an understandable desire to go to college out of town. Mother took this as a personal insult.

"What? After everything we've done for you? I've never asked you to do anything and now the one thing I do ask you to do, a simple thing like going to Western Reserve which is a perfectly fine university, you say you don't want to. Of all the selfish, self-centered, ungrateful people."

We were sitting at the dinner table, and while it was unusual for the conversation to revolve about me, whenever it did it meant I was in trouble. Generally, during mother's tirades, I imagined I was enclosed in a glass cage and couldn't hear a thing. It amused me that she acted as if I could hear her, and I thought how surprised she'd be if she found out the glass cage was entirely sound-proof. Daddy intervened.

"Your mother's right. She did everything for you. Not me, but your mother. She really looked after your education up to now – and pretty well, I'd say. So you'd better listen to her when she tells you about college."

There was cake for dessert, chocolate cake covered with coconut. Three slices of it were set out on a plate.

ME
"But Daddy, can't you understand I want to live away from home for a while?"

MOTHER
"If you don't go to Western Reserve you won't go to college at all."

I reached for a piece of cake.

DADDY
"If you lived away from home you'd be eating all three pieces of that cake."

I got a firm hold on the cake, squared away and heaved it at my father. It splattered over him, and the drapes, and the wall and the painting of cockatoos that Uncle Isaac had brought back from South America. My God, what had I done? Horrified, I ran to my bedroom and locked the door. Never in my life had I done anything like that before, and to my father of all people. I held my breath, listening for sounds of anger. When my father got really angry he banged on things. I waited for him to come and pound on the door of my bedroom and maybe break it down. But nothing happened and there was silence. Then I heard the sound of the vacuum cleaner. Mother came to the door and asked me if I wanted to come out. So it was Daddy who was running the vacuum cleaner.

Nothing more was said about the incident, but we made a deal. I agreed to go to college in Cleveland, and they bought me a pair of loafers and a Navy pea jacket.

Was it my new accoutrement that worked the miracle? Why else should the same people who hated me in high school suddenly adore me in college? I was still as fat and sarcastic, but instead of being ostracized, I was sought out as being witty and amusing. In the ivory tower of college, the students were no longer afraid of people who were different. Even a few black students found a temporary haven of friendship.

Thus it was that, for the first time in my life, I became part of a group. Our group was made up of the six class leaders, and we had given each other animal nicknames. Owl was the intellectual, the one who made Phi Beta Kappa. Beaver was the all-round organizer, Bambi was the most popular girl and Colt was the class president. Then there were Sparrow and Bear – that is, Mary Jane Perkins and myself.

Sparrow was my best friend, and two more unlike people you will never see. I was big and tall and dark and Jewish, and Sparrow was tiny and blonde and Episcopalian. But we had immediately recognized each other as sisters – today people would say soul sisters. Her voice was soprano and mine alto, she drew beautifully and wrote a little, I wrote a lot and drew a little, we acted as catalysts on each other. Whatever one would start the other would finish. People couldn't tell our handwriting apart. Once, when we were walking down the street and not saying anything, we both started singing the same song on the same note in the same key – in the middle of the song.

What I particularly loved about her was her fingers – or rather, what came out of them. Whenever she put a pen or pencil to paper, lush vegetation seemed to flow from her hand onto the page. Fanciful flowers and leaves, succulent buds and squiggly vines filled every blank space with burgeoning life. I was astounded by her creativity – no two flowers or leaves were the same – but she dismissed it as mere doodling. Later, in her junior and senior years, her academic training allowed her to harness that "doodling" and incorporate it into whatever she was drawing, thus creating a style of illustration that was uniquely her own.

At the beginning of our sophomore year, our group began to receive invitations to sorority parties – the rushing season had begun. I didn't want to rush, I didn't see the point. All the other girls in our group were Gentile, and no Jewish girl had ever made a Gentile sorority, even though our sororities were local and not national. My friends tried to persuade me to go to the rush parties anyway but I didn't want to. Frankly, I was afraid of the humiliation when I wouldn't be invited to the last party, the one that means they've chosen you.

That's when Sparrow spoke out in Quad Hall where the president of the Student Council was explaining to us about sorority rushing and asking if we had any questions. Mary Jane Perkins stood up, all 5'1" of her, in front of the whole school, and looking me straight in the eye, she said,

"I have a question. Is there any specific rule that forbids a Jewish girl from joining a Christian sorority?"

The president of the Student Council got red in the face and said that no, just because it had never been done didn't mean there was actually a specific rule about it. And I thought, God, if Sparrow had the guts to stand up and defy the whole school, the least I could do was to risk a disappointment. And then all the girls in our group decided to stand together, and if I wouldn't rush they wouldn't either.

So I became the first Jewish girl in the history of the college to belong to a Gentile sorority. The president of the Jewish sorority came to see me and said that for once there was somebody good who would qualify to belong to their sorority, I went and joined the other side. She said I was a traitor to my people.

I didn't feel like a traitor. I felt great. There I was a member of the best sorority on campus, and editor of the college paper, with a group of real friends. I'd never had it so good.

Sparrow and I made plans. After we got out of college, we would take summer jobs to earn enough for our passage, and we would go to Paris. I would write and she would illustrate, and we'd set the town on its ear. She was majoring in Art Ed and me in French Lit, but neither of us had any intention of becoming teachers. That was for lesser talents than ourselves. We were destined for Paris.

In our senior year, our group was running the sorority and each of us was in charge of one of the social events. Owl organized a Flapper Party for which she researched each historical detail. Bambi set up a Hayride. Beaver and Colt gave an Alumni Brunch and Sewing Bee, respectively. As for Sparrow and me, we were in charge of the Graduation Dinner. It was an important event, the last event before the Commencement Exercises themselves, and it was also the last time the sorority sisters and their parents would be united.

The dinner was to be held at the Wade Park Manor, and Sparrow and I went to a lot of trouble. We planned the menu, made ceramic placecards, painted decorations, wrote and rehearsed one of the skits we had become famous for on campus – the works.

The night of the big event, the dining room of the Manor looked really great the way we'd fixed it up, and all the girls and their parents seemed pleased. Daddy didn't come, he hated what he called socializing, but mother was there.

Sparrow and I hardly had time to eat, we were so busy supervising everything and preparing ourselves for the skit we were putting on right after dinner. It was another of those lampoons we did on the school and its administration. This one was entitled "Alice in Blunderland" and it featured me as the Mock Turtle (hardly any stuffing was needed) and Sparrow as Alice, all done up in a blue dress and white starched pinafore and patent leather slippers. She was also supposed to be wearing white gloves which she couldn't find and was looking for rather hysterically.

"Never mind," I said. "No one will ever notice the difference."

That's when I looked at her hands and saw the ring.

"Good God, what's that? Not Robert, I hope?"

"I didn't know how to tell you, Bear."

Robert was a humorless, totally uninteresting guy who'd been hanging around Sparrow the past few months. He was such a nothing, you didn't feel like calling him Bob. Even Sparrow called him Robert.

She launched into a whole spiel about how, after due consideration, she'd decided she couldn't refuse his proposal. I had to admit she had a point. In Cleveland, any girl who graduated from college at the age of 21 and still wasn't married was virtually condemned to remain single. We were in the Last Chance Café.

"But what about us? What about Paris?"

"You go to Paris, you're made for that, not me. I don't have the guts. I was always protected and taken care of by my father. Now it'll be Robert."

I straightened my Mock Turtle shell.

"So when's the wedding?"

"Next month in Detroit. That's where Robert's folks live. Listen, Bear, they have a big house, we can spend the whole month there preparing the wedding. It'll be our next big production."

"Our last big production."

"You will be my maid of honor, won't you?"

We were both near tears. How we managed to put on the skit I'll never know, but I guess that shows what good troopers we were. Everybody applauded and congratulated us like mad, so I decided it would be a good time to tell mother I couldn't go to Florida. Mother's plans called for us to be in Miami Beach just at the time Sparrow needed me in Detroit to help prepare her wedding. Mother didn't like her plans to be interfered with, but I figured in front of all those people she wouldn't dare have a fit.

I figured wrong. I had hardly stated my case when mother started yelling, not at me but at Sparrow. Everyone stopped talking to stare at us. Sparrow stood up. Mother lunged at her and started shaking her like a sapling. In front of all those people whose friendship and respect meant so much to me. I couldn't believe it was happening. My glass cage broke and her words flooded through.

"All your fault... selfish and self-centered... stealing my daughter away... putting ideas in her head... she's mine..."

I ran.  Ran from the Wade Park Manor, from mother, from Cleveland.

Oh, I went to Miami Beach all right.  My last act of total subserviance to my mother.  I turned 21 in Miami Beach.  And I arrived in Detroit just in time for the wedding.  Some well-meaning person had had my dress made, a strapless tulle affair in which I looked like a huge ball of cotton candy.

Sparrow looked like the kind of perfect bride whose pictures you see in the Sunday New York Times.  Even Robert looked handsome.  Watching them walk down the aisle of the wood-paneled church, bursting the seams of my tulle dress, I realized with utter dejection that they were right and I was wrong.

Robert's friends, his fraternity brothers, were all clean-cut goyish types who looked at me as if I had just arrived from another planet and might contaminate them if they let me come too close.  I couldn't blame Sparrow for not bailing me out.  It was her show, not mine.

That night she got pregnant.  And I won't allow any smartass insinuations that it might have happened earlier.  Sparrow was as innocent as they come.  Why, she didn't even know what a man looked like – that part of him, I mean.  Beaver and I fished around in the bushes in front of the dorm and found a used rubber.  After we'd washed it we attached it to a hair dryer and told Sparrow to look.

"You see, when it's at rest it's about that big.  And when it's in erection…"

We turned on the dryer and the rubber ballooned out at poor Sparrow who nearly fainted.  So don't tell me she wasn't a virgin when she got married.

We talked, as often as I could afford and she could get Robert's approval, from Detroit where they were living to New York where I was working. Our plan, remember? I'd gotten a job that was boring but was earning me enough money to get to Paris. I tried to write and she tried to draw, but without our catalytic action on one another, nothing came out right. I asked her if she was happy and she said yes. I was miserable but didn't say so.

By the time her baby was born I had made it to Paris. The child was a little girl. Sparrow sent me a baby announcement she had painted, but the painting was constrained. I was shocked to see that it didn't contain any leaves or flowers. Then at Christmas she sent me a card, again un-adorned, in the shape of an old-fashioned telephone. Overseas phone calls were considered a terrific luxury in those days.

She died of post-partem depression. That means having the blues after having a baby. Apparently it got her bad one day and she swallowed a whole bottle of aspirin. I never considered aspirin particularly lethal and I'm sure she didn't either. I'd swallowed half a bottle myself, one day in New York, and nothing happened. It was more a gesture, an empty form of theatrics.

She immediately regretted it and called the doctor. But aspirin enters the bloodstream very quickly, and can be lethal in the right quantity. Before the doctor arrived she was dead, while her infant child watched, incapable of acting or comprehending.

And I wandered around Paris like an unhappy bear kicked out of hibernation, still looking for a way for my life to begin.

## II

# "AHA," SHE CRIED, WAVING HER WOODEN LEG ALOFT IN FIENDISH GLEE, "SO THIS IS PARIS!"

(One of my father's favorite expressions, a line he'd gleaned from one of the old vaudeville acts he loved so much)

I got my first glimpse of France at 5:00 in the morning. We were landing in Southampton but first the boat docked briefly at Le Havre. I stayed up all night in order not to miss the sight.

It was so French. It was dawn, and it was raining. An intricate French lamppost threw its uncertain light on the perfectly rounded French cobblestones, making them shine with that peculiarly greasy quality of wetness that exists nowhere else. To top it off, there was actually a French policeman doing his rounds on a bicycle. He wore a képi and a cape, and his bicycle wobbled as he rode past the lamppost.

Satisfied by this brief vision, I went back to my cabin, still shivering from the cold, and slept until we reached Southampton.

The boat was the S.S. United States, which is too bad because it bore a closer resemblance to a troopship than to the Normandie. The walls were painted in drab tones of beige and grey, and the food was unspeakable, even for my uneducated palate. I always intended to make up for it by taking one of the really lovely ocean liners. But they have disappeared one by one, and now the only way I can evoke the luxury trans-Atlantic travel of that period is by visiting the Queen Mary at its permanent berth in Long Beach.

Being in Southampton, I naturally continued on to London, but I felt like a foreigner there – which I was, of course, but that's not how I'd wanted to feel. To use an expression that didn't exist then, I wasn't getting good vibes. There was no way I could disguise my American accent, although I'm ashamed to say I tried. Too much of the city had been bombed out and rebuilt for me to get the feeling I'd hoped for of being awash in history. And I didn't know a single human being, which in some places doesn't matter but in London it does. Also, the slight cold I had developed during my early morning observation of Le Havre was quickly turning into bronchitis. The weather in London was wet and dreary, and as I coughed in the chilly room of my boarding house, it seemed to me that the sun must surely be shining in France.

My plan was to buy a bicycle in Paris and then bike down the Rhone valley to Milan, in time to catch the season at La Scala. Before leaving New York I had bought a double canvas knapsack that was supposed to fit over the back wheel of the bike. I was also equipped with a list of youth hostels. On the boat, a nice young man named François (married, unfortunately) had prudently suggested I buy a motorbike – it would be less fatiguing – but to me that seemed like cheating. In my mind, the Rhone valley was all downhill anyway, and no one had bothered to tell me about the Alps.

I decided to take the day crossing – by train to Dover, then a ferry boat across the Channel, and another train from Calais to Paris. It was more fatiguing than the night crossing, in which you and your railroad car are carried on and off the ferry in toto, but it was cheaper and more scenic.

In Dover we all got off the train and shuffled onto the ferry, which as it pulled away towards France afforded us a nice view of the famous white cliffs. I was standing by the railing of the lower deck, watching the cliffs, when I became concretely aware of the Finnish student who'd been looking at me in the train. He was standing behind me and talking to me a blue streak, trying to fascinate me at all costs.

Some of my best friends are Finnish students, but those who aren't are the most determined and single-minded of any predatory males. This guy didn't seem particularly appealing, but how to shake him off? I must add that by this time I could barely speak, my bronchitis having turned into laryngitis. I croaked a few discouraging phrases but it didn't do any good. Worse yet, the more he followed me around talking to me, the more people assumed we were travelling together.

I went up a flight of stairs, but there was the lounge bar. Nix on that. Up another flight, and I was on the top deck. Lousy for my cold, with the wind buffeting us, but there was more room to maneuver. There were a number of wooden folding chairs, almost all of which were occupied. To my great delight I spied an empty chair, with a man sitting next to it. Even though his back was turned, I could tell he was a priest. I popped onto the chair, and swallowed the temptation to stick out my tongue at the Finnish student.

The priest turned toward me and smiled. He was about 25 and looked like an Italian movie star. "I yam Padre Federico," he said, his teeth flashing at me. Oh well, a priest is a priest, right?

I allowed Father Federico to accompany me on the train from Calais to Paris. By this time he had found out about:
my laryngitis
my name and nationality
whether I was married
whether I was Catholic
where I was going and why.

He spoke almost no English and I almost no Italian, so we conversed in French, to the greater enlightenment of our fellow travelers, especially a kind looking old man with a beret who was sitting opposite me and drinking in every word of our conversation.

I looked disconsolately out of the window at the flat, totally uninteresting countryside. It was raining in France, even harder than in England. Father Federico took hold of my arm to attract my attention. "In italiano, questo è la pioggia," he said, pointing to the rain, and flashed his teeth again. "Oggi piove molto. Piovere, pioggia."

He still hadn't let go of my arm. "Why did you become a priest?" I asked. He proceeded to tell me a story I have since learned is a common one, especially in Italy. A poor family with many children, and no money to pay for their studies. A bright child, apt for learning, but the only free classes are at the seminary. The mother's joy, the father's pride. And at age 12, there are certain things a boy doesn't realize.

Father Federico told me all this in measured terms, but the old man in the beret started worrying about me. "Where will you stay? How will you get by, with your voice no more than a whisper? Who will look after you?" (A stern look at the priest.)

"Have you ever seen the church of the Madeleine?" asked Father Federico as if that would solve all my problems. "No, of course, you've never been to Paris. Ah, but you must see the Madeleine. I will take you to see it. We will pray together."

"In a few minutes we will arrive at the Gare du Nord," interjected the old man in the beret. "There I will take you to the office of the Hostesses of Paris. They will find you a nice place to stay." The others around him nodded their approval. Father Federico smiled at me.

When we reached the Gare du Nord it was a few minutes before 6PM, and the Hostess of Paris who was on duty was obviously in a hurry to get off duty. She threw me an exasperated look and snapped, "What do you want, a hotel or a pension de famille?" The "family" part of the latter sounded appealing to me after my dreary London boarding house, and in that instant I chose my destiny for all the years to come.

"A pension de famille, please." She made a brief phone call, scribbled an address on a piece of paper, and turned her back to me. I thanked the old man in the beret and we said goodbye. Father Federico, who had hovered behind him, shook my hand endlessly and said, "I'll pray for you, I'll pray for you."

I walked out of the Gare du Nord and into Paris.

I have developed a personal criterion, my own crazy idea, about which cities I like best and why. The idea is that the city must have its own unique personality – one which pleases me, of course – and (this is the hard part) wherever I am in the city I must be able to recognize that I am there and nowhere else. Very few cities pass muster. There are parts of Geneva that look like Lyon, parts of Rome that look like Detroit, and parts of Los Angeles that don't look like a city at all. The winners, according to my criterion, are three cities built on islands : New York, Venice and Paris.

Take that first taxi ride from the Gare du Nord to my pension de famille on the rue d'Assas. The stretch between the station and the river, a cheap commercial area which in so many cities would have been ugly and uninteresting, was straight out of Zola. Goods were literally pouring out of the shops, which seemed too overflowing to contain them. In front of the bakeries were tables heaped with candies and cookies. In front of every "charcuterie" (the French delicatessen-with-a-difference) chickens roasted on spits. On the corner of every street, passers-by good-naturedly jostled the waiters of sidewalk cafés who bobbed among the tables with their long aprons, a round tray balanced on one raised arm.

There was a predominance of clothing stores on the Boulevard Sebastopol, and all their contents seemed to have been transported onto the sidewalk, racks and racks of overcoats, raincoats and suit coats lined up like headless soldiers. As so often in

Paris, the area had once been fashionable, so that behind the painted signs saying "giant sale – don't miss it" were beautiful stone buildings with carved portals over portes cochères[1], and wrought iron balconies in front of high shuttered windows – that wonderful style of architecture that is the signature of the city.

At Châtelet we crossed the Seine, and I nearly wrenched my neck out of joint, not knowing which way to look first. To the right, the Eiffel Tower, to the left Notre Dame. To the right, the conciergerie and its famous clock tower, to the left the flower market. To the right the Sainte Chapelle, to the left the Place St. Michel. In the midst of all this, the driver wanted to know if in my opinion number 78 was at the Sèvres-Babylone end or the Observatoire end of the rue d'Assas. I had no voice and certainly no opinion. He laughed and touched his throat, saying "Extinction de voix" which was an expression for laryngitis I didn't know. "Je suis enrhumée," I croaked, which launched him into a diatribe about the weather, a very edifying conversation he sustained alone until we reached our destination.

Number 78 turned out to be precisely in the middle of the rue d'Assas, on the corner of the rue Vavin, just opposite the Luxembourg Gardens. Of all the places for an English and French literature student to land, and by accident yet. Hemingway and Ezra Pound had lived on the next street over, the rue Notre Dame des Champs. Gertrude Stein's studio was on the rue de Fleurus a few blocks away, and the Pension Maupommé, which

---

1    Porte cochère means carriage door and is a very high, very wide double door meant to accommodate a horse-drawn carriage, which was the usual conveyance when most Parisian houses were built. A smaller door in one of the double doors lets pedestrians in and out, and if there is a covered passageway to the courtyard there are generally narrow sidewalks on either side so the pedestrians don't get crushed by the high wheels of the carriage. In the courtyard were stables which are now transformed into apartments or garages. In particularly old houses it is moving to see, worn into the pavement, the narrow ruts made by the carriage wheels.

was where I was going, turned out to have been the model for the Pension Vedel-Azaïs in André Gide's "The Counterfeiters". Hem's beloved Closerie des Lilas was three blocks to the left, and the famous Coupole and the literary cafés of Montparnasse, Le Dôme and Le Sélect, were three blocks to the right.

I handed the taxi driver a 500 Franc note, the equivalent of 5 New Francs, at that time worth even less than $1.00. I know it was a 500 Franc note because I remember seeing the familiar face of Victor Hugo and thinking, "How nice that the French think enough of their writers to put them on money". I didn't know then that the French slang term for that bill was "un misérable". But I handed the driver the misérable anyway, and when he opened wide eyes I thought it wasn't enough, until I heard him say it was too much. I insisted he keep the change (big spender from the West –one whole dollar) so he insisted on helping me up with my suitcases.

For people who have only come to Paris more recently I must explain that as a general rule, Parisians were far nicer then than they are now. I attribute this to two main factors: the arrival, with the collapse of the colonies, of hordes of pieds noirs; and, with de Gaulle, an increase in material well-being. For some reason, consumer goods do not sit well with the French character. In 1957, only the wealthiest families owned a refrigerator, a television set or a car – to name only those – but nobody missed them because they'd never had them. What they had instead – a community life based around the local market, the local café and the people they met as they walked there – made them more naturally friendly than they are now. Modern technology has been alienating for the French. Maybe it is for everyone.

As for the pieds noirs, or black feet, that is the term for non-Arabs who were either born in or emigrated to North Africa. Most of them were of French origin but there were also a lot of Spaniards, Italians and Portuguese mixed in. These people then became citizens of whatever country their North African colony belonged to. For instance, the actress Claudia Cardinale was born in the French colony of Tunisia. Although her family is Italian and she naturally speaks the language perfectly, plus Arabic, she is a French citizen and her true mother tongue is French.

So here you had this great mass of people, hundreds of thousands of them, from all walks of life, some of whose families had lived in North Africa for over a century. When the Mahgreb started to revolt against French colonialism in the late 1950's, the pieds noirs began to return to what the French call the Metropolis, a term they prefer to the germanic Fatherland (although in French it is, naturally, Motherland), and a decade later all but a handful of them were living in the Métropole. This caused overcrowding, inflation and a general outbreak of bad temper, particularly in Paris and Marseille. But in 1957 the big exodus had not yet begun, and Parisians were much nicer than they are now.

If my taxi driver hadn't been so nice, I might never have found the Pension Maupommé even though I was at the right address. Once through the porte cochère, the dark hallway was a warren of doors and stairways, and I had no idea which to take. The taxi driver found the door behind which the concièrge was lurking, and she indicated a stairway (the one farthest away) up which he lugged my suitcases to the 4ème étage. That, as everyone probably knows, is the 5th floor to us, since the French call the ground floor the rez-de-chaussée and their first floor is the one above that, and so on.

We rang the bell and for a long time nothing happened. It had to be the right door – the name was engraved on a large bronze plaque. Maybe the bell didn't work. We rang it again and were able to hear it ring. Finally there was the shuffling of feet and a harassed serving girl opened the door.

"I'm Barbara Glass," I whispered. "Madame Maupommé is expecting me. I'm whispering because I have an extinction de voix."

"Just as well," the girl whispered back. "She's cross enough as it is." Taking over for the taxi driver, who left with my grateful thanks, she dragged my suitcases down the hall to my room. Before I could enter the room myself, she took me by the arm and led me back up the hall. "Dinner first, and I'm late with my service."

I found myself standing at the entrance to a room that looked like a railway car crossed with a greenhouse. The room was so narrow that the long table plus the surrounding chairs filled it completely. The last third of the room was a metal structure with glass panels which jutted out into the courtyard. It looked as if it had been tacked on at the last minute, or as an after-the-fact attempt to house a table long enough for all the boarders to sit at. I had the distinct impression it might fall off.

At the head of the table sat a person who could only be Madame Maupommé. More than a person, she was a type. Even today, Paris is full of such women. A sallow face surmounting a wide, shapeless body; a thin-lipped mouth, always tightly shut; drooping eyelids, and wrinkles that indicate a permanently disagreeable expression.

These ladies hover at the edge of the upper middle class, struggling either to creep upwards or to keep from slipping downwards. They are always dressed alike – severe, amply cut coats and dresses, made of long-wearing material. The colors vary between black, dark blue and dark grey. And inevitably a close-fitting turban, made of either wool or fur. An occasional fur collar or silk scarf, perhaps intended to lighten the dreariness, only makes the total effect more drab. These women never smile in public and always look at others reprovingly.

At that moment the one she was looking at reprovingly was me, because I had rung the doorbell just as she was saying grace.

"Excusez moi, je suis Mademoiselle Glass."

She took my whisper to be a sign I was well bred, and cracked what was supposed to be a gracious smile, one of the few I ever got from her. "You will try to be more punctual in future." She squinted toward the greenhouse end of the table and spied a free chair which I eventually reached after much shuffling and murmuring "Pardon, excusez moi," etc. like when you go to the movies after the film has begun.

A plate of vegetable soup was handed down to me and everyone looked at me while I ate it because they had already finished theirs. After I'd gulped it down, all the heads turned expectantly toward the hall where the serving girl was standing with two platters, one for each side of the table. Since this was my first meal in France I was pretty excited, although the vegetable soup had warned me not to expect too much from boarding house cuisine, even in France. Still, I wasn't ready for what was on the platters: thin slices of cold ham, period. Each person took a slice of ham, passed the platter, and dug in. Jeez, the war had been over for more than a decade and people were still eating like that. I couldn't believe it. My little slice of ham looked so lonely on the plate, I felt guilty about eating it. Just as I'd steeled myself for the sacrificial act, I raised my head and saw great steaming bowls of mashed potatoes and Brussels sprouts being brought in to fill the space around the fast diminishing slices of ham. What a relief.

Having recovered from hunger and shock, and while waiting for the cheese course, I was able to observe Mme. Maupommé's seating arrangement. She was alone at the head of the table, whereas the table was wide enough for two to be seated at the other end. The space around her was filled with little bells to call the cook and the serving girl, a bottle of mineral water, several glasses, bottles of pills and vials of medicine.

The seats to her right were reserved for visiting dignitaries; that evening it was a Korean missionary and his wife. All the other seats in the first third of the table were occupied by a clutch of little old ladies, with one exception. Mme. Maupommé's daughter Camille sat to her mother's left. An exquisite girl with a high forehead framed in heavy black hair, her eyes were huge, dark and tragic, and her delicate mouth was petulant as befitted a sixteen year old girl condemned to spend every meal making polite conversation with little old ladies. I wondered who her father was, and where he was. Her beauty was marred by a vivid red welt on the left side of her neck, between the chin and the ear, which identified her to me as a fellow violinist. Mine was already fading to brown, but she saw it anyway and we smiled at each other.

The bottom third of the table, the greenhouse end, was for the other young people. In between was a sort of wasteland in which sat a potpourri of people who were neither worthy enough to sit at the first third of the table, nor expendable enough to sit at the last third. The way I figured it, Mme. Maupommé also expected the greenhouse end to fall off one day, and since the young people were all potential troublemakers anyway, they should be the ones to go. Also, one didn't need Mme. Maupommé's eminent sense of practicality to figure out that since the food arrived at the head of the table and was passed along from there, those sitting nearest her were the best served.

After that first dinner, I was classified as an unworthy adult and seated in the middle third, between Mademoiselle Metzinger and the Verdiers. If hard pressed, Mme. Maupommé would admit that Mlle. Metzinger was "un peu étrange" but the fact was, the poor woman was insane. The French are more tolerant of madness than Americans. In the States, anyone with means who shows signs of mental imbalance is immediately carted off for psychiatric care. A boy I knew in marionette class was sent to an insane asylum by his parents when he was twelve, and to the best of my knowledge he's still there. But in France a crazy person is allowed a normal life as long as he's considered harmless. Roughly, there are three social classes of madmen. The poorest ones generally join the ranks of clochards, or tramps, who according to legend sleep under the bridges of Paris. In actual fact they sleep on the sidewalks, covered with newspapers and lying on the vents that send up hot air from the Métro. During the day they sit on public benches and shake their fists and rant and rave.

Middle class madmen live with their families, dress nicely, and are given a bit of pocket money. Later, when I lived in the 17th arrondissement, I knew a middle class madman who walked two miles to the Champs-Elysées every day to buy a certain kind of lollipop he liked, and then drooled all over his shirt front as he ate it on the way back. There was also a middle class madwoman who sat in front of the neighborhood church and shouted obscenities at all the passers-by. These people were tolerated as being part of the local scene.

Your upper class madman is more difficult to spot, being better hidden away. Since the families have money they can get rid of their crazy members by sending them off to rest homes or, if they're stingy, to pensions de famille.

Such was the case with Mlle. Metzinger. None of her relatives ever came to see her, so the pension de famille became literally that for her. Perhaps it was her real family that had driven her crazy in the first place. Be that as it may, her need for human warmth, her inability to communicate, and her uncontrollable reactions to the wrong human contacts had been transferred to her new famille. She spent most of her time in her room, and there her behavior was fairly normal except that a hundred times a day she would ring for the maid and when the girl finally arrived, she had forgotten why she rang. Ten minutes would go by, and then she would ring again.

The best and most difficult times for her were meal times. At the beginning of the meal she seemed genuinely happy to see us, and an outsider would have difficulty discerning her madness. Coming, as she did, from a good family, she was always well dressed and well groomed. Strangely enough, you did not notice her eyes until she opened her mouth. Closed, her mouth looked normal enough. But she couldn't open it to speak or laugh without it taking on grotesque distortions, and there were several front teeth missing. Then you looked again at her eyes, and saw that what you had taken for a sparkle was the reflection of nothingness, the opening to an abyss.

I think she knew this, and at the beginning of each meal made an effort to control it. She would exchange a few polite remarks, and keep her nose pointed toward her soup plate. But as the meal progressed she became more agitated, and on bad days had to leave the table before the meal was over.

The day I arrived was a bad day. The Verdiers were new arrivals too, and had not been forewarned about Mlle. Metzinger. Monsieur Verdier, who was sitting next to her then, was an inveterate joke teller. Since his wife and daughter were no longer an appreciative enough audience, he tried his entire repertory on her during the course of the meal.

She didn't understand his jokes, but as soon as she realized she was expected to laugh, she did so, politely at first. As her laugh became wilder, Mme. Maupommé tried to intervene and involve Monsieur Verdier in the conversation she was having with the guests of honor about the upholding of the Christian faith in northern Korea. But M. Verdier, excited to have a good listener for once, remembered another irresistible story he had to tell. And Mlle. Metzinger, distracted by the interruption, forgot she was supposed to laugh. So M. Verdier repeated the punch line several times, each time with more insistence. As the tone of his voice rose, her eyes became wider and emptier.

It was the cheese course. The platter being passed around contained some French gouda, plus little glass pots of yogurt, and petits suisses – tiny cylinders of soft white cheese (two per person) around which pieces of paper are rolled. I had chosen a yogurt, and was wondering whether to put sugar in right away or taste it first, when I noticed the silence. I looked up, and saw that everyone was staring at Mlle. Metzinger. With her left hand she had tipped her dessert plate on end, and with her right hand she was pushing one of her petits suisses, still wrapped in its paper, up one side of the plate and down the other, humming tunelessly to herself. Then she pushed it along the edge of the plate, chugging like a locomotive. The little cheese oozed out of its paper cylinder and plopped onto the oilcloth that covered the table.

No one moved or said a word. We were all mesmerized. She cupped the second petit suisse in her hand, and delicately took hold of one end of the paper. Then, with a raucous cry that sounded like "whoopee", she yanked hard on the paper. The cheese went flying across the table and splattered all over poor Mme. Grandet, a nice widow who sat among the unworthy adults. Mlle. Metzinger was laughing uncontrollably now, but it was not a human sound.  It began as a low gurgle and built in waves and gasps to a desperate shriek.

Mme. Maupommé rang both her little bells.  The cook and the serving girl arrived to lead the madwoman away to her room.  M. Verdier got red in the face, collected his wife and daughter, and left the table.  Mme. Grandet went to wash up, helped by the ladies sitting on either side of her.  Mme. Maupommé invited the Korean missionaries for a cup of tea in her office where they could admire her photos of Gide.  They trooped off, followed by the little old ladies.  That left us at the greenhouse end with the whole platter of fruit to ourselves.

"Welcome to Maupommé's Madhouse," said Nicole, a plump, pleasant girl who was sitting next to me.  We each helped ourselves to a pear, an apple and an orange, and Nicole introduced me to the others.  There was Michel, an ugly, bespectacled boy my age; Kenzo, who looked every bit as inscrutable as the Japanese are reputed to be; and there was Hansli.  Sixteen years old, with a beautiful, sensitive face.  I couldn't hear the Swiss German accent in his French, but I guessed at his nationality because he was wearing a cotton plush sweater.  I'd tried to buy one in New York and it cost a fortune, imported from Switzerland.  Under a fringe of straight dark hair, his big brown eyes were as bright and inquisitive as a squirrel's.  His attitude was aggressive, yet everything about him seemed fragile and defenseless.  Neither of us knew it then, but it was the beginning of a long story.

With the exception of Michel, who was a student of Oriental languages, they were all musicians.  Nicole was a pianist, Hansli a cellist, and Kenzo a composer.

"I wish she'd had her fit during the meat course," said Hansli.  "Those slices of ham were paper thin."

"We've got to get her better organized," said Nicole.

"I'd say she's better organized already," said Michel. "Why, with one fit she initiated four new boarders – Barbara and the three lovely Verdiers."

They began gossiping about the Verdiers in rapid whispers and giggles. I was having trouble following the conversation, and suddenly realized how tired I was. I said good night to my new friends and went off to finally have a look at my room.

I have to laugh when I think of all those Cleveland Heights matrons who say they've decorated their homes in French Provincial. Obviously they've never seen the real thing. The rooms of the Pension Maupommé were the real thing.

The walls were simply painted white. The wooden floor shone with the gleam of years of waxing. The curtains and bedspread were made of an inexpensive but charming beige cotton printed with little blue flowers. The massive, carved wooden furniture consisted of a bed, a table and chair, and that indispensable item in every French bedroom, an armoire à glace[2]. Also, to my delight, there was a marble-topped dressing table on which sat a washbasin and pitcher. Next to the bed was a night table with three little drawers and a door which, when opened, revealed a chamber pot. Basin, pitcher and pot were in white porcelain decorated with a blue flower motif.

Not that Mme. Maupommé was striving for any decorative effect, French Provincial or otherwise. She had simply bought the least

---

2    Old buildings were designed without closet space, and an armoire is what replaces the closet. Over six feet high, at least four feet wide, and two deep, with a single or double door depending on its width, the armoire contains either shelves, or a rack from which to hang your clothes, or both. If it is an armoire à glace then there is a full-length mirror framed in the door. In French bedroom comedies, the lover always hides in the armoire.

expensive and sturdiest stuff you could find, which at that time was beautiful at no extra cost. Today the French still use washbasins and chamber pots, but they are made of plastic. If you want to get the old kind you must hunt through antique shops or, better yet, the flea markets.

I put on a clean nightgown in honor of my first night in Paris, slipped between the rough linen sheets which smelled of lavender, and sank into a deep, dreamless sleep.

I awoke to a knock on the door, and the maid came in with my breakfast on a tray. That was over half a century ago, but the taste of that first French breakfast is something I'll never forget. The secret of French cuisine, for me, is not in the elaboration of its most complicated dishes but in the fact that its simplest basic ingredients are so delicious.

It was only coffee and bread, basically. But if masterpieces can be said to exist on that level, then it was a masterpiece. The coffee was strong and freshly brewed. Since it was café au lait, I was served a pitcher of coffee and a pitcher of milk. Both were boiling hot. This was not intended to please me, although it did. It was meant as a punishment for being a new boarder. Most of the others preferred to sleep a bit longer and be served their breakfast later, although the coffee and milk were by then lukewarm. As long as I remained at the Pension Maupommé, I continued to be the first one up and had my café au lait boiling hot every morning.

It was the bread and butter that made the real difference. When great chunks of baguette, still warm from the baker's, are served to you with immoderate quantities of sweet dairy butter, the taste is something it takes more than fifty years to erase.

I felt exhilarated by my first encounter with French gastronomy, and couldn't wait to get a closer look at the city I had only glimpsed from the taxi the evening before. I washed summarily in the basin with the pitcher of warm water that had been brought to me, and rushed out to conquer Paris. It was, of course, the contrary that happened.

As everyone knows, Paris is a woman – and a coquettish woman at that. Like all good coquettes, she takes a long time to reveal herself to her lovers. I had imagined I could engulf and possess the city all at once. But she – or fate – decided it should be otherwise. I ended up living in Paris for over twenty years, and there were still secrets she withheld from me.

The first thing I knew I had to do was to set off by foot, at random. No guided tours for me. No groups, no explanations, no dashes through museums with thirty seconds per picture and two minutes per masterpiece. I prefer to stay at home and read about a place in a book, or look at pictures of it, rather than visit it with a guided tour. If, on the other hand, you set out to visit a place alone and by foot, your experience will be like no one else's. The monuments you come across in your wanderings will seem to be your own discoveries. Hopefully you will get lost, which means that you will meet people in the process of getting back on the right track again. And you can mingle with crowds, in streets and in cafés, listening to how they talk and getting an idea of what it's like living there.

My father adored travelling that way. Every year he had three weeks vacation, which was his sacred time to be alone wherever he wanted, and the place he loved best was Havana, Cuba. He spoke first rate Spanish which he had learned as a young man from a Catalan friend named Rafael Ferrer. I saw pictures of the two of them together. Rafael was tall and good-looking with clear eyes which Daddy said were blue. I never got to meet him, though, because Rafael went back to Spain to fight in the Republican army and was killed.

Daddy had a natural aptitude for Spanish as I later had for French. We used to bicker over which language was preferable. "What's the point," he used to say, "of learning a language in which half the letters aren't even pronounced?"

"If you were capable of speaking French," I would retort, "you'd see how superior it is to your crass old Spanish."

We compromised on Italian as being a great Romance language. As his ill-fated Italian teacher used to say," Italiano eesa beautiful, eesa beautiful, juice lika de music of Giuseppe Verdi." But Daddy had never been able to pursue his Italian studies, so he concentrated on Spanish, and in successive trips to Havana even became proficient in Cuban slang.

His way of visiting Havana was to slouch around in old clothes, his bare feet in sandals, a straw hat riveted to his head. In his favorite bars and working class restaurants he was known as Eriberto Vidrio, not Herbert Glass. His greatest satisfaction came one day when a well dressed Cuban woman stopped him on the street and asked for directions. He provided them, and she thanked him and went off without giving him a second glance. She hadn't realized he was a foreigner.

I wanted to have the same relationship with Paris that my father had with Havana. And I had to make it snappy, because I couldn't afford to spend more than two weeks there.

I sauntered out of the Pension and across the street to the Luxembourg Gardens, trying to make it look like a daily habit. Once in the park, though, I realized that everyone there, habitués and tourists alike, harbored the same silly smiles of enjoyment. One could even enjoy being sad there. The trees, at that time of year, were a bouquet of autumn colors and yet the park immediately conjured up for me the image of Verlaine's poem,

"Dans le vieux parc, solitaire et glacé". The impeccably designed tree-framed paths, studded with statues, were filled with lovers and old people and children rolling hoops. Still I could see Verlaine's couple, alone under the barren trees, exorcising the ghost of their love. I felt overcome by the French spirit of order and beauty and love for love's sake.

I sat by the fountain pool in the center of the part where every child in Paris has, at least once, sailed a little boat, and saw other children taking donkey rides. I saw little tots wearing white gloves and velvet-collared coats gravely shake hands with their playmates before digging into the sandpile. Guignol, holding forth in the tiny marionette theatre, drew shrieks of encouragement and gasps of amazement from his young admirers. Old men sat by the flower beds playing chess or just dreaming. How happy Sparrow would have been here, sketchbook in hand. It seemed so wrong, so unfair, that I should be here without her. Worse yet, that she would never be here, that her young life had ended – why, for what?

 A beautiful young man in bronze near the Medici fountain held up his fallen comrade, tenderly and defiantly – a monument to all the young people who had fought and died in the Resistance. Looking at it, I felt that mixture of guilt and wonder I would often experience at such reminders. I knew why these kids had died. There had been a terrible war, right here. While I was flattening tin cans and buying war bonds and collecting the foil out of gum wrappers, kids my age were being heroic and getting arrested and shot. And now the ones who survived were young lovers, as beautiful as statues, kissing in the classic décor of the park. Maybe one of them was for me. Maybe a handsome young Frenchman would ask me to marry him and I could stay here forever.

The whole morning had gone by and I hadn't gotten any farther than the Luxembourg Gardens. Where to go? What to see first?

Being my father's daughter, I opted for public transportation. It turned out to be a good choice.

In those days, the best and cheapest way to see Paris was from the platform of a bus. Paris busses today are rectangular and stream-lined, the kind you can see anywhere. But at that time they were rickety affairs with the motor sticking out in front and an open platform on the back. The platform was enclosed waist-high, with a wooden railing you could lean over to gawk at the sights, as I did, or to yell at passing motorists, as some of the passengers did. The entrance to the platform, where a gate should have been, was symbolically opened and closed by a leather-covered chain. The *receveur* stood next to the non-gate and let people on and off, since the only entrance to the bus was via the platform. When the *receveur* decided the bus could start again, he pulled on another chain that hung from the roof over the platform, rather like an old-fashioned toilet chain. This chain rang a bell that was a signal to the driver – one pull meant start, two pulls meant stop. The driver sat in a separate cubicle up front, and he got in and out by a little door over the front left tire.

Normally people queued up at the bus stop and filed on in an orderly line. But at rush hours, when there were huge crowds waiting for every bus, you had to take a number written on a slip of paper which you got by pressing a lever on a box attached to the pole of the bus stop. When the bus came, the *receveur* asked for the first number and then called out as many successive num-bers as there were places in the bus, while the people shouted and jostled and waved their little bits of paper. Sometimes a smart aleck would find a much lower number that had fallen to the ground and would try to get on first with it, provoking loud protestations from the others.

Once inside the bus, you paid according to how far you were going. The route of each bus was divided into sections – roughly four stops per section – and you gave the receveur a ticket per section. The bus tickets – fragile things no more than a quarter of an inch wide – could be bought individually or in an accordion of twenty which at that time cost about fifteen cents. People gave their tickets to the receveur, who put them into a little metal box attached to his waist and turned a crank to stamp them with mysterious markings. Most people then slipped the tickets under their wedding rings so as not to lose them in case a controlleur came on board. The mysterious markings enabled the controlleur to see whether or not you had given enough tickets. If you hadn't, he made you pay a fine.

The Parisian's favorite sport in those days was platform-jumping. When the *receveur* was inside the bus obliterating tickets, he couldn't prevent passengers from jumping on and off the moving bus, either as a convenience or just for the fun of it. And when he was on the platform, standing under his toilet chain, the most he would do was to frown at people jumping off while the bus was in motion. When the bus was at a standstill, people could get on and off as they pleased. As for running after and jumping on a moving bus, it was considered a mark of bravura. Middle aged businessmen did it as a work-out. Young men and women did it to show their agility. Older people and women with high heels only did it when they felt they had a reasonable chance of succeeding.

The would-be platform jumper surged out of a side street or a café or even a car and hurtled down the street oblivious of other traffic, intent on the elusive platform. Seeing him or her coming, the *receveur* would drop the chain of the non-gate and, like the people around him, stand at the ready, arms outstretched. The breathless jumper was hauled aboard and, if his or her exploit had been particularly noteworthy, was even congratulated. Sometimes, in the process, belongings were lost such as gloves or glasses or a briefcase or a shoe, but this didn't seem to deter the jumpers. It was still their favorite sport.

Paris looked particularly beautiful from the platform of a bus. For one thing, it made you aware of how visible the sky was. Coming from New York, this surprised and delighted me. Before the zoning laws were changed to accommodate such unnecessary monstrosities as the Montparnasse Tower, no building in Paris could be more than eight stories high. The avenues were broad and tree-lined, and what you saw was one-third city and two-thirds sky, like in a painting. The platform wasn't more than two feet off the ground, giving you the sensation of being in direct contact with the street and yet floating strangely over it on a noisy wooden flying carpet. The streets then were paved with rounded cobblestones or with cubic paving stones set in patterns. In May 1968 the demonstrators pulled the stones out of a lot of streets to throw them at the cops, and afterwards what was left was covered with asphalt. Now Parisians who visit the provinces where there were no demonstrations get emotional at the sight of paving stones in the streets.

Paris seemed elusive from the platform of a bus, slipping away from me like a film being run backwards. And I gained there, on those floating trips around the city, a feeling I've never lost since. A feeling of being a foreigner, a stranger, a non-entity, interested but not concerned. I didn't feel alienated but strangely invulnerable, as if nothing in this city could hurt me the way I'd been hurt before. I had finally managed to become invisible.

And it was on a bus that I had my first Parisian adventure. It was so rainy and windy that I'd beaten a retreat to the first seat, nearest the platform, on the aisle. Seated opposite, facing me, were two middle-aged Frenchmen wearing drab business suits, engaged in a desultory conversation about percentages of something. Down the aisle staggered a little old lady, trying to reach the platform despite the lurching of the bus. There was a rather high step between the bus and the platform, and the R.A.T.P. had thoughtfully installed long metal rods on either side of the doorway. The little old lady grasped them and began easing herself down.

The only trouble was, with one hand she was grasping the metal rod and with the other hand she was grasping me. She began with my shoulder and, as she lowered herself to the platform, her hand slid down my arm and clutched that part of me it was easiest to grab hold of. Aside from turning red in the face, I didn't know what to do. A little old lady was feeling me up in public. Had anyone noticed? Although they appeared to still be absorbed in their discussion of percentages, I felt certain my two Frenchmen hadn't missed a thing of what was going on.

Finally, to my relief, the little old lady reached the platform and let go of me. The bus went on, the men went on talking, and it was as if nothing had happened. Then it came time for the men to get off. The first one got up and went to the platform without a word. But the second one hesitated, turned around, and said, "No, mademoiselle, I won't do it. But... je regrette!

# III

# ET VOILÀ!

In which a Hungarian-American Jew is effortlessly transformed into a Swiss-American Protestant.

I was lying in bed sick, and had been for a week. For someone who'd only been in Paris ten days, I wasn't doing so well. I was sick when I arrived, but the excitement of being in Paris made me think I'd get better automatically. Instead of which, the more I stood on bus platforms the more I coughed. The last straw came one evening after dinner when Nicole and I were being pursued by Hansli who was trying to throw a carafe of water on us and managed to throw it on my bed instead. The next morning I awoke with a sharp pain in my back, and while waiting for the doctor to arrive, Mme. Maupommé cheered me up with a detailed description of how her young niece had died of pleurisy.

Had I told him my sob story, my father would have asked, "Well, so did you die of pleurisy?" No, but I nearly died of frustration when the doctor ordered me to stay in bed for a week.[3] Was the Pension Maupommé all I'd ever see of Paris?

Hansli sheepishly brought me a bouquet of chrysanthemums, a flower I love for its connotations of football games and crisp autumn days with the leaves turning all colors. When I was a little girl, mother would pin chrysanthemums from our garden in my hair on my first day back to school. I told this to Hansli, who gleefully informed me that in Europe, chrysanthemums are inexpensive because they are considered flowers for the dead and are generally laid on tombs.

To complete the jolly effect, Camille lent me her record player but the only record available (she said she'd lent the others to a friend) was Mozart's Requiem. So I listened to the Requiem and to Nicole practicing Beethoven and to Hansli practicing Boccherini and to Camille practicing Mendelssohn. When they all practiced together, I closed my door and drowned out the cacophony with my Mozart.

---

3    Doctors in France made house calls then, and they still do now.

The day my transformation began, I had just zipped through the Dies Irae and was about to settle into my favorite part, where the basso sings "Tuba mirum spargen sorum" and really sounds like a tuba, when Hansli popped into the room.

"Sit down," I said.

"The contralto on that recording is lousy," he replied.

"Yes, but the tenor is great." As if to prove my point, the tenor burst into "Mors stupebit et natura."

Hansli smiled broadly, sincerely for once, and sat down. "The tenor is Swiss. I know him." To reward me for my good taste, he told me about the Lacrimosa in the Requiem, how it was the last thing Mozart ever wrote, and how the long ascension of notes from the fifth to the ninth measures, written on his deathbed, seemed to reflect his own passage from this life to the next.

We were thinking about that when Annick came to the door, grinning conspiratorially, to announce that I had a visitor. Annick was the maid; she was from Brittany, and from that day on she was very friendly to me. That much I knew. There were two things I didn't know: 1) the people of Brittany are very devout Catholics and 2) the Pension Maupommé was Protestant. I was equally oblivious to the repercussions of those facts, namely that the majority of French people are Catholics, making the Protestants as paranoid as any other minority group. Mme. Maupommé being no exception, it made Annick paranoid in turn, having to be the only upholder of the true faith in a house full of touchy heretics. So she swore allegiance to me on the day my transformation began, because my visitor was none other than Padre Federico.

I suppose I shouldn't have, but I panicked. It was a situation I didn't know how to handle. I had too much respect for the priesthood to tell the Padre to get lost, but I was still mistrustful of his intentions. By the time I'd have explained things to him nicely – and in my room, in my nightgown, yet – who knows what would have happened? The fact that he'd managed to track me down was in itself unsettling. At least, I thought, if I have to have a visitor it's a respectable (looking) person. That should improve my standing at the Pension. But how was I to cope?

Hansli was intrigued. "Why on earth is a priest here to see you? Do you think you need extreme unction?"

"I don't want to see him. Hansli, you go out and talk to him. Tell him I'm sick. Tell him anything, but send him away."

Looking intense, Hansli headed for the door, then turned to me abruptly. "Is your family Bohemian or Hungarian?"

"Hungarian." Before I could ask him why, he had gone. Oh well, at least I'd coped.

When Hansli came back he was smiling broadly. "It's all worked out. He's gone, and next Tuesday when you're better he's taking us to visit the Madeleine."

"What??"

"That was the only way to get rid of him, and besides, what better way to visit a church?"

So much for the way I'd coped with the Padre Federico situation – a total disaster. Not only had I failed to get rid of him, but Annick soon spread the good word all over the pension that a priest had come to see me. When she heard that, Mme. Maupommé immediately vowed to herself to get rid of me as soon as possible. And to think I'd hoped she'd be impressed. In my innocence, I'd painted myself into a corner.

Every new arrival at the Pension was put through a careful interrogation by Mme. Maupommé. Even if you weren't subjected to it on your very first day, before your first week was out you were invited into her office where you found her reclining on a turn-of-the-century lounge chair. She showed you her pictures of Gide, began discoursing on human nature and morality, and then slipped in some questions about your education and background. Finally, ever so casually, she asked about your religion.

In my case, it was the subtlety of her question that put us both on the wrong track. She asked if I was Catholic and I told her, truthfully, that I was not. I thought the crucifixes on the walls and the air of religious fervor denoted a Catholic pension, and supposed she was disappointed by my negative answer. So I decided not to add insult to injury by saying, "No, I'm not Catholic, I'm Jewish." She, on the other hand, decided that since I was American I had to be either Catholic or Protestant.

I learned later, from Hansli who had a wealth of such gossip, why it never occurred to her I might be Jewish. Jews were her bête noire, and she tried to block them out of her mind completely.

Tempted as she was to hate them, Jews were nevertheless the heroes of the Old Testament. Unlike many Christians, she even recognized that Christ was a Jew. French Protestants in general consider themselves much closer to Jews than Catholics.

But Mme. Maupommé had made a fatal mistake. She had married a Protestant pastor named Klein, who was actually a converted Jew. Or at least was thought to be of Jewish origin.

This atavistic incompatibility became her justification of the marriage's ultimate failure which she couldn't have otherwise reconciled with her strict religious principles. As if to erase any trace of her misadventure, she reverted to her maiden name preceded by Madame. The one trace she couldn't erase, namely Camille, was rebaptized as well in order to completely eliminate the contemptible name of Klein which, although not necessarily Jewish, could be assumed to have Semitic undertones. The good pastor was considerate enough to die shortly after the divorce, thus avoiding the Maupommé ladies any further embarrassment. If Camille missed her father she was careful not to show it. And Mme. Maupommé tried never to think about Jews at all.

Luckily, the above information was relayed to me before my second "interview" with Mme. Maupommé to which I was rapidly convoked. She accused me darkly of having lied to her. I assured her I was indeed not Catholic and that I was just as annoyed as she was by the untimely appearance of the Padre.

"So you are Protestant, then?

Of course I gave up and said yes, thus changing my classification in Mme. Maupommé's mind from "undesirable and unretainable" to "undesirable but retainable" and prolonging my imperiled stay at the Pension.

As it turned out, my second encounter with Padre Federico was less eventful than the circumstances surrounding it. On the fateful Tuesday, Hansli and I trooped off to the Madeleine where the handsome young priest stood waiting for us on the steps, nervously fingering his prayer book. It was my first day out since my illness – a fine sunny day, too. I felt exhilarated, and the situation made me giggly. Everything the priest said sent me into fits of repressed titters.

I wasn't particularly wild about the austere, neo-Greek Madeleine, but there was an enchanting flower market clustered against one side of the church. When Chopin died, his funeral mass was held at the Madeleine because it was then the chic-est church in town, and its high steps and the square surrounding it were flooded with weeping, hysterical women. At the end of de Maupassant's "Bel Ami" the social-climbing hero stands on the steps of the Madeleine after his marriage and surveys Paris like a feudal lord standing on the ramparts of his castle to survey his domain. The church is named for Mary Magdalen, patron saint of the *dames de petite vertu* who work the streets around it. I have been told more than once that many of the "ladies of small virtue" in the Madeleine area are upper class women who turn a few tricks in the afternoon to help pay for that country house or second fur coat they otherwise couldn't afford.

Those bits of information were not provided by the Padre, of course. He was chattering blithely about ogives and naves and stations of the cross. Every time he got too close or negligently took my arm to show me something, Hansli who was forewarned asked him about something on the far side of the church while I giggled.

"She is so charming, your cousin, so gay," said the Padre to Hansli.

I wondered how on earth the priest knew Hansli's cousin in Paris. All I knew about her was her name (Ursula) and her age (the same as mine). Hansli wanted me to meet her. When did he introduce her to Padre Federico, and why?

We had run out of things to visit in the Madeleine and Padre Federico was fidgeting with his prayer book, trying to get up courage to ask us to have coffee with him. I saw him coming and immediately declared that I felt weak and had to go home. He asked for and obtained permission to send me an image of

St. Anthony from his home town of Padua which, he said, would protect my health. Strangely enough, it always has.

Hansli and I didn't go straight home. I felt fine and he wanted to buy some Gregorian music he'd seen at a *bouquiniste*'s stall along the Seine. On the way, I riddled him with questions. What was the story between the Padre and Ursula? And why (now that I thought of it) had he asked me whether my family was Bohemian or Hungarian?

"Because Glass is a German name and I thought your family might be Swiss. I asked my father about it when he called – he's a professor – and he said that the Swiss Glass families are of either Bohemian origin, in which case they're Catholics, or of Hungarian origin, in which case they're Jewish. Before seeing Padre Federico I wanted to know if you were Catholic or not. When I saw him I immediately understood he was trying to seduce you so I told him I was your cousin and like that he was obliged to take me along too. And I was able to protect you."

The above, in essence, is what Hansli told me and I've written his meaning but certainly not his words because at that point in our lives there was no one language we were comfortable in. My French was better than his then, but my German was weak. When he restated in German what I'd just said in French, I couldn't always be sure the translation was correct and we'd sometimes get all mixed up. In the years we subsequently spent together, French became the language we spoke the most because we were living in France. I also improved my German and learned some Swiss German and Hansli got very proficient in English and we both learned Italian. But in the early days we were always adrift in a linguistic potpourri, and the language we really communicated best in was music.

The Gregorian chants he'd wanted to buy turned out to be large sheets of real parchment with the music painted on both sides. They must have been taken from old church books. They were beautiful and cost fifty cents so we each bought one and carried them triumphantly back to the Pension.

My friends at the Pension each had some special after-dinner activity. Nicole and Camille read symphonic scores together. Kenzo and Michel, who spoke Japanese, munched dried seaweed and listened to Japanese vaudeville records that sent them into gales of laughter. Hansli heated water in the kitchen and made himself tea which he drank alone in his room. That evening he invited me to share his private tea ceremony so we could sight-read the Gregorian chants. He had a theory, which he said Padre Federico had confirmed, that when reading Gregorian music you should count an interval of a note and a half of our scale to every note of their scale. I have no idea if either he or the Padre knew what they were talking about, but the music thus produced was very haunting and oriental. It took a lot of concentration, though, and we often slipped back into the wrong scale. Pretty soon Mme. Maupommé barged in to see what all the noise was about.

Mme. Maupommé never knocked before entering. She just burst into her boarders' rooms whenever she felt like it. After all, the rooms belonged to her and so, in a way, did the boarders. She felt absolutely no compunction about intruding on them. Generally her excuse was that she was checking on how much electricity we were using. "Vous ne faîtes absolument pas d'économies d'électricité," she would say, switching off lights and leaving us in semi-darkness.

That evening, her excuse was different. "It's after ten o'clock." It was, in fact, three minutes past ten and she had probably been counting the minutes. There is a law in France that you can make all the noise you want between eight in the morning and ten at night. But if after ten your radio is blaring or your stereo is booming, your neighbors can call the cops. Except that one night a month you can have an all night party ("un surboum") and make a racket provided you've obtained permission before-hand from your local police station.

"Is that solfège you're doing, Hans? A boy your age should be in bed at this hour." She glared at the two lamps lit in the room and let out a perfunctory "Vous ne faîtes pas d'économies d'électricité" but decided against turning one of the lamps off because of my provocative presence in the room. "Haven't you anything else to do?" she asked me, with a look that added, "Besides seducing teenage boys." Hansli and I smiled at her angelically and she stomped out of the room.

The next day we bought candles, and practiced a lot in the café downstairs. By the time dinner was over we were ready. At exactly three minutes past ten, we burst loudly into the now har-monic strains of the Gregorian chants. When Mme. Maupommé yanked the door open she found us holding our parchments, lost in the music and oblivious to her presence. She couldn't even make any cracks about the electricity because there were no lights on. We had put a lace doily over the bedside table, propped a large wooden cross on it (there was one hanging on the wall of every room) and surrounded it with lighted candles in the best imitation we could muster of a Catholic altar. We knelt in front of it while we sang, and for an added touch Hansli waved his teapot around as if it were incense.

From then on, war was declared. Each side had advantages. Mme. Maupommé could of course have thrown either or both of us out. But she felt morally responsible for Hansli, and she was making me pay through the nose. Besides, we were a chal-lenge to her.

On our side, we had Hansli's spunk combined with my long experience as a prankster. I had practically taken a B.A. in Pranks. The situation in college had been nearly the same except that it was Sparrow and me against Mrs. Jamison, our housemother. Mrs. Jamison had a strict set of rules and was maniacal about enforcing them. No men, not even relatives, were allowed in the dorm other than in the drawing room. Girls were to be neatly dressed at all times. No one could sit down at table until grace had been said. Girls had to be in the dorm by 10:00 every night except Saturday when they had to be in by midnight. The list went on and on.

Mrs. Jamison was a squat, fat woman with dark hair that looked like a wig. She always kept a scowling eye on what was happening and, like Mme. Maupommé, had a habit of popping up where she was least expected. Her surveillance was enforced by a "counselor" on each floor. There were always seniors servile enough to want to be counselor-spies. If the threat of the spies and the scowls of Mrs. Jamison did not suffice, then she called in Miss Wilkes, the Dean of Women.

Silky Wilkes, as we called her, was as smooth as Mrs. Jamison was coarse. She was slim except for piano legs, dressed in impeccably tailored clothes, and a small ironic smile always played on her lips. She never shouted or pounded her fist like Mrs. Jamison. But her grey eyes were cold as steel, and her unspoken threats were meant to intimidate. The point of their combined efforts was to treat us to an action replay of "Jane Eyre".

None of the girls expected it to be any different, and few of them resented it. We did. I mean Owl, Beaver, Bambi, Colt, Sparrow and me, known to the other girls as the Animal Crackers. We resented the repression but didn't know what to do about it. Posters, slogans, demonstrations and marches were things the steel workers did, in one of those other worlds we lived a million miles away from in Cleveland. Never in our wildest dreams would we have thought of applying such tactics to our college situation. We fought back with pranks.

While we could still get into Mrs. Jamison's rooms with the key Bambi had managed to copy, we did things like putting pennies in her lamps so they'd short-circuit when she turned them on. We twisted upright a copper tube in the tank of her toilet, so that when she flushed it the water gushed out like a fountain, drenching everything within a six foot radius. Her rooms, on the second floor, opened onto a terrace that was in fact the roof of the veranda that ran across the front of the dorm. One day when Mrs. Jamison was attending an Alumni Picnic for the class of '26, we moved all the contents of her rooms – the bed, the tables and chairs, the lamps, the knitting machine, everything – out on the terrace, arranged in the same order. Instead of being grateful it didn't rain, she forbade all of us to go out for a week and put extra locks on her doors.

That didn't deter us. There was a particularly hideous rubber plant in the front hall that Mrs. Jamison doted on. Owl, who was studying chemistry, developed a mixture which, when poured regularly on the rubber plant, caused it to die by degrees. Thinking the hall was too drafty, Mrs. Jamison moved it into the drawing room where its yellowing leaves were the subject of amused twitters between the girls and their visitors.

Things didn't really come to a head until our junior year, which was ironic because by then we had stopped paying much attention to Mrs. Jamison and her repressive ways. We had found a modus vivendi that allowed us to lead our own lives despite the dorm rules. Bambi had turned her talents as a locksmith to obtaining a key to the back door, so we could go in and out at any hour of the night.

Some of the girls, involved in heavy affairs, used the key to return from a late night date. Sparrow and I used it quite differently. We had gotten into the habit of staying up all night, generally one night out of two, just for the hell of it. We never did much studying. It wasn't a tough school, and we were both able to graduate cum laude without any particular effort. But during the day we were involved in a hundred activities – classes, of course, and dramatics and the newspaper and school government and endless bridge games. Those quiet nighttime hours, when we were virtually the only people awake in the dorm, were when we could be creative. We wrote poetry, painted, dreamed up our next skit or vaudeville act. A hundred mad schemes bounced off the walls of our room.

It wasn't hard to stay awake. We had an electric enameling kiln (we made and sold cloisonné jewelry to earn our pocket money) and always kept a pot of coffee brewing on it. Then there was No-Doze, and those little "pep pills" our family doctors gave us to help us with our studies. But around three or four in the morning, we would come down with a terrible case of what is now known as the munchies, and not even hoarded candy bars or potato chips could quell it. No, the only way we could get through the night was to slip out of the dorm and go to Manny's Diner for hamburgers. We did this at the risk of being expelled, not only from the dorm but from the university. And yet that risk never really impressed us. Watching the dawn break, our minds zinging with ideas while everyone else lay in their beds asleep and unaware, we felt exhilarated and very superior.

We no longer concerned ourselves much with Mrs. Jamison, but she had not stopped resenting us. Nor had Dean Wilkes, and for good reason. There was hardly a newspaper article or skit signed by one of the Animal Crackers that didn't lampoon some failing, great or small, of the school's administration. That wouldn't seem like much of a crime today, but in those days we were regarded as dangerous radicals.

The big showdown occurred when we least expected it, simply because we hadn't done anything. There was a big water fight in the dorm, on the floor below us, but we weren't involved. It was the sophomores, and they made a terrible mess. Silky Wilkes came storming over and to our surprise she called us, the juniors, into Mrs. Jamison's office.

Whenever Dean Wilkes bawled us out, her diatribes followed the same toccata-and-fugue pattern my mother's did. That is, a few favorite themes were stated and then embroidered upon in the fugue part. As we stood around her reverently, the theme words of Silky's toccata rang out – responsibility, young womanhood, thoughtfulness, character. She then launched into her fugue and my mind wandered as it sometimes does at a bad concert, when suddenly she hit a wrong note that jarred me back to consciousness. "I'll make you pay for this – literally. The damages have been estimated at $600 and I expect each of you to contribute her share."

That was grossly unfair. How dare she? And how dare the girls just stand there open-mouthed and speechless? To my relief, someone spoke up. "That is totally unacceptable, Dean Wilkes. First of all we had nothing to do with the water fight. Second of all, the dorm is insured and we also happen to know you planned to redecorate next summer anyway."

The tension broke. All the girls began talking at once, and it was only then I realized that the person who had spoken up first was me. I couldn't believe it. A shiver of shock ran up my spine, but my mouth went on talking.

Dean Wilkes fought back, of course. She tried to argue that the repairs had nothing to do with the redecorating. When that didn't work, she tried to get us to say who was behind the water fight. Finally she glared at me, snapped "You haven't heard the last of this," and strode out of the office.

The girls all crowded around me to say "Wow, you were great" and things like that, but far from feeling proud and courageous, I was just plain stunned. Me, the coward. Being a coward was one of my major obsessions. I never dared to tell people straight out what I thought. I never dared to do things that might shock people, and I admired girls who could even pose for ads like "I dreamed I went horseback riding in Central Park in my Maidenform bra". My worst obsession of all came from the endless World War II movies I'd seen. I felt certain that in the next war I'd be a spy and have to do all sorts of courageous things, and I worried about it terribly. I projected myself into various scenes involving clever duplicity, foreign disguises and intrigue, and there I felt pretty sure of myself. But when it came to facing up to a Gestapo interrogation or crossing enemy lines under fire, I knew I'd collapse into cowardly inertia.

No, I've never been courageous. But occasionally, as on that day with Dean Wilkes, my mind goes blank and when I come to, I realize I've done something reckless.

Dean Wilkes soon made it clear to me just how reckless I'd been. Her revenge was subtle but precise. She had Mrs. Jamison keep an eye on me, and waited for me to make a false move.

One night I suddenly fell ill. I'm one of those people who can be feeling fine one minute, and have a 103° fever the next, which is exactly what happened that night. I was getting pneumonia and I knew it because I'd had it before. The nurse in the infirmary gave me two aspirin and said I could see a doctor the next day, but I panicked and had Sparrow call my parents. Daddy drove down to the dorm, bundled me up and took me home while my mother got the doctor. I was sick a couple of weeks but recovered nicely, thank you.

When I got back I found I'd been kicked out of the dorm because of my false move. What? I had left the dorm in the middle of the night with a man, and I hadn't signed out. To leave the dorm and not sign out was the most dreadful thing a girl could do.

The report did mention that I had left with a man "alleged to be" my father, but only signing out in Mrs. Jamison's book could have proved that beyond a doubt. Signed statements by my parents, my doctor and Sparrow were brushed aside. I had brought shame and sin to the dorm, and I was out.

The Animal Crackers raised a stink, the thing became a cause célèbre and a compromise was reached. Either Mrs. Jamison would campus me for the rest of the term or I was out.

To campus a girl meant she was not allowed outside the dorm except to the library next door after 7 PM every night, seven nights a week. Silky felt this was a pretty safe alternative. The end of the term was more than two months away, and there were lots of proms and parties in the interim. She was certain I wouldn't sacrifice my social life just to stay in the dorm.

But I cleverly outwitted her. I didn't have any social life. In other words, I didn't have a boyfriend. Proms were anguish for me anyway, because I had to scrounge for a date and either find no one, or spend the evening with some creep. The only parties I enjoyed were sorority doings, and my sisters immediately transferred those to the dorm.

My two months of confinement turned out to be quite pleasant. Not only did I acquire a slight aura of martyrdom and mystery (was the man I'd left with really my father?) but we also gave our enemy ladies a hard time. Mrs. Jamison especially, since I was always in the dorm – where else?

Sparrow painted a larger-than-life-size picture of Mrs. Jamison as a jailer brandishing her bunch of keys at the girls dressed in striped prison suits. This was pasted to her door frame, and she had to punch her way through it the next morning to get out of her room. One night after a party we got hold of every roll of toilet paper in the dorm, stationed ourselves along the four flights of main stairs and festooned the huge stairwell with gay streamers from top to bottom. It looked very decorative, and even having to tear it down later was fun. Another time we opened the hundred or so dorm windows and hung a chair out of every single one. That too looked decorative, but was less fun to dismantle.

Dean Wilkes would have loved to get back at us scholastically, but we were all honor students. Mrs. Jamison's punishment was to not speak to us any more, for which we were duly grateful. All in all it was a lovely war.

I should probably have gained a sense of caution and self-protection from those experiences but I didn't. I was ready to start all over again with Mme. Maupommé. She, however, did not want to play games with me. After my first salvo of introductory pranks (coating her bar of soap with clear nail polish so it wouldn't lather, etc. etc.) she made a move intended to neutralize me completely.

With one of her "gracious smiles" and language so polite I knew something was terribly wrong, she explained to me that a little old lady was about to arrive in Paris for her yearly visit. Not only did this little old lady stay at the Pension every year, but she had to have precisely the room I was living in. No other rooms in the Pension were available, but Mme. Maupommé didn't want to lose me (she meant my money), so she herself went to the trouble of finding me a room nearby in an establishment whose owners she knew. I would go on having my meals at the Pension and go on paying her for my room and board. Like that I could still be one of the "family". She even sweetened it a bit more and found me a job teaching English to a six year old child, to bolster my swiftly sinking funds. Thus it was that I moved into the American Hotel.

I'm afraid to say that was, and still is, its name. Not l'Hôtel Américain or even l'Américan Hôtel. My dismay was such that I refused to change my address and continued to have my mail sent to the Pension. The offending name appeared in red letters on a neon sign over the narrow doorway. Everything about the American Hotel was narrow – the tiny entrance hall, the steep stairway, and my room six flights up where, with the help of a string someone had attached to the light switch, I could reach across the room from my bed to turn the light off. The only thing that wasn't narrow was the mind of the owner, Monsieur Claude. He didn't seem to care when the hotel residents, most of whom were women, lazed around the halls in dressing gowns or bath-robes. The American Hotel was, in fact, an hôtel de passe. But I didn't know what that was, and the amused allusions of people like the Verdiers escaped me.

What I did know was that I didn't feel like spending a lot of time there. Mornings were all right. Breakfast was not only brought to my room but even included croissants. I would daydream while looking out my narrow window at the pigeons on the chimney-studded roofs of Paris – the classic view you see in every American film. It took a restful morning to prepare me for the day's exertions, not the least of which was getting to lunch. That involved going down six flights of stairs, walking two blocks to the Pension and then up five flights. At the rate of eleven flights per meal, I began taking off weight.

Once I'd left the American Hotel I was in no hurry to get back. After lunch I would walk in the Luxembourg Gardens until it was time to take the Metro to the Ile St. Louis for my daily session with Jean-François. My pupil was only six years old but he already had a very clear idea of how he wanted to spend his afternoons, and it did not include learning English. I didn't care how much English he learned beyond one new phrase per day – enough to keep me from losing my job. We made a deal. The autumn weather was still crisp and sunny, and Jean-François' mother saw no objection to our holding our lessons in the park. On the way to and from the park, I drummed the day's phrase into the child's head. Once in the park, our roles were reversed and he became my teacher, filling an important gap in my French language education – how to play hopscotch, tag and hide-and-seek in French.

The park was a little public square, idyllically situated behind the flying buttresses of Notre Dame. As everyone knows, Notre Dame is built on the Ile de la Cité, so called because the tiny island was the site of Lutetia, the first city of Paris. Once Jean-François' grandmother, one of the first French women to become a lawyer, walked me around the Ile de la Cité, showing me bits of iron and stonework that were the last vestiges of the wall that had surrounded the old city a thousand years ago.

The Ile St. Louis is an even tinier island which is now linked to the Ile de la Cité by a small footbridge. Even in those days you had to have a lot of money to live there. I didn't know that Marc Chagall had his studio there. I did know Jean-François' parents were rich because they had both a refrigerator and a television set. Once a week I would forfeit my walk in the Luxembourg Gardens and go to the Ile St. Louis earlier than usual. French children go to school on Saturday mornings but have a day off during the week. Now it's Wednesdays. In those days it was Thursdays. When I arrived at Jean-François' on Thursdays I would be shown into the salon, where the brocade drapes were drawn shut and the Louis XV chairs were carefully arranged in rows in front of the black and white TV set. Thursdays were special – the only day there were afternoon programs on television. The rest of the week, programs were only shown in the evening.

Children and grownups alike sat enthralled as the opaque glass lit up and music was heard. The screen was absolutely blank, however. Then an image appeared – a large clock with a second hand. The clock ticked away the ensuing 300 seconds, five interminable minutes until the program began. No one seemed bored or impatient.

Thus, at the munificent rate of 50 cents an hour, my afternoons ticked away until it was time for me to take the Metro back to the Pension for dinner. That was the meal that reunited the whole *famille* around an inevitable tureen of vegetable soup. The atmosphere was as joyful as ever, despite the fact that Mlle. Metzinger had been temporarily removed to a rest home. Whenever a visiting missionary was present, which was often, we were treated to Mme. Maupommé's two mandatory jokes. They were:

Two foreign tourists are in front of a Paris theatre, studying the program. They go to the box-office and say, "Give us two tickets to 'Relâche' please." Ha ha. Relâche is a French word meaning "no performance".

The second joke was intended to counteract the aggressive chauvinism of the first.

Two French women are travelling through Germany. Their train stops in a station. "Where are we?" asks one. The other looks out the window, sees a sign and says," We must be in Abort." Ha ha ha. Abort is a German word, accented on the first syllable, which means toilet. Of course no one understood that joke except the few people who spoke German and those of us who had already heard the story twenty times, so she had to explain what it meant after telling it, while throwing us sharp looks if we didn't laugh on cue.

The ensuing silence was generally broken by Monsieur Verdier who had a repertory of puns. Since he was seated next to me, I generally bore the brunt of them. Once, after he had spent some time rolling crumbs of his bread into little balls, he joyfully threw them into my glass of water, exclaiming "Quelle sale eau!"

"Very funny, Monsieur Verdier," I said. "The water is dirty. Very funny."

"You don't understand," Madame Verdier interjected kindly. "Salaud is a French word which I think in your language you say bastard. Salaud. Sale eau. That is the joke."

Madame Verdier was Albanian which I found interesting because she was and is the only living proof I had ever encountered that Albania really existed. She and her husband were pieds noirs of sorts, having owned a radio and appliance store in Algiers. The Algerians had made life so unbearable for them that they were forced to sell their store at what they considered a very bad price and move to Paris. They were living in the Pension while their new house was being built. Their tales of harassment and injustice at the hands of the Algerian upstarts drew exclamations of sympathy from the top third of the table. To me, however, the urge to make life unbearable for Monsieur Verdier seemed understandable.

The most objectionable of his puns were the physical ones. He would grab my hand and say, "Name the five principal condiments. Count them on your fingers." The first time he did this

I just gaped at him, so he helped me. "Salt, pepper," he recited, bending two of my fingers down.

"Onion, parsley," I ventured, turning down two more fingers.

"And here's the last one!" He wrenched my little finger out of joint.

"Ow!" I screamed.

He looked disappointed. "That's not it. You're supposed to say 'Ai'." Ail means garlic in French, and when Frenchmen bump their knees on furniture or have their fingers wrenched out of joint they don't say "ow", they say "ai". That is the joke.

Hansli had a theory about Madame Verdier. He had discovered that she spoke perfect German and he decided she must have collaborated with the Germans in North Africa during the war. He even suspected her of being a German pretending to be Albanian, which of course substantiated my suspicion that Albania doesn't really exist.

Hansli and I would exchange theories over tea in his room after dinner. He had passed the entrance exams to the Paris Conservatory, and his days were divided between classes and practicing. The few hours after dinner before bedtime became a time we enjoyed spending together. Sometimes we would just sit and read. On Tuesdays and Fridays between 9:30 and 10:00 we would listen for the telltale squeak of bedsprings in the Verdiers' room next door. Once in a while we would take the 83 bus to the Rond Point and walk up the Champs-Elysées to one of the big movie houses. Not only did we enjoy the glitter and elegance of the Champs, but it was the only place we could see American films in English. Elsewhere they were dubbed into French.

When we couldn't afford movies and didn't feel like reading we would invent other amusements. Once, standing on the balcony of Hansli's room and making bets about the number of times each 58 bus would downshift in order to make the turn into the rue Vavin, we accidentally made up a new game. It was a blustery fall night and I was holding the amusement page of the newspaper, looking for films. The wind blew it out of my hands and down the street where it whirled gracefully before fluttering to the ground in front of the bakery. Hansli immediately rushed to the kitchen to collect the old newspapers, and our contests began. Anything short of the bakery didn't count. Papers that got as far as the toy store counted double, and one particularly windy night Hansli even managed to send a folded sheet of newsprint all the way to the corner of the rue Notre-Dame-des-Champs. When bedtime rolled around I would follow a trail of papers down the rue Vavin to the American Hotel, up six flights to bed, and on to another day.

A lot of days went by like that. Autumn gave way to the pinkish greyness of Paris winter. When I had to write my parents to ask them to send me a trunkful of winter clothes, the realization came to me. I was no longer visiting Paris. I had begun to live there.

# GENERATION GAP

## I

## *The Silent Scream*

People born in the United States between 1929 and 1942 are often regarded as members of a failed generation. Unlike the generation that preceded them, they didn't go to war in Europe or the Pacific and return as glorious heroes. Unlike the generation that followed them, they didn't dream of a world-changing revolution. What they did dream of – job security in a large corporation, a single-family home with a two-car garage – is considered today to be a despicable goal, a sell-out. Even at the time, the monotony of a newly built housing development and the drabness of its principal inhabitant, the Man in a Gray Flannel Suit, were objects of derision.

The dynamics of the twentieth century say it all. The Jazz Age was known as the Roaring Twenties – a roar that ended in October 1929 with the resounding crash of Wall Street. The silence that ensued lasted through the hard times of the Depression and the pain of World War II, finally ending with the explosion of the Baby Boom. It was a silence that the historian William Manchester aptly recognized as the characterization of the generation itself. He described American youth of the period as "withdrawn, cautious, unimaginative, indifferent, unadventurous – and silent." The label stuck, and it became known as the Silent Generation.

Can an entire generation be forgiven for its shortcomings, simply by virtue of the circumstances into which it was born? It can be argued that in this case there were mitigating circumstances that more than explained the disappointing nature of the Silent Generation.

Anyone who was born into the Great Depression was marked by it forever. In the decade beginning with 1929, hardship was the rule. Less than ten percent of the American population escaped the rigors inflicted by massive devaluation, unemployment and disenfranchisement. Farmers were evicted from their lands and swelled the ranks of the homeless. Factory workers, when they were fortunate enough to get a job, worked fifty-hour weeks for slave wages. Those who protested were met with armed repression.

The middle class shrank to less than twenty percent of the population. In 1930 and 1931, some 3,646 banks failed. In those days, savings were not insured, and the bank failures caused over two and a half billion dollars of deposits to disappear overnight. Businesses failed by the thousands, and even large corporations ran up huge deficits. People felt that they had been betrayed, and for over a decade they lived in constant fear.

The children of the Great Depression had no sense of entitlement – far from it. Being given a nickel to buy an ice cream cone was a special treat, memorable because it was so rare. Toys were durable, built to last for years, and children were thrilled to receive gifts of clothing and shoes.

Basically, people were grateful for anything they had, no matter how little it was. The Depression-era lifestyle of the middle class can be summed up as "bruised fruit, patched clothing and an old car". Almost no one owned their own house. City dwellers huddled together in tenements or as roomers in boarding houses, while a fortunate few rented duplexes. Soup kitchens were everywhere, and eating three meals a day was considered a luxury.

Is it any wonder, then, that the Silent Generation who came into the world during this grim period was "withdrawn and cautious"? What was there to be exuberant about?

With the advent of World War II the Great Depression ended. Unfortunately for the children of the Silent Generation, deprivation was replaced with wartime restrictions and caveats. "Loose lips sink ships." "Even the walls have ears." "Uncle Sam wants you!"

There was more money now, even though Daddy was probably away at war and Mommy was holding down a job for the first time. Children could enjoy Disney feature films, and a ten-cent Saturday matinee double feature generally included a Flash Gordon adventure. But youngsters were expected to pitch in to the wartime effort, too. They dutifully peeled the tinfoil lining from chewing gum wrappers, collected flattened tin cans in their Radio Flyers, and were pleased when their parents gave them gifts of savings stamps that could be turned into U.S. War Bonds. In their spare time, everyone in the neighborhood pitched in to turn back yards and empty lots into Victory Gardens. And everyone prayed for the war to end.

When it finally ended, the oldest Silents were still teenagers. They watched admiringly as returning GI's enrolled in college and applied for subsidized housing. The nation, caught up in postwar euphoria, was experiencing unbridled economic expansion. Patched overalls and tenement housing were things of the past. Now it was time for ranch wagons parked in the ample garages of ranch-style homes. The word "ranch", redolent of the wide-open spaces of the West, imparted a notion of freedom and romance.

For people who had spent decades in a boarding house, the idea of living in a free-standing or semi-connected house with a yard was a lifelong dream. An iconic image of postwar America is the aerial view of a Levittown – named for its creator, David Levitt – showing street after street of identical homes crammed together in a housing tract.

The ironic disconnect between the perceived glamour and the colorless reality of Levittown living was lost on the Silents. For them, anything that bespoke prosperity was a good thing. Well-being was something they had never known before, and now they were willing to brave the "rat race" in order to attain it. As they graduated from college, the jobs offered by large corporations seemed irresistably appealing.  Students (virtually all of them male) vied for opportunities to become "company men".

Conformity was viewed as a positive value.  The bigger the corporation and the more uniform its employees, the stronger they would be.  Like Scarlett O'Hara raising her fist to the sky, they vowed to "never be hungry again".  In unity there was strength, and everyone wanted to belong.

"Everyone" did not include women or minorities.  The Silents were blissfully unfettered by notions of sexual, ethnic or racial equality.  What they feared was a repeat of what they had experienced in the past – another depression or another war, this time with atomic weapons.  To assuage their fears, they flocked to the reassuring environment of housing tracts.  There, among their peers, they could establish a new rule of law, the law of "nice".

In a "nice" community, Daddy worked as a company man and Mommy stayed at home to raise 3.3 children.  There were no conflicts, and whatever conflicts arose were settled by problem-solving meetings.  No one rocked the boat.  A perfect example of "nice" can be found in the cardboard carrying cases often provided by veterinarians for pets that had just been operated on.  Inside the case was a shivering creature with matted fur, probably howling in pain.  But on the outside of the case was the picture of a smiling doggie or kitty with a word balloon saying, "I'm feeling much better, thank you."

Even as their perfect lifestyle disintegrated, as corporate employment lost its charm and divorce rates soared, the Silents never complained.   Unlike feminists, blacks and other minority groups, they never organized.  There was never a support group for "Adult Children of the Great Depression".  On the contrary, some analysts claimed that the Silents were the most fortunate generation. Because birth rates had plummeted during the harsh years of the depression and the war, it was argued that there were fewer people in the Silent Generation to compete for good jobs and achieve economic success.

As a generation, the Silents became used to never being acclaimed or admired, and they themselves recoiled from being critical of others. But they were happy to be helpful whenever possible. Although no Silents ever became president of the United States, they have been top presidential aides for the past four decades. They flocked into the Peace Corps, whose activities were a perfect match for their value system. As professors, psychiatrists and technocrats, they excelled as interpreters, mediators and facilitators of American society. The most imaginative and voluble of them (Bob Dylan, Martin Luther King) paved the way for the revolts of the Boomers.

Today, more than ever, it is easy to look back with scorn at the Silent Generation. All that conformity seems despicable in retrospect. Those Silents who are still alive today are, in general, prosperous and well-off, often living in retirement communities not unlike the Levittowns of their young adulthood. History hasn't given them much to point to with pride, but not much to be ashamed of either. Then as now, the Silents aren't talking. But they know that behind the door of every "nice" ranch house lived people who, at birth, were branded with the mark of humiliation and despair.

# IV

# HANSLI AND
# SCHATZLI PLAY HOUSE

In the late 50's, the Rue Fromentin had a Jeckyl-and-Hyde personality. By day it was a petit bourgeois residential street, its apartment buildings fronted with small shops. But as soon as night fell, the shoemaker and grocer and butcher closed their shutters. Other storefronts – anonymous panels, not noticed by day – were opened to reveal garish neon signs and photos of naked women. The Rue Fromentin was a tiny part of the Paris phenomenon known as Pigalle. Around the corner, the Boulevard Clichy was lined with cabarets, the most legendary of which was the Moulin Rouge. The sex tourism business was then in its infancy in Pigalle, and it would take another decade for it to graduate to a full-fledged international industry of tour busses, sex shops and high-tech peep shows.

In those days, little bars like those of the Rue Fromentin provided watered-down but reasonably priced drinks, along with bump-and-grind striptease. Then as now, other pleasures could be had for a price. Randy Legionnaires and wide-eyed ex-GIs, roaming the streets of Pigalle at night, were lured into the bars while they still had some money left. Once they were too broke or too drunk, bouncers kicked them out onto the street again, where they picked fights with each other or with the small-time gangsters whose turf they were on. They were a fairly self-contained bunch, and we never felt threatened by them.

Why, you might ask, was a nice Jewish girl from Cleveland hanging out in such a disreputable neighborhood? I was there to visit Ursula, Hansli's cousin. She was living in sin on the Rue Fromentin, sharing a cold water flat with her German lover, Fritz. It was the scandal of Hansli's family, of course, and they wouldn't let their son so much as set foot in Pigalle. But he arranged for Ursula to come and meet me at the café outside the Pension Maupommé, and when I showed her the American Hotel she burst out laughing and said I might as well come to see her in Pigalle from then on.

We hit it off right away. For one thing, we had the same name in a way – she was Ursi and I was Bear – and it fit us both. She was a chunky, jolly girl. Fritz's chain smoking hadn't dimmed the Swiss pinkness of her cheeks. She spoke openly and animatedly in German, French and English. Her straight black hair, shoulder length with bangs, shifted with every movement and her dark eyes sparkled.

Fritz, on the other hand, was perpetually gloomy. When I got to know him a little, I began to understand why. Fritz was born just before the Anschluss and his father, a German Communist, was killed by the Nazis in 1938. Fritz spent the war years trying (successfully) to stay out of the Hitler Youth. But postwar Germany was no easier for him to take, and as soon as he completed his Gymnasium education he felt compelled to leave the country. He was glad he chose to come to France, and he loved living in Paris. But he had to put up with the scorn and hostility of the French whenever they found out he was German. Even his name was a slap in the face for them – "Fritz" is one of an extremely long list of pejorative terms for "German" the French have developed over their many years of hostilities with them. And to top it off, he fell in love with Ursi whose Swiss German family ardently detested the Germans and threatened to disown her if she married him. Being German was even more of a problem for Fritz than being Jewish was for me.

The overwhelming discomfort of the *chambre de bonne* that Fritz and Ursi lived in was not unusual in those days – the majority of people lived that way. By that I mean that refrigerators were virtually unknown, not to mention any of the other "mod cons" that were the pride of every American housewife. Walking up five or six flights of stairs was the accepted lot of all but the most favored classes in Paris. When you did encounter an elevator in an upper-class building, it was either a rickety fin-de-siècle affair or a one-person contraption that Hansli and I called a "vertical coffin", in which you barely had room to lift your arm to push the button.

No building on the Rue Fromentin contained an elevator. To get to Fritz and Ursi's flat, you walked down a narrow hallway next to the grocery store to reach a courtyard with stairways marked A, B and C. You chose stairway C, then walked up seven flights to the 6ème étage, the floor where the maids' rooms were. In the 18th and 19th centuries, apartment buildings were built with servants' quarters on the top floor – one small room per servant. As Mimi says in "La Bohème", it's a long way up but the view makes it all worth it.

When maids' rooms were built, no one was too concerned about the comfort of the maids. The room was for sleeping and sitting only. Cold water could be pumped from a small fountain at the end of the hallway. The Turkish hole that passed for a toilet was located halfway down the stairs to the next floor, and there was only one for the whole floor. Fritz and Ursi had added a hot plate in one corner of their room, plus a gadget I'd never seen before – an electric coil that you placed in a cup or pot to boil water. That coil was always at work, heating cups of tea or coffee that we drank while Fritz chain smoked, Ursi knitted and we all had endless, eager discussions in a variety of languages.

It took me a while to realize that none of their friends were French. There were French Swiss and German Swiss and Germans and even an occasional American other than me. All of us loved being in Paris, but none of us had the impression the French were reaching out to welcome us. Christiane, a tall, slim, sedate girl from Geneva, liked to laugh about the fact that when her landlord asked her where she was from and she said she was Swiss, he complimented her on how well she spoke French. Rolf was a serious young man from Berlin who wore jackets with leather at the elbows and smoked a pipe. Pauli, who came from

Zurich like Ursi did, had a soft spot for anyone who seemed to be down and out in Paris. Since he himself hardly had two misérables to rub together, his solution was to invite them to Fritz and Ursi's, where there was always something warm to drink and new friends to be met.

And then there was Vali. Tall, dark and rather fierce looking, Vali was of undetermined origin. He spoke many languages, all of them with an accent. When I asked him where he came from, he waved his hand behind his back to indicate somewhere in Eastern Europe, and said he was more interested in where he was going. Vali was a painter, and he did good stuff. He had a studio on another side of the building – two connecting chambres de bonne with skylights. He was serious about his work, but occasionally when he needed money he would go up to the Butte Montmartre to "be a whore", as he put it. That meant painting *poulbots* (wistful big-eyed gamins) for the tourists.

Vali was always "in gallant company", as the French say. Usually his companion was one of the Bluebell Girls, a dance troupe from the Moulin Rouge around the corner. They were all young and leggy and gorgeous, and most of them were British. Vali would make fun of their accents and taunt them if they weren't very bright, which was often the case. But they kept showing up, and he kept treating them badly. I definitely did not approve of Vali.

I said as much to Hansli when I told him about the goings-on at the Rue Fromentin. He was never allowed to go there himself. His parents were well aware of their niece Ursula's lifestyle and intended to preserve him from it. Logically, this should have made him anxious to go there anyway, but in fact he showed indifference and even scorn. Ursi's friends were of no interest to him, and Vali, who he had never met, was clearly a scoundrel. Hansli had his music, and that was all he needed.

Well, not exactly all. He also needed more room, better food, more flexible practicing hours and a place to live that was closer to the Conservatory. It would be cheaper and far more convenient for him to leave the Pension Maupommé and share an apartment with someone. After intense conversations with his parents, they decided the "someone" should be me. I was older but not crazy like Ursi. I sounded nice on the telephone. And they somehow seemed impressed by the fact I was American. Hansli had taken to calling me Schatzli, "little treasure", and I guess they agreed with him.

Why in the world did I agree to keep house for a teenage Swiss cellist? Let's just say my options at the time seemed somewhat limited. They included: 1) going back to Cleveland for a high-paying job my mother found for me in an ad agency; 2) finding a fiancé or at least a boyfriend to move in with; and 3) setting off on a new, unknown adventure. #1 represented everything I hated and had gone to great pains to distance myself from. #2 was unfortunately out of the question – none of Ursi's friends was boyfriend material, and if Mr. Right was out there waiting for me somewhere, he should have sent me better directions. As for #3, that was exactly what I was doing, even though it was working out in ways I hadn't expected. There is a lovely French expression for what I was doing – *la fuite en avant*, which means escaping from something through forward movement.

Another reason I agreed to share an apartment with Hansli was that I could actually afford it. Jean-François' parents referred me to a friend of theirs, Samy Valentin, who was looking for a bilingual secretary to work in his office. The office was located at the Place des Ternes, a forty minute ride on the 83 bus from the Pension Maupommé, but only a few blocks away from our new apartment on the Rue Laugier. And my new salary of $300 a month made it possible. Hansli and I told our landlady (who told the concierge who told everyone in the neighborhood) that we were cousins. I didn't feel as if I was actually living in sin with someone. The innocence of our relationship made the cousin story so credible that we even began to believe it ourselves.

A series of special delivery letters from my mother expressed my parents' displeasure. No use trying to sell them on the cousin story, but I did my best to convince them that my relationship with Hansli was strictly platonic. For them, I guess the real sin was not getting engaged or married to some nice young man, preferably Jewish. However I was greatly relieved to see, scribbled at the bottom of one of my mother's typewritten diatribes in Daddy's slanty hand, the words "I trust you, DD". DD stood for "darlin' dotter", a form of expression we gleaned from the comic strip "Pogo" that we both adored. The important part of his message came from The Frank Incident, as it came to be known to Daddy and me.

My relationship with Frank could be defined by the music we played together. That might make it sound romantic, but I now realize the romance was only in my head. When I entered Heights High in tenth grade, I found myself sitting next to Frank in orchestra. Even at age fourteen, Frank was tall and slim with straight ash-blond hair that fell onto his forehead whenever he played intensely. We were in second violins that year, both tackling a major symphonic work (Beethoven's Pastoral) for the first time. We also had the same French teacher but at different hours, and when we discovered we were sitting at the same desk – him at 10 AM and me at 1 PM – we took to writing notes to each other that we hid in the radiator next to the desk.

Our growing complicity blossomed in eleventh grade when we were promoted to the first violin section, still sitting next to each other. Competition in the orchestra had grown tougher for us. In first violins we had try-outs twice a month, not once a month like the second violins. Frank and I held down the second stand, sitting behind the concertmeister Mike and his assistant Dave. We had no ambitions to oust them, they were just too good, but it was still a job holding on to our second stand, with Norman and Julia breathing down our necks behind us.

It was Frank's idea for us to do the Bach Double on our own, just to sharpen our skills. Bach's Concerto for Two Violins is an exquisite dialogue between two equal voices. It was the second movement that did it to me – the sweetness of the melody, the interweaving of harmonies, me and Frank looking at each other for cues, each responding to the other. I fell hopelessly in love.

The Bach rehearsals took place at my house, which was right across the street from Heights High. Since my parents both worked, there was no one home but us. When we weren't playing violin or exchanging timid kisses, he told me about his interest in electronics, which was then a new field. I found everything about him fascinating. My newly discovered passion turned me into a fetishist, and I collected every scrap of anything related to Frank, such as a napkin from the ice-cream parlor where he invited me for a soda one day after rehearsal. I had visions of us being George and Emily in the drugstore scene from "Our Town". But our town of Cleveland Heights had a different vision of us.

It wasn't long before Frank's mother informed him that "Barbara is a nice girl, but she's not in our circle." What that really meant was, "I don't want my son Franklin Edmund Hartford III being seen in public with some Jewish slut." What it meant to Frank was, "OK, I can still hang out (i.e. make out) with Barbara as long as we're never seen in public."

So we continued getting together at my house to "practice the Bach Double". Timid kissing led to light petting which in turn led to the end of the school year and an abrupt "goodbye for

the summer" from Frank.  My music and drama camp summer was spent overeating and commiserating with the woes of
Emily Dickinson and Edna St. Vincent Millay.  When I was finally
released from hell and allowed a fresh glimpse of my beloved, I
found him to be taller and handsomer and the proud possessor
of a driver's license.  Over the summer my weight problem had
begun in earnest, but Frank didn't seem to mind.  Why should
he, if we were never seen together in public?  Now that he had
occasional use of the car, a sharp-eyed observer would have spotted us together in drive-ins at the far end of town, or amid the
dense foliage of the Arboretum.  As we approached graduation
from high school, we also graduated from light petting to heavy
petting.  That's when The Frank Incident occurred.

It all stemmed from our need for a bed.  Making out in a car was
cramped, and in the foliage it was uncomfortable.  One Thursday
night, which was Daddy's night to play poker with his office bud-
dies, mother was out of town.  That was our big chance.  Frank
came over and we went to my room, which was next to the living
room.  I lay down on my bed and he lay down next to me.  I was
afraid to go "all the way" and perhaps Frank was too, but before
the issue could be addressed we heard the back door slam.  We
froze.  Daddy called my name.  While I was trying to figure out
whether to die of embarrassment or to die of shame, Frank was
realizing that his folded trousers were draped over the living
room sofa.

I came out of my room first, in tears.  I threw my arms around
Daddy and swore up and down that nothing had happened.  He
handed me Frank's trousers and said very quietly, "Tell him to go
home."  After Frank left, Daddy and I had a long talk in which
he said, in essence, that having a physical relationship with someone you love and respect can be a wonderful thing.  But at my
age he wasn't sure I was mature enough to handle it, and perhaps Frank wasn't the ideal person for me.  I couldn't explain

to him how Frank was the only person for me, so I concentrated on the fact that we had never gone "all the way". That's when he told me he trusted me.

We didn't betray his trust until we were in college. Frank went to Kent State to study electronics. He didn't call me often, but just often enough to keep me dangling. And I was more interested in being strung along by Frank than in finding a new boyfriend. Although I was really in love with love, I thought that Frank was the only one I would ever love. No matter how badly he treated me, I couldn't imagine ever being interested in anyone but him. In those days there were no assertive young women singing those "I'm outta here, you piece of shit" songs. I might have bene-fited from that approach, but all I ever heard over the radio was "I'll love you forever" and "without you I'm doomed". So I told myself I'd never stop loving Frank, and no one else could ever replace him. I didn't have a real relationship, but at least I had the intensity of my obsession with him. The only irreverence I allowed myself was to chuckle wickedly at the fact that the initials of Franklin Edmund Hartford III's fancy monicker spelled the derisive Yiddish word "feh". In fact, triple feh!

The summer after our first year of college found us both in New York for a few weeks. We each had other engagements, but we managed to spend two days together. We met at a Horn and Hardardt Automat, and even before we said a word we both knew that that night was when we were finally going to do it. It was dark when we left the Automat and neither of us knew New York very well, but we had to find a hotel. I was too embarrassed to go hotel hunting with Frank, so he left me in a drugstore for a while and soon came back looking pleased. He'd found it – a kind of upscale flophouse called the Alpine Hotel. It looked like such a forlorn and remote place, I figured I could never find it again if I tried. We spent the night there, earnestly going about the business of losing our respective virginities. For days afterwards I kept staring at myself in the mirror, looking for outward signs that I had changed, but there were none. Both Frank and I were so overwhelmed by guilt that we didn't lay a hand on each other until another whole year had gone by. A few years later, when I was working in New York, the bus that took me to my job every day drove right past the Alpine Hotel. Feh!

There were now a lot of sour notes in the music of my relationship with Frank. During our junior and senior years of college we got over our guilt and started meeting in motels near Kent State or hotels in downtown Cleveland. I continued to be slavishly devoted to him, but my idealized dream world had become more real and more comfortable to me than those sordid get-togethers. Still, when the music stopped altogether it was a shock. He was visiting New York and had come to see me in my tiny midtown studio. We had just made love and were lying in my bed when he announced that he was about to be engaged. I didn't know the girl, some friend of his mother's family, obviously someone who was "in their circle". I never saw Frank again. My college friend Bambi sent me a clipping about his wedding just before Hansli and I moved into our apartment.

It was a bonbon of an apartment, done in soft fabrics and pastel colors. A small entrance hall opened onto two adjoining rooms of equal size, a living/dining room with a day bed where I slept, and a bed/sitting room that became home to Hansli and his cello. There were working fireplaces in each of the rooms, and Persian rugs on the parquet floors. Two other doors off the hall led to the kitchen and bathroom respectively, plus a third door for the WC. Those letters stand for the French words "water closet" (pronounced "wattère clohsette") and no matter how small the apartment, the French have always preferred to build a separate room for the WC where, as they say, *même le roi va seul* – even the king goes there alone.

We had a real bathroom, a "salle de bains" where you can soak in a tub rather than a "salle d'eau" where you come into contact with the water, but far less comfortably. At the Pension Maupommé not only was it a salle d'eau but it was a cramped space at the end of a narrow hallway that also contained the coal-burning heater, and if you weren't careful you got smudged right after you'd washed. In my room at the American Hotel, the plumbing consisted mainly of the bidet. So as simplistic as it was by American standards, our Rue Laugier bathroom seemed like a great luxury to us. The same was true of our kitchen, which actually contained a small refrigerator.

The kitchen was completely equipped with pots, pans and utensils. There was a full set of dishes and silverware, and virtually all the linens we needed. We had an eerie feeling of being Snow White discovering the dwarfs' house, or Goldilocks *chez* the three bears. When we asked our landlady why the apartment was so fully furnished, she explained tearfully that it had been the dwelling of her son and daughter-in-law, a young couple who adored each other but had died tragically young. We didn't dare ask her for details. The French are very close-mouthed about personal subjects like age, income and death. But it became clear to us that we had stumbled into an abandoned love nest.

We were soon joined by Frou Frou, who had been living at the concierge's since his masters' untimely demise. Frou Frou was a Sidney Greenstreet of a cat – handsome and surprisingly agile, but also quite rotund. Once he got whiff of the fact that his apartment was again inhabited, he immediately reclaimed his favorite armchair where he spent most of the day snoozing. In the evening after dinner, he was the audience for our shows.

We started putting on shows when we discovered, at the back of a closet, a large wicker basket that contained costumes. There was an Alpine dirndl and a Spanish mantilla and a wispy fairy costume for me, and lederhosen and a Zorro outfit (black cape and big hat) and fake armor for Hansli, and Roman togas for both of us. Frou Frou devotedly sniffed the costumes, and made a nest of whatever we weren't using, so it wasn't hard to figure out that they had once belonged to the ill-fated couple. But why? Halloween is big in France now but it was unknown then. Were they carnival fanatics? Or maybe something kinkier?

As we got to know more people in our neighborhood, we were gradually able to fill in some of the blanks. It seems that Monsieur Vincent was a singer, a second tenor at the Chatelet – a theatre that performed operettas. He had been well reviewed in supporting roles and had a promising career. Before his wife became Madame Vincent she had been an aspiring soprano, and after her marriage she was made part of the chorus at the Chatelet. It was at that point that the stories diverged. Monsieur Grégoire the upholsterer, whose shop was on the ground floor of our building, claimed that the Vincents – wishing to earn extra money with a concert tour in Tierra del Fuego during the Chatelet's off-season – contracted a fatal disease that killed her first and then him.

But Monsieur and Madame Piot, who owned the *charcuterie* at the end of our street, had a different, darker version. According to them, Monsieur Vincent was a very jealous man who suspected his wife of flirting with the first tenor and eventually killed her. They claimed he wasn't dead at all but was serving a long prison term.

We were tempted to believe them because 1) it made a good story and 2) the Piots seemed to know a lot about the theatre. Even though they had to get up at 5 AM six days a week to pre-pare the food they sold, and though their shop was open until 7 PM, they somehow managed to find time to attend all the new theatrical productions. They were self-styled critics who, when we showed up to buy some *vol-au-vent* or *boudin blanc*, readily voiced their opinions of the shows and the performers they had recently seen.

The shows from Hansli/Schatzli Productions, which no one but Frou Frou ever saw, had titles like "Revenge of the Roman Senorita" and "The Yodeling Prince". Our Gregorian chants weren't easily adaptable for these masterpieces, so I started pinching old sheet music from the office. Before and after World War II, Samy Valentin and his Sophomores had been one of the most popular bands in France. As silly as they were, his songs were very appealing and lent themselves perfectly to our needs.

Another thing I proudly bore home from the office, and which is still one of my most prized possessions, was a thick cookbook entitled "Cuisine et Vins de France" by Maurice Curnonsky. An itinerant book salesman convinced me to buy it, and I signed an agreement to pay for it in six monthly installments. Until the time of that purchase, our meals had been simple affairs. Ursi had given me some Swiss recipes such as barley soup and rösti (a fried potato dish), and Hansli's favorites included chocolate oatmeal (very filling if you eat it at night, and very inexpensive if you're broke) and an elaborate multi-fruited version of what was then the Swiss national dish, unknown elsewhere – muesli, which they called Birchermuesli in honor of its inventor, Dr. Bircher.

It hadn't taken us long to convert to the French habit of eating a large, elaborate Sunday lunch. But eating such a meal in a restaurant was too expensive to be affordable very often. Once Curnonsky became a member of our household, so to speak, we undertook to prepare fancy meals at home. The book was a collection of recipes from the greatest chefs of France, with clear instructions and beautiful color photos. We started with simple dishes and when they turned out well, we gradually moved on to more complicated ones. I did most of the cooking. Hansli prepped for me, set the table with flowers and fanciful decorations, and created elaborate hand-written menus. One of the best open-air markets in Paris was just around the corner from us, so finding the right ingredients was not a problem.

At the end of every recipe, Curnonsky gave a list of wine suggestions. Of course I knew nothing about wine. At home my parents drank whiskey, but that was such a rarity in Paris that it was totally unaffordable. In New York I'd drunk gin – in fact, far too much gin. I would have been happy to keep on drinking as much hard liquor in Paris as I had in New York, and in fact there were many evenings when I really missed the soothing effects of alcohol. But it was a luxury that was simply out of my reach. Wine was never served at the Pension Maupommé and the first time I found myself actually drinking wine was shortly after Hansli and I moved into the Rue Laugier apartment. I was terribly depressed about Sparrow's death and I would have given anything for a good stiff drink. Since I was broke, the best I could do was to buy a liter of red table wine, which I downed after Hansli had gone to bed. It made me terribly sick and he had to help me clean up. I was mortified, and swore I'd never drink the stuff again, but he assured me it would be all right for me to drink a few glasses of nice wine along with a meal. In Europe, families are used to drinking wine with meals, even the kids.

Monsieur Grégoire startled me when he first asked if I'd be interested in buying good champagne at a bargain price. I had assumed champagne was as unaffordable in France as it was in the States, and indeed the biggest brands of Rheims champagne were pricey in Paris too. But Monsieur Grégoire came from the Epernay region and every so often his relatives shipped him a few cases of a brand I'd never heard of that cost less than two dollars a bottle. He told me that Epernay champagne is better than Rheims champagne and when I was able to compare the two, I agreed with him. Epernay is less acidic and never gives you a headache. Champagne is a wine that can be drunk with virtually any dish, from appetizer to dessert, and Monsieur Grégoire's champagne was within our budget. But before long we became curious to try some of the exotic sounding wines suggested by Curnonsky.

Monsieur Grégoire gave us the address of a wine store in our neighborhood that had been owned by the same family for three generations. I went there to buy one bottle a week to go with our Sunday meal, always looking for something we could afford from the list of Curnonsky's suggestions. After a few visits the owner became so curious he couldn't help asking me why I was asking for those particular wines. When I explained to him about the cook book, he apparently took pity on me – an American girl who couldn't even pronounce "chassagne montrachet" correctly much less appreciate it fully – and proceeded to take me downstairs to his wine cellar. It was an amazing sight. Casks and crates were stacked everywhere amid cobwebs and dust. Nothing was marked but he seemed to know just where to find anything he wanted.

From then on, whenever I came to buy a bottle of wine, we would go down to the cellar and he would pluck a bottle from under the stairs or out of some remote corner. He explained that wine collectors buy only by the case, but since over the decades odd lots of bottles in smaller quantities had accumulated, he could sell them to me at very low prices. He told me I was taking a risk, because bottles as old as the ones he was selling me could have turned to vinegar. Since he never laid a hand on me, I believed him. Now, in retrospect, I wonder what his motives were. Maybe he just enjoyed having an appreciative pupil. His own children were not interested in continuing his profession. But I know that never again in my lifetime will I acquire a 1914 Sauternes or a 1923 St. Amour for a few dollars a bottle. And I know that wine collectors will pay high prices for rare bottles, even at the risk of having them turn to vinegar when they're opened.

After Sunday lunch we would go on an excursion. We had resolved to go up in every Paris monument that had stairs or an elevator – not just the Eiffel Tower and the Arch of Triumph but also odd-ball monuments like the Bastille column and every church tower from Notre Dame to the Armenian Protestant church in our neighborhood. Other times we were able to get inexpensive tickets for Sunday matinee concerts or the opera.

Our domestic tranquility was soon shattered by the news that my parents were coming for a visit. Their presenting reason was that mother had a real estate convention to attend in Paris, but I knew they really wanted to check up on me. Maybe they thought Hansli was some sort of gigolo who was taking advantage of me or besmirching their daughter's honor. In actual fact, he looked more like a pre-teen than a teenager with his wide eyes and pink cheeks. As preparation for my parents' arrival, we decided to improve his English. He wanted to speak "real American" so I taught him advertising slogans like "the pause that refreshes" or "a little dab'll do ya". He was a quick learner and soon was chattering away merrily. He claimed that after German, English was easy as pie. So I didn't hesitate to make fun of him when he said things like "I brushed my teeth but the yellow didn't went".

As soon as Daddy laid eyes on him, they both relaxed and started speaking German. Mother was a tougher nut to crack. She was bound and determined to get upset about something, and when it clearly couldn't be Hansli, she set about finding something else. I thought the apartment was too cute and well furnished for her to find fault with it, and indeed she did approve of everything that was there, but then she started fussing about what wasn't there. In those days dishwashers were rare even in America, but every self-respecting U.S. household had a clothes washer and dryer. That's what we needed too. When I explained that they were still rarer than hen's teeth in French homes and dreadfully expensive to boot, I figured the matter was settled.

Hansli and I prepared a fabulous meal of Curnonsky's finest selections for them, and although the food was richer and more copious than what they were used to, they seemed to enjoy it. We refrained from putting on one of our shows, but Hansli proposed a "pause that refreshes" and played cello for them. That was a big success. Then we whisked them off to the Jeu de Paume Museum to look at impressionist paintings. Daddy was particularly fond of Renoir. He said you could feel the warmth of the sunlight coming right through the canvas. I think what he really meant was the warmth of the flesh of Renoir's women. Mother kept pacing back and forth with a preoccupied look, until suddenly she stood still and nearly shouted, "That's it!" Then she rushed up to me and said "Let's go, we're going to find you a laundromat!"

We managed to complete our visit of the museum, and it was nearly dark when we got out. Hansli had to go home to practice, so I took my parents for a walk around the Latin Quarter. Daddy discovered with delight some of the streets that Elliot Paul, one of his favorite authors, had described – and mother discovered that the Latin Quarter contained no laundromats.

The next day mother's real estate convention started. Hansli was busy at the Conservatory and I managed to get a few days off work, so I was able to show Daddy my Paris. He admired the audacity of the platform-jumping bus riders, and the sleek efficiency of the Metro system. He bought himself a beret which he wore with panache. It made him look like a European roué. We giggled, remembering the Peter Arno cartoon showing an American co-ed sitting on a Frenchman's lap while her friend exclaims, "Mary Ann, you mean you're never coming home?"

We hung out in cafés, taking in the local scene and getting caught up. At home mother's presence was so intrusive that we could never have private talks, but once I turned eighteen we got into the habit of meeting in bars from time to time. We both loved the fact that nobody took us for father and daughter. In Paris, of course, nobody cared. We were just two Americans, one of whom spoke French. Daddy found he could read French, and I'm sure he would have learned to speak it too if he'd had the time. Mother was exactly the opposite. Resolutely monolingual, her idea of how to communicate with the French was to speak English very slowly. She had no feeling for language, not even English – Daddy always teased her by calling her Mrs. Malaprop. And she had none of the instincts that saved Daddy and me when we were trying to come to grips with a new language. Standing on a Paris street corner trying to flag down a passing vehicle, she could have shouted "Taxi" which is almost universally understood. But no, she stood there and yelled out "CAAAB!"

Her determination expressed itself in other forms. Once her real estate meetings were over and I had returned to work, she and Daddy visited my office. I was very fond of the little room in which I worked, with sheet music piled up all around me, but mother declared it to be a fire trap. She also predicted that I would soon have scoliosis if I didn't sit in a better chair. Samy Valentin, my boss, who was a man of parts, immediately grasped the situation and suavely promised my mother that the sheet music would soon be sent to storage. As for the chair, mother decided she would buy it for me herself. So we went off to neighborhoods I'd never visited before, places that specialized in import-export, and stores that sold restaurant equipment and building materials and office equipment. She found the chair all right, a sturdy leather affair which I still use to this day. And she also found a laundromat, probably the only one in Paris in those days and impossibly far away from my apartment, but I faithfully promised to use it too.

The last big event of their visit was our birthday celebration. Mother and I were born only a day apart, her on April 8 (which had also been her mother's birthday) and me on April 9. She said I was born a day late and had been late ever since. That year, 1958, she was turning 59 and me 23. Mother wanted to spend an evening at the Lido, so that's what we did although Daddy, Hansli and I had no particular desire to do so. Ironically, we would have had more fun if mother hadn't been there. We could have made cracks about the girls, which Daddy hesitated to do in mother's presence, and we could have spoken other languages. But mother had a good time, so we were satisfied.

As my parents said goodbye after a visit we all agreed was a big success, things were happening in France of which we were only dimly aware. The Fourth Republic, characterized by a multi-party system that caused the government to change several times every year, was on its last legs. It was an extremely democratic system, but its very fairness made it too unwieldy to cope with the problems France was facing. They had lost their Vietnam war. Two other French colonies, Tunisia and Morocco, had successfully negotiated to obtain their independence as well. Now things were volatile in Algeria, where the National Liberation Front had begun its struggle. The French army in Algiers threatened to revolt unless General de Gaulle took charge. Since the end of World War II, de Gaulle had chosen to stay out of politics, but now he declared himself ready to take over as Prime Minister if he could change the system and create a new constitution. President René Coty agreed to his terms, and de Gaulle's new government was the beginning of the Fifth Republic, the one still in force today.

De Gaulle's rise to power caused great euphoria in France, and I was able to experience it first-hand a few weeks later on the 14th of July. It was my first Bastille Day in France. Events were planned for the entire day and night, and I wanted to attend as many of them as I could. The first of the day's festivities was a military parade down the Champs-Elysées. Hansli probably would have attended it with me, but he had returned to Switzerland for his summer vacation. No one at the office wanted to go, and Ursi *et al* were disinclined to get up that early in the morning. So I went all by myself.

The parade went from the Arch of Triumph to the Place de la Concorde where a grandstand was set up for General de Gaulle and other French and foreign dignitaries. I got off the Metro halfway down the Champs-Elysées where I figured I'd have the best view. Almost an hour before the parade was scheduled to begin, the street was already jammed with people, many of whom were holding periscopes made of cardboard and mirrors. I found myself standing next to a man who had brought along a stepstool, the kind you use in the kitchen to reach high cupboards, for his young daughter. When he found out I was American, he put his daughter on his shoulders and urged me to stand on the stepstool so I'd be sure to see everything. This was a historic occasion, he said, and the people of Paris hadn't been this elated since the Liberation fourteen years earlier, in 1944.

As if to emphasize this, the parade began with the silent rumble of tanks creaking and grinding their way down the avenue. They were from the armored division that General Leclerc had led victoriously across Normandy to Paris, and some were the actual tanks that had taken part in the Liberation. The crowd recognized their names and shouted them out. Each of the units that followed had a fanfare playing their special music. The Garde Républicaine were all on horseback, wearing sabers and shiny metal helmets with red horsehair plumes. Their musicians were on horseback too, and their drummers had two small kettle drums astride their saddles.

Wave after wave of colorful uniforms marched by, with equally colorful music. The cadets from St. Cyr, the military academy, wore plumed hats and marched to a sprightly tune. The students from Polytechnique, in dark uniforms with three-cornered hats, were in military formation even though they weren't soldiers. The paratroopers could be recognized by their red berets worn at a slant. There were armored units and infantry and airforce and naval units. The French sailors all wore white berets with red pompoms which are said to bring good luck if you touch them. There was a motorcade of smartly uniformed motorcycle police, and a unit of firemen. One of the units that drew the most attention was the Foreign Legion. Wearing khaki uniforms and white képis, the Legionnaires loped along in a slow, deliberate step, their arms swinging in unison to the sound of their familiar march, irreverently known as "Tiens, il y a du boudin" (Say, there's blood sausage.).

The Bastille Day parade still takes place every year, and each time the military hardware on display becomes more intricate and impressive. A few years after de Gaulle came to power, he began the practice of sending three jet fighters over the Champs-Elysées spewing plumes of red, white and blue smoke over the parade, which always makes a big impression. But on July 14, 1958 I saw a sight that was soon to disappear forever, and that I will never forget. As the last military unit marched by and their music faded, a hush fell over the crowd. Suddenly, before I could see anything, I heard hoof beats thundering toward me. In a cloud of dust, like a vision from another era, came a horde of men riding purebred Arabian stallions. They were the Spahis, an Algerian cavalry unit that in those days was still part of the French army. They wore pale blue djellabas and white headdresses that floated out behind them as they galloped along, shooting their rifles into the air and whooping. The most amazing thing was that they were standing up in their stirrups, their bodies absolutely immobile as the horses raced beneath them.

We all went crazy, yelling "Vive les Spahis" and "Vive la France" and "Vive de Gaulle". Then the man and his daughter shook my hand, and it was over.

The plan for the afternoon was to go to the Comédie-Française, the national theatre that presented works by classic authors such as Corneille and Racine. The theatre was as beautiful as an opera house, and tickets were quite expensive. But every Bastille Day, all over France, national theatres and museums are open to the public for free, so that everyone can participate in the *patrimoine* or cultural heritage.

I found Ursi and Fritz in front of the Comédie-Française, standing in a line that was already quite long. In keeping with the elegance of the place, I was wearing my "New York career girl" outfit – a tight-fitting slate grey sheath dress with three-quarter length sleeves and a jewel neckline completed by a fake pearl choker, and a small velvet hat with a veil. I needn't have bothered to dress up, as most of the people standing in line were too poor to afford fancy clothes and some were street tramps wrapped in blankets.

When the doors opened we all trooped in and sat in the best seats we could find – it was first come first served, but very orderly. The play being given was "Le Bourgeois Gentilhomme" by Molière. The sets and costumes were opulent and the acting was superb. I had studied the play in college, which was lucky because my French still wasn't good enough to keep up with every line of Molière's elegant verse as it tripped off the actors' practiced tongues. But it didn't take any knowledge of the language to delight at Monsieur Jourdain, the gullible "middle-class nobleman". Ridiculously overdressed and prancing awkwardly to the music of Lulli, he beamed with pride as his unscrupulous entourage told him how handsome he was and how well he danced. The audience loved it, and it was a wonderful tribute to

Molière's genius to see a roomful of disenfranchised 20th century spectators revel in his spoof of snooty 17th century pretentiousness.

After the theatre we had an apéritif in a café near the Louvre, a building that has special meaning on July 14th. Of course Bastille Day commemorates the storming of the infamous Bastille prison, but the prison was then torn down and all that remains is an outline of the walls and towers in the pavement of the Place de la Bastille, and old lithographs displayed in the Bastille Metro station. Whereas the Louvre, still an imposing group of buildings containing not only the museum but also the government's Tax Collection department, had once been the royal palace where kings lorded it over their subjects until the subjects decided it was time for a change.

The French take as much pride in their revolution as Americans take in theirs, and that particular Bastille Day they were also feeling good about their future. Recovery after World War II had been slow, and although there weren't as many privations as in, say, Great Britain where rationing continued well into the 1950's, the man in the street didn't have many luxuries to enjoy. The feeling was that de Gaulle, the general who kept France's honor intact during the war, would now take the country to the next level.

As we strolled over to the Left Bank to join Rolf and Pauli for dinner, we could hear music coming from every street corner – either people singing in cafés, or small bands warming up for the *bal populaire* that night. Kids were running around setting off firecrackers, and people who would usually look grim had silly smiles on their faces.

We were meeting our friends at a student restaurant called Roger la Frite. It consisted of one huge room with many rows of long tables where people ate family style. The place was always rowdy, and that evening it was chaotic. As we stood there looking for the others, the people at the table nearest us started banging their silverware on the table in a pounding rhythm. They were yelling something – it sounded like "Chapeau! Chapeau! Chapeau!" Oh, something about a hat. Someone was wearing a hat and they were all poking fun at that person. Now everyone in the place was doing it. "Cha-peau, cha-peau, CHA-PEAU!!" Ursi looked at me, and I realized – oh no, it was me!

Paralyzed with embarrassment, I couldn't decide whether to keep the hat on or not. The matter was decided when someone reached out, took it off my head, and threw it to someone else. Soon my little velvet bowler was flying around the room. A tall, gangly young man put it on, stood on the table, and began dancing the cancan. Everyone burst out laughing, including me.

We squeezed in next to Rolf, who was with a studious looking young woman with glasses, and Pauli who had brought along two girls from Rumania. Everyone that night was eating the same meal served from big platters of food being passed around. It reminded me of the Pension Maupommé except that the food was much more fun – heaps of crisp French fries and piles of steaming sausages served with mustard and *baguettes*. Beer and wine flowed freely. We began singing that wonderful French drinking song, "Chevaliers de la Table Ronde" where the Knights of the Round Table are asked to taste the wine to see if it's good. They are of two opinions – some say "yes yes yes" and others say "no no no". There are endless verses, and with every chorus of *ouis* and *nons* we pounded our glasses on the table.

I felt a tap on my shoulder and turned around to see a young man holding my hat. "I believe this belongs to you, Mademoiselle." By this time I had completely forgotten about the hat, but I was happy to have it back and thanked him profusely. Rolf was just making room for him to sit down with us when a shout went out. "The fireworks are about to begin!" We all rushed outside and ran down the street to the nearest bridge over the Seine.

It was dark now, and when the rockets started exploding the people cheered. Everyone's favorites were the ones that burst into one color, then another and another. We counted them, shouting out the numbers – there were always four or five different colors, sometimes even six or seven. As a change from the rockets, they shot off sparklers and Roman candles that streamed into the water. After that they lit up a display that was floating on a raft in the river. It was in the shape of one of those round-hulled boats you see in medieval tapestries and it was the symbol of Lutetia, the ancient city of Paris, whose motto is "Fluctuat nec mergitur" – it rocks but does not sink. Then people started exclaiming, "Ah, le bouquet, le bouquet" as a profusion of rockets were shot off all together. It was indeed a grand finale.

In the darkness that followed the fireworks I suddenly saw a string of bobbing lights coming toward me, and I heard the blaring of a trumpet. Led by a man wearing a red mobcap who was blowing the trumpet, a string of revelers was winding its way toward us. They were dancing a *farandole*, a kind of line dance in which a group of people hold hands and skip around, following the leader. Before I knew it, the fellow who had found my hat grabbed my hand and we were part of the line of dancers. We all followed the trumpeter down a series of streets until we found ourselves in front of two very tall, very wide doors that were usually closed but had been opened for the occasion. It was the *caserne des pompiers*, the fire station, where the firemen were having their Bastille Day ball.

The fire trucks had been removed from the huge courtyard, which was surrounded on three sides by stairways and corridors that reached up four stories high. From the upper floors, strings of paper lanterns, striped in bright colors, were criss-crossed over the courtyard.  It looked as if the firmament had gone mad and replaced the stars with a crazy-quilt of colored paper.  In one corner a little band – an accordion, a drum, a clarinet and some strings – was sitting on a makeshift platform, cranking out polkas and waltzes.

We danced and danced.  I had no idea what time it was, where my friends were, or who I was dancing with.  Finally we paused to catch our breath, and he told me his name was Philippe Dutoit.  When I told him my name, he said asked me if I was related to "that modern American composer."  I wasn't, but I found it reassuring that Philippe knew something about modern music.

The next thing I knew, we were walking down the narrow streets to where he'd parked his Vespa.  I wanted to hop on behind him the way I'd seen French girls do, but my dress was too tight.  I had to hitch up my skirt and climb on as best I could.  I hoped he wouldn't notice, but just then he turned around and asked me where I lived.

The night air as it rushed by felt deliciously cool.  Philippe had to zigzag past empty wine bottles and piles of streamers littering the nearly empty streets.  I hung on to him with my arms around his waist.

When we got to my building, I wasn't sure what to do next.  He settled the matter by taking me in his arms and kissing me.  All those "one kiss and I'm yours" love song lyrics raced through my mind.  It was true.  I felt weak in the knees, unable to resist.  We went upstairs.

He led me to the nearest bed, which happened to be Hansli's bed but I wasn't about to protest.  Once we were lying on it, he encountered some surprises with my underwear.  I wouldn't have dared to wear a sheath dress without a panty girdle with garters and a waist-length bra. His reaction made it clear to me that French girls dressed differently, but he bravely went about the business of removing the various layers of latex. All I could do was lie there and worry about whether he would think I was a good lover or not.

I needn't have worried. Philippe was unstoppable. There was none of the hesitation and shyness I'd experienced with Frank. Philippe's unfamiliar touch thrilled me all over, and I gave myself to him joyfully. We smoked afterwards, like in the movies, and then he said he had to leave. I asked him if he'd call me and he said "Sure, what's your number?" He wrote it down, put it in his pocket, kissed me and left. I fell blissfully asleep.

The remaining weeks of July dragged into the hot beginnings of August. I waited to get a call from Philippe, and I waited to get my period. I got neither.

# V

# A CERTAIN IDEA OF FRANCE

"Toute ma vie je me suis fait une certaine idée de la France."
(All my life I've had in mind a certain idea of France.)

– Memoirs of General de Gaulle

Whether you took the elevator or walked up the two flights of stairs, the first thing you saw upon entering Valentin Productions was Germaine the telephone operator. Although she was tucked away in a small cubicle just off the waiting room, it was hard to take your eyes off her. Germaine had complete mastery of the switchboard, *le standard* – she was *la standardiste*. The *standard* consisted of a large vertical panel full of holes, into which a series of phone lines with tips like miniature fire hoses were plugged and unplugged. Her arms flailing as she criss-crossed the lines across the board, she looked like a crazed weaver following a pattern known only to her.

Amazingly, alongside her frenzied activity of connecting and disconnecting calls, she was able to hold a lively conversation with whoever was in the waiting room. She had a wealth of information about a wide variety of topics – the comings and goings of the people in the office, of course, but also the weather, politics and movie stars. She worked a ten-hour day uncomplainingly, juggling phone lines and gossip with equal gusto.

She seemed to know everything about everybody, even me. The first time I walked in and gave her my name, she knew I was the bilingual secretary who'd been recommended by the parents of Jean-François, the little boy I'd taught English to. I had been equivocal about taking the job. I needed the money if I wanted to stay in Paris, but I didn't like being a secretary. I'd done it in New York, at least long enough to earn the money to get me to Paris. And now here I was, being introduced to everyone as "the bilingual secretary".

I didn't really mind, though, because this was no ordinary office. It looked and felt more like a music store. The walls were decorated with record jackets and posters featuring Samy Valentin and his Sophomores smiling down on us. I didn't know what had become of the Sophomores, but Mr. V in person still looked good, now wearing business suits instead of a white tuxedo but as dapper and debonair as ever. His mellow but chirpy music – like Guy Lombardo peppered with Spike Jones zaniness – was no longer "top of the pops" but he was still a household name. Once an artist has created something that touches their hearts, the French are forever grateful and admirative. I was working for a famous man, and it was fun.

Since then I've learned that many famous people are no fun, so I'm glad I started out with Mr. V. A modest, soft-spoken man whose bald head and pleasant expression made him seem like a benign Buddha, he made his employees feel as if we all belonged to a special club. When I looked at film clips of Samy and his Sophomores, I got the impression that was how his musicians felt too. In business dealings he was shrewd and self-assured. The only time he would lose his cool was whenever his wife Lucienne, known as Lulu, showed up. Then he became tense and uncertain. Lulu was the mother of his two children, cute little girls dolled up like princesses. He doted on the girls, but Lulu seemed to turn him into a nervous wreck. Was he afraid of losing her to another man? Or was he having an affair himself?

Raoul, Mr. V's driver, hinted it was a game they played. She enjoyed making him suffer, and he needed the suffering to counterbalance his celebrity and success. Raoul was a master of innuendo. He never actually came out and said things that you could quote him on, he just dropped hints and you had to piece them together. He seemed to have definitely been in the Resistance during the war, and perhaps he'd gotten to know Mr. V at that time although I couldn't be sure.

The only thing straightforward about Raoul was his love of puns and corny jokes. He was overjoyed when I came to work for Valentin Productions because I gave him an opportunity (which he used endlessly) to pull the following stunt. He would ask me,

"Do you speak English?" and when I said "Yes" he would then say something (presumably something very vulgar) in French slang that I couldn't understand. That made him laugh uproariously. After a while I wouldn't answer him when he asked if I spoke English, but I would still fall for another of his gags. Just like anywhere else, the people in the office would greet each other with the formulaic "Bonjour, ça va?" (Hi, how's it going?). It wasn't something you thought about. You'd ask "ça va?" and the other person answered affirmatively, "ça va". But not Raoul. If you fell into his trap and asked "ça va?" he'd answer "ça varie" (it varies).

It varied for me too. I was happy with my job and thrilled to be living in Paris, but the aftermath of my Bastille Day fling was beginning to worry me. I had never dealt with the concept of pregnancy before, and I had no idea what to do. My corner drugstore had a special counter for lab tests and I hung around it, afraid to ask but hoping I'd overhear something useful. My strategy paid off when I saw a young woman bring in a bottle containing a urine sample. She asked for an albumin test and they told her to return the next day for the results. Summoning my courage, I asked the pharmacist what the albumin test was for. "It's for pregnancy," she replied. Bingo! The next day I brought in my bottle, and the day after that I was told the results were negative.

After work I went over to the Rue Fromentin to celebrate. I told Ursi and Fritz that the bottle of champagne (Monsieur Grégoire's special reserve) was because I'd had a winning lottery ticket. But later that evening, when Fritz went out to buy cigarettes, I told Ursi the real reason. Her jaw dropped – and a moment later mine dropped too when she told me the test I'd taken was only to measure albumin in pregnant women's urine. It didn't mean anything – I might very well be pregnant.

It was the first week of September, and Hansli was due back from his summer vacation in a few days. I was too preoccupied with my dilemma to even notice I'd forgotten to celebrate the anniversary of my first year in Paris. What was I going to do? Ursi had been in a similar situation and had tried all the usual tricks like drinking quarts of Schweppes Tonic – quinine is supposed to make you abort. She even took the extreme measure of climbing all the stairs to the top of the Eiffel Tower, but it didn't work. She finally had to go back to Switzerland to have an abortion there, unbeknownst to her parents. It didn't cost her anything because she was covered by Swiss health insurance. She had no other choice because in France abortion was illegal.

If indeed I was pregnant, a Swiss abortion would cost me a fortune – money I didn't have. I had to find a solution in France. Running a quick inventory of the French people I knew who could help me, the only one I could come up with was Claire Lagrange, Mr. V's personal secretary. I found Claire somewhat daunting. Her manner was pleasant, not aloof, and she seemed to be about my age. But she was always so perfectly dressed, coiffed and made up – not a hair out of place as they say – and her self-assurance was such that she made me feel messy and inadequate. Still, if she could cope so well with Mr. V's affairs, maybe she could help me too.

I took a deep breath and invited her for coffee at the café on the ground floor of our office building. I couldn't help looking at her intently. There she was, her blonde hair curving into the turtleneck of her white cable-knit sweater which was neatly tucked into a dark skirt topped off by a patent leather belt to show off her tiny waist. I could see myself in comparison, overweight and overwrought, and I didn't know where to start. She leaned forward expectantly, as if to make clear that she knew we'd come here for a reason. So I blurted it out.

When she frowned my heart sank, but I wasn't prepared for her question. "Are you a good liar?" Without waiting for an answer, she went on to explain that her family gynecologist could help me, on one condition. He must never find out how I got his name. Performing abortions was illegal in France, and a breach of confidentiality could put him in prison. He wouldn't take me as a patient unless I was absolutely trustworthy, and convincing him of that was up to me.

As I thanked her profusely she added, "Don't let him scare you. He's got a gruff manner, but he's a wonderful guy." I kept her words in mind when I found myself in Dr. Guichard's office. As he glared at me across his desk, I kept telling myself I shouldn't let him scare me. His bushy eyebrows and shaggy downturned mustache were off-putting, but when I explained that I needed to know if I was pregnant or not, he merely nodded.

Then the tricky part began. Why had I come to him? His office was in Passy, the upscale neighborhood that was miles away from where I lived and worked. I had to tell him I just happened to walk by and saw his nameplate on the door. But why was I there at all? As luck would have it, Dr. Guichard's office was right around the corner from a store I'd heard about that sold American sheets at reasonable prices. For some reason, bed linens were incredibly expensive in France. A few stores imported American sheets but they were expensive too – except in that store in Passy. I'd never actually shopped there because my parents sent me sheets from the States. But it convinced Dr. Guichard who almost smiled when he said, "Ah yes, the American sheets. You are American yourself, are you not?"

Having gotten past the confidentiality hurdle, he agreed to examine me. His examination showed that I was two months pregnant. "Gee, he's good," I thought to myself. "That's it, right on the dot."

He looked at me quizzically. "Does this news make you happy?"

This was the really tough part. I had planned on telling the truth about how I got pregnant, but when I looked at him I suddenly realized the truth might not work. Performing an abortion was risky for him, and he might not want to take a chance on an idiotic girl who got knocked up during a one-night stand with a total stranger. So I found myself telling him about a doomed relationship I'd been having with an older man who I thought was serious about me until I discovered he was married. I'd already decided to break up with him, but now... I felt so sorry for myself, it wasn't hard to burst into tears.

It worked. He cautiously asked me if I wanted to keep the baby and I shook my head, sobbing. Then we moved on to the next stage – discussing the abortion procedure itself. It wouldn't cost me a fortune but it would take all the money I'd saved up, in cash. I'd need two appointments with him. The first one could take place during the day when his assistant/receptionist was in the office. The second one had to take place after hours, when only he and I were present. Once the appointments were set up, he gave me a form to take to work so I'd be excused for three days for medical reasons.

I was so busy getting my money out of the bank, setting up my medical leave at work, thanking Claire and generally feeling relieved that my problem was about to be solved, that by the time I showed up for my first appointment I hadn't given any thought to what I was actually doing. The purpose of the first visit was to place something called a *sonde* (a probe) the purpose of which, he said, was to widen the opening of my cervix so he could operate better.

The day the *sonde* was placed, I didn't have to go back to work and I didn't want to go home because Hansli was there and he didn't know what was going on. So I went for a walk in the park near Dr. Guichard's office. It was a warm, sunny afternoon and the park was full of young mothers pushing baby carriages or watching their toddlers play in the sandbox. Motherhood suddenly seemed like such a magical state, a privilege bestowed only on the fortunate. Today I was among them, but tomorrow it would be over.

I tried to imagine what the child I was carrying would look like, and realized with a shock that if the baby didn't resemble my side of the family I would have no way of knowing who he or she did look like. I would never see Philippe again. I didn't even remember his last name. How could I ever explain that to my child? How could I raise a baby in those conditions? Yes, but was that a justification for killing the child?

I tried to reason with myself. This pregnancy was merely a biological accident, the product of a casual encounter that resulted in an involuntary fertilization. I couldn't feel impersonal about my baby, but I couldn't feel good about being pregnant either. I had no particular ambitions for my own future. But that very aimlessness, combined with a total void on the father's side (not to mention my own family – my God, how would they react?) didn't augur well for the little person in my belly. I shook my head sadly as the weight of the realization swept over me. I had made the correct decision and I had no other choice. In Dr. Guichard's hands I felt certain I would come out of this all right, and go on to have another child in the future under better circumstances. As I walked out of the park I said goodbye to the baby I would never have. I didn't know it, but the *sonde* had already entered the uterus and killed the foetus.

The next evening Dr. Guichard received me as if it was the Occupation and we were Resistance fighters. Once he'd locked the door behind me, he explained the procedure. He couldn't give me a heavy anesthesia because he was working alone. He would give me a shot that would deaden the pain somewhat, but

I would have to remain conscious. The D&C procedure consisted of carefully removing the contents of my uterus without causing any permanent damage. For this he would use a small, long-handled tool, "rather like making melon balls with a melon-cutting spoon".

When the shot had taken effect, he began. It was hard work for him and excruciating for me, even with the pain killer. It seemed to go on forever. He told me I had an unusually large placenta. "When you have a baby you can keep, he'll be well fed," he said with a wry smile. I felt like my guts were being ripped out, spoonful by spoonful. When it got so bad I was afraid I'd scream he sensed it and stopped, patting the inside of my thighs and telling me how brave I was. Once we took a cigarette break. I usually didn't smoke but I really needed that cigarette.

Finally it was over. He gave me a hug and a short speech about how I should keep in mind the biological unfairness between men and women. I promised to return the following week for a check-up and to be fitted for a diaphragm – although at that moment in time I would have gladly signed a contract agreeing never to have sex again. Then Dr. Guichard called me a taxi and I went home.

With Hansli back in Paris, home was not a quiet or restful place. During the day when he was practicing I was normally at the office and didn't notice it. But our upstairs neighbor Madame Nozet hated it, and it turned her into our sworn enemy. I had first sensed hostility in Mme. Nozet shortly after we moved in and she slipped the following note under our door: "Sachez, Madame, que vous êtes en France et qu'ici on a des lois. On ne jette rien par la fenêtre." (Madam, I want you to know you're in France and here we have laws. We do not throw things out the window.) I didn't feel compelled to thank her – I knew where I was, and the fact that the French had laws was not a surprise either. As for throwing things out the window, I had no idea what she was talking about – or where she got her information, given that she lived upstairs of us. So I simply ignored her missive.

Piqued, perhaps, by my lack of response, she took to expressing her outrage in other ways. Whenever Hansli started to practice, she would turn on her radio full blast to drown him out. Evenings, when we listened to music on our radio, she would drop heavy objects that landed with a disruptive thud above our heads. Sometimes her husband would creep downstairs and suddenly pound on our door, shouting imprecations. At first we were terrified, feeling as if we were being arrested by the Gestapo. After a while we got used to it, and pushed our temerity to the point of jerking the door open while he was pounding on it. He got red in the face and wordlessly rushed upstairs. From then on he made only sneak attacks, and escaped before we could confront him again.

The daytime cacaphony (Hansli vs. Mme. Nozet) and evening poundings did not create a relaxing environment in which to recoup from my abortion. So after a day of attempted rest I gladly returned to the office. It had gradually dawned on me how fortunate I'd been to stumble into a job at Valentin Productions. For one thing, it allowed me to get work papers, and that in itself was a huge piece of luck. Starting, as I did, to work in France at the same time de Gaulle came into office, I was barely able to squeak through before it became virtually impossible for Americans to get work permits.

De Gaulle's attitude toward the USA was not exactly friendly. He referred to NATO as "ce machin" (that thingamabob) and he made all American troops stationed in France since the end of the war leave the country. His "France first" approach was apparent everywhere. Whenever Hansli and I went to the movies, the feature was always preceded by a short film about the French building a new bridge or a supersonic plane or a spacecraft or whatever – we grouped them under the general heading of "yet another triumph of French technology." De Gaulle took to appearing on TV and speaking to the nation as if they were all members of a private club. His speeches always began "Françaises, français" and ended with a resounding "Vive la France!" Despite his nationalism, he was pro-European and was often seen in public with "Der Alte", Germany's chancellor Adenauer. Both men seemed anxious to erase their countries' past differences in an effort to build a new Europe.

The new Europe ultimately emerged, of course, and as it did, Americans were increasingly excluded. Luckily for me, when Samy Valentin decided to hire me, he was able to pull strings to get my work papers. I was never able to find out exactly what strings he pulled, but I knew it had to do with the Resistance. My instructions were clear. I was to go to a certain government ministry, ask to see a Monsieur Jardin, speak when spoken to, and say yes to everything he asked me. Mr. V assured me the rest would take care of itself.

When I went to the address I'd been given, I found myself standing outside a building with high walls guarded by soldiers. Inside was the courtyard you always saw in newsreels where important people arrive and depart in black limousines. A few steps led inside to an impressive hallway lined with mirrors, guarded by a uniformed official. Shortly after I announced the purpose of my visit, a mirrored door opened and I was ushered into an elegant room that was Monsieur Jardin's office. It was gorgeously furnished in Louis XV furniture, and beyond the brocaded drapes I caught glimpses of huge flower beds. I would have loved to rush to the window to see more, but restrained myself.

Monsieur Jardin greeted me effusively. "Mademoiselle Glass, I understand you are the cousin of Jack Curtis." Following instructions, I said yes. He embraced me and kissed me on both cheeks. "Ah, ce cher Jack", he mused as if lost in remembrance. "He was a great friend of France." I assumed he was referring to the war. "And a great friend of ours too." Did that mean he and Mr. V and this Jack Curtis were all in the war together? "And now you want to work here?" I assented. He complimented me on my excellent French – puzzling in view of the fact that I'd said little more than "oui" – and assured me it would be taken care of. I barely had time to murmur "merci" before I was shown out of the office. What in the world was that all about?

Whatever it was, it worked. Within days I was issued a permanent work permit, and my temporary sojourn permit was extended to "privileged resident" status. Obviously, Mr. V had clout. And there was more to him than the jolly smile on his famous face hinted at. Quite by chance, I was given a rare glimpse into another side of his personality. One fall day I volunteered to buy office supplies at a shop down the street. It was located opposite a concert hall, but that morning the hall was occupied by large numbers of people in dark clothes holding prayer books. When I saw the yarmulkes it clicked – today was Yom Kippur. Holding my purchases and looking discreetly through the shop window, I observed the scene. I was curious to find out more about French Jews.

Jews in France kept a very low profile. Less than twenty years after the end of the war, their memories of militia roundups and extermination camps were still vivid. In a Catholic country with a long history of anti-Semitism, Jews were not tempted to flaunt their presence. There were no Jewish comedians on TV, no delis serving bagels and lox. I did discover a *charcuterie* selling gefilte fish and corned beef, but the sign on their window said "Oriental specialties". So I was not surprised when the men who had attended Yom Kippur services in the concert hall took off their yarmulkes as soon as they reached the street. But I was surprised to recognize, among the newly bared heads, the familiar bald pate of Mr. V.

Was it really him? The face I saw was sunken and subdued. His head was bowed. He stood in isolation, as if weighed down by the woes of the world. On Yom Kippur, the Day of Atonement, he had taken on himself his own failings and those of his fellow humans. From that moment on, I felt I had an insight into the real Samy Valentin. Whenever I saw his famous smile, I knew it came from a wellspring of suffering and compassion.

The work I did at Valentin Productions didn't put me in contact with him that often. As his personal secretary, Claire Lagrange handled his correspondence and day-to-day business. I was brought in as a bilingual secretary because Mr. V had contacts, usually in English, with foreign publishers who bought the rights to the many tunes he'd composed for his Sophomores. After Mr. V discovered that I had a background in music, he enlarged my job. My small office was stacked high with sheet music that included not only Sophomores tunes but also film music and popular songs that Mr. V had composed for other singers. The stuff had piled up haphazardly, and he asked me to make sense of it. So I would sit there, scanning the lyrics and humming the tunes, and then file the piece in one of the numerous categories I'd created such as "love song – serious", "love song – humorous", "nonsense song – real words", "nonsense song – fake words", etc. This filing system made it easier for me to locate a piece when someone requested it, or to offer it to a buyer when an opportunity arose. I also kept an alphabetical list of all the titles, mostly to placate Louise the file clerk. At first I felt sure it was her disapproval of my fanciful classifications that made her scowl at me all the time. She seemed nice enough with other people, but whenever she saw me her face darkened. Even after I created the alphabetical file, she would still cluck and mutter and shake her head at me, like a crabby old librarian who wants you to shush.

Far from looking like an old librarian, Louise had the fragile charm of a china doll, with blonde curls and pale eyes. Her attitude toward me didn't make any sense. Since Claire and I were now in the habit of having lunch together several times a week, I asked her about it. Claire burst out laughing.

"She resents you, all right, and there isn't a thing you can do about it. It's because you're American."

I still didn't understand, so Claire patiently explained that Louise was a card-carrying member of the French Communist Party. As such, she was committed to the defense of the working class and the overthrow of imperialism. In that context, the good guys were the Russians and the bad guys were the Americans.

That was something I could understand. The Cold War was well underway when I left the States, and there were even repercussions in my family. My cousin Bert, who was a professional jazz musician, hung out with people my mother didn't approve of. She said darkly that those people were "pinkos", and Bert risked getting the reputation of being a "fellow traveler". Now that I was living in Paris, I often met Americans who had been blacklisted by McCarthy and couldn't find work in the States. Since many of those exiles were artists and musicians, it gave me the impression that being a leftist was a sign of creative merit.

Not being an artist myself, I felt no need to get involved in political matters. But it didn't seem right that Louise should dislike me – or, for that matter, any other Americans – just because of our nationality. I tried to reason with her. I knew better than to mention the Marshall Plan; since arriving in France, I'd learned that for every French person who felt deep gratitude to the

Americans for their aid, there were equal numbers of people who resented it as an attempt to "buy them off". But warts and all, every American I could think of was basically a nice person. I said as much to Louise, whose expression changed from scorn to pity.

"How naïve you are," she said. "But just you wait. Right now you think you're invulnerable, but it won't last. Imperialism will be crushed. Just you wait." She trembled slightly as she spoke, and I could see how passionately sincere she was. I was about a foot taller than Louise and probably twice her weight, but she looked up at me fearlessly and resolutely. Unable and unwilling to come up with a snappy rejoinder, I shrugged my shoulders and let the matter drop.

In the States, I had never given much thought to politics. When I became old enough to vote, everybody I knew liked Ike so I liked him too. At the time, the smart-alecky egghead Adlai Stevenson didn't seem as appealing as smiley old Ike. But once I got to France, I began to realize that for the French, politics is a big deal. This struck me particularly forcefully when Claire invited me home for dinner and I met her parents. Her father, Jean-Paul Lagrange, was a journalist who looked strangely familiar to me until I realized that he looked a lot like Adlai Stevenson – smart, bald and short. His wife was slightly taller than he. It was obvious from the way they looked at each other that they loved one another, but their dinner table conversation was witty and acerbic. Hélène Lagrange was particularly fond of giving her husband barbed replies. When, during the cheese course, he cut open the camembert and declared it to be under-ripe, she retorted, "I wasn't inside it when I bought it."

Politics was a favorite topic of conversation in the Lagrange household. The women – Claire and her mother – tended to be more moderate and less critical of the current regime. The men – Claire's brother Alain and their father – seemed to love sniping at De Gaulle, although for different reasons. From his inside vantage point as a journalist, Jean-Paul was wise to what he called "De Gaulle's tricks". He told a wonderful story of how the General behaved in a press conference. When he was asked a question he didn't want to answer, he would respond grandly, "*Je vais grouper les questions*" (I am going to group the questions) and of course he never got around to the bothersome ones.

Alain's criticism of the General was based on the events taking place in Algeria. Alain was in his last year of studies at the prestigious HEC (*Hautes Etudes Commerciales*), the French equivalent of Harvard Business School. He and his classmates felt that Algeria was a prized possession, the last colonial jewel in France's crown after the loss of Indo-China. Although de Gaulle had been brought into office with the expectation that he would maintain *l'Algérie française*, there were now suspicions that his real intentions were quite the opposite.

I had been in France for over a year but I had never been invited into a French home before, and I had trouble following the conversation. It sounded to me more like a televised political debate than family chit-chat. As I struggled to master the vocabulary, I realized I had no political views of my own. So when the Lagranges turned to me expectantly, I decided to ask them for help in solving a mystery. Why was Louise so hostile to me?

Louise? Claire quickly explained that she was "that CGT activist at the office". Again I didn't understand. I thought Claire had told me she was a Communist. That was when I learned that in France, labor unions have political affiliations. If for instance you are a mechanic, you can belong to a Communist union or a Socialist one or a Center-Right one or a Christian one, all of them mechanics' unions. The CGT was the Communist union, with branches in factories and offices throughout the country.

"They're all hard-line Stalinists," added Alain. "They all think Papa Joe is their savior, and they refuse to admit that he's turned into a ruthless dictator." Joe Stalin a ruthless dictator? I remembered seeing pictures of him at Yalta with Roosevelt and Churchill, and he looked nice enough. Oh well.

I was relieved when the dinner table talk turned to gossip, the kind the French call "*qui-baise-qui*" or "who's screwing who". There again I had nothing to contribute, but it was more fun to listen to. Claire turned out to be quite an authority on movie star scandals (I suspect her source was Germaine the receptionist, but it could have been Mr. V himself) whereas her father, understandably for a journalist, had the latest poop on public figures. It seemed to me that the sexual peccadilloes of the stars only increased ticket sales, while those of the politicians ended up costing taxpayer money. "Did you hear they're building a new highway from here to the Dordogne? Do you know why? It's because the Minister of Justice has a *résidence secondaire* there where he's keeping a mistress and two illegitimate children."

That was something else I learned about from the Lagranges – the Parisians and their "secondary residences". The idea was to get out of town – not just for summer vacation, Christmas and Easter but as often as possible. Since France is a Catholic country there are a lot of three-day weekends such as Good Friday, Easter Monday and Ascension Day which afford owners of country houses in far-flung regions like Normandy and Brittany an opportunity to get away from Paris. Now that France is crisscrossed with freeways and superhighways you can get farther much faster, so even more people have country houses now than they did before. But even then, the roads leading out of Paris were clogged every Friday evening with people whose country houses were close enough to be used on weekends.

The Lagranges were in that fortunate category. Their "country house" was in fact a full-fledged estate of nearly 300 acres, less than 100 miles from Paris. The first time I went there I was overwhelmed, not because it was fancy or pretentious but because I found it so incredibly appealing. It was, in fact, a working farm complete with animals, crops and a family of tenant farmers, the Martins, who ran the place. They lived in an adorable cottage like you see on postcards, with blue shutters and geraniums on the windowsills. Next to their cottage was a small henhouse, in which the chickens nested at night although during the day they pecked busily around the house. There was also a pigsty with its own enclosed courtyard containing a trough for the swill and a mudhole for the happy swine to roll around in, and separate small barns for the goats and sheep. During the winter the livestock stayed in their barns, eating hay that had been harvested for them during the summer, but as soon as winter was over the sheep and goats were allowed to graze outside in the fields, along with the cows.

The estate had been in Madame Lagrange's family for four generations. Her mother, Madame Villeret, known to everyone as Mamie, still lived in the manor house, a large stone structure that was unpretentious but imposing – like Mamie herself. The building was shaped like a squared-off U, with the family residence occupying the base of the U and the two wings reaching out like arms to embrace the courtyard. One wing had been transformed by Mamie into a series of playrooms for her children and grandchildren – there were books and toys in one room, a billiard table in another, and the third room had card tables and games. The other wing was still used as a barn, providing housing for the farm's three milk cows in winter as well as storage for the bales of hay. Perhaps because of the intoxicating smell of the hay, Alain and I loved horsing around in the barn as if we were kids. We would play hide-and-seek, leaping out from behind a haystack, or tussling in a mock wrestling match. This was uncharacteristic behavior for me, and even more so for him, the serious intellectual and HEC student, but it provided a nice release for both of us. There were sexual undertones, of course, but from time to time we'd stop, out of breath, and he'd look at me with such a wise, knowing look. It reminded me of the man in the bus who'd said, "No, mademoiselle, I won't do it. But... je regrette!"

Being at Mamie's farm transported me into another world. As much as I loved Paris, I discovered that I loved rural France even more. I loved the house itself, with the musty smells of its seemingly endless nooks and crannies. I loved the way the back of the house opened onto a ramshackle garden that sloped down to a river. Not just any river – the Seine! But most of all I loved the farm itself. It introduced me to a whole new concept of the relationship between humans and nature, a harmonious concept in which beauty and practicality were intermingled.

The farmers were extremely orderly and ingenious– every scrap of land was used, and each crop was set out in neat rows. The string beans literally grew on strings that were laced onto wooden frames. The peas grew more riotously, wrapping their tendrils around bushy stakes – the tips of tree branches stuck in the ground. Asparagus shot up from raised beds. Other asparagus spears – the fatter, white kind – were hidden under carefully tended mounds of dirt, as were Belgian endive, with only the tips showing. Many of the vegetable patches were edged with parsley, both practical and attractive. Others sported nasturtiums, which I thought were merely decorative until I discovered that everything about them is edible – the leaves taste like watercress, the flowers can be added to salads, and the seeds can be pickled in vinegar like capers. Surrounded by such exuberant vegetation, I felt as if Sparrow's "doodling" had come to life all around me.

The fruit orchard was a marvel. Grape vines were gracefully trained over a long arched tunnel with benches underneath, making a perfect place to read. Various species of apple and pear trees were espaliered to make harvesting easier. The harvesting of cherries was often left to the farmers' children, who clambered merrily in the branches to pick the ripe fruit. I discovered a new kind of peach, called *pêche de vigne*, particularly delicious when poached in wine. I also discovered that in France a plum is more than a prune waiting to dry up. French plums can be big or little, round or oval, and come in various shades of green, yellow, pink and purple. Some are best for jam, some for pie, while others are distilled into liqueurs.

The farm also grew berries of all kinds. Sophisticated Claire turned out to be a first-rate berry picker, and she initiated me in that skill. The currents – red, white and black – were grown on bushes planted close enough together for cross-pollination to occur. The fruit hung down in inviting clusters, but I soon learned that if you pulled on a current it was likely to crush between your fingers. Claire used a small knife to cut off the clusters, and then later in the kitchen the stems were carefully removed.

Picking blackberries provided a different kind of challenge. The vines grew in a wild tangle that was trimmed to form a hedge, but the biggest, most delicious looking berries always seemed to be deep within the thorny hedge or so high as to be just out of reach. I tried to pick them anyway, snagging my clothes and pricking my berry-stained fingers, while Claire judiciously gathered the more accessible ones. The berries I liked picking the most were the raspberries. They grew more or less in rows, and although the canes had thorns, they didn't hurt like the blackberry thorns did. The raspberries were better behaved, too. If you pulled on them gently and they resisted, that meant they weren't quite ripe yet. A raspberry detaches itself perfectly from the whitish cone it grows on when it's ripe, and if no one picks it then it just withers up. Whereas a ripe blackberry will often fall to the ground just as you reach for it, because you've bumped the vine. But in my opinion those pesky blackberries make the best jam in the whole world, and the taste of that jam (or even the thought of it) instantly transports me to the French countryside.

Those wonderful weekends at Mamie's farm – and there were many of them, thanks to the generous hospitality of the Lagrange family – were very therapeutic for me. I gradually began to heal from the pain of my "interrupted pregnancy" – the French medical term for what had happened. To use another French expression, "*Je me sentais bien dans ma peau*" – literally, I felt good in my skin. Life was good – not perfect, maybe, but certainly not bad. I had a job and work papers, enough money to get by, and a new circle of friends who were making me feel welcome in France. I also continued to see Ursi and Fritz, and I still shared the apartment with Hansli, but now they were in a separate world. I learned that it's quite easy in France to lead several lives. Their whole way of being leans in that direction. Being nosy is considered extremely rude, and people choose to be vague about their personal details. If you don't want to introduce a person you're with, you can just say "This is a friend" and no one will press for the name. I instinctively chose not to mention Hansli to the Lagranges, and so the matter never came up. By this time Hansli was involved with his own circle of new friends from the Conservatory, so it worked out well.

One thing was still noticeably lacking from my life, and that was a boyfriend. A few times, through the office, I went on dates with Americans. But they were either interesting people who were just passing through, or people I found to be a drag ("Us ex-pats gotta stick together, huh, kid.") Where Frenchmen were concerned, I was still wary about getting involved physically, and that's all that most of them were interested in. I did notice, however, that I was attracting more interest than before. Not only I'd lost most of the weight I needed to lose, I'd actually begun to pay attention to my appearance. The person I had to thank for that was Claire's mother. Hélène Lagrange was a tall, big-boned woman who was less attractive than her daughter but she always looked incredibly chic. At first I thought she spent a fortune on clothes, but gradually I learned her tricks. She had a basic wardrobe of beautifully made suits and dresses that were copies of *haute couture* models made for her by a dressmaker. The real secret was accessories – simple gold jewelry which you can wear over and over again, silk scarves used in a variety of ways to make an old outfit look new, the use of color to draw attention to your face rather than your clothes. As soon as I could afford it, I had Mme. Lagrange's dressmaker make a suit for me too, a Chanel knockoff whose straight skirt and boxy jacket hid my remaining "problem areas" and showed off my legs, which had always been slim. I began getting compliments on my tiny ankles. I loved the idea that some part of me might be considered tiny.

I also began to realize that the way you dressed showed what class you belonged to. Workers were usually seen in *bleus de travail*, blue cotton overalls. Students wore oversized sweaters and tight pants. The kind of clothes I had begun to wear marked me as a member of the *bourgeoisie*. And when I paid closer attention to the Martins, the farmers at Mamie's, I realized their clothes—and their whole lifestyle—showed them to be peasants. The peasant class in France exists even to this day, and they are a proud race. Like farmers anywhere, they work virtually around the clock and their fortunes are tied to the uncontrollable forces of nature. In France, their feudal status was prolonged well into the 20th century, as most peasants were tenant farmers for wealthy landowners. Banks only began to lend money to farmers to buy their land after World War II. Perhaps because of this, they banded together to form a distinct class, with their own customs and dress. The Martins still looked like those peasants you see in 19th century

French paintings with their wooden clogs and straw hats. Every Sunday they dressed up to go to church. In the old days the peasants of each region had special dress-up clothes, usually consisting of a long skirt, an embroidered blouse and a white, starched lace coif for the women and velvet pants and an embroidered vest or jacket for the men. In modern times these costumes gave way to a far less attractive dress code – the men in ready-made suits (usually ill-fitting) and the women in flower-printed nylon dresses and white shoes, which seemed to represent for them the ultimate in chic despite the fact that they were wildly impractical. I figured those white shoes were a modern-day interpretation of the traditional white lace coifs – a symbol of the pristine purity that is considered to be a feminine virtue, and a proof of the owner's ability to keep them clean and new-looking.

These realizations came to me when I was far from Mamie's farm. There is a wonderful French expression, *l'esprit de l'escalier*, which literally means "staircase wit". They use it to refer to those times (often, in my case) when you can't think of a clever answer to something, but when you're on your way downstairs (i.e. after it's too late) you think of what you should have said. I have a personal variation of staircase wit. When I'm in a place or situation, I usually let events wash over me without reacting too much. But later, in another time and place, the meaning of what I had previously experienced finally dawns on me. Thus it was that my reflections on the dress code of French peasants occurred in a place that was very far from Mamie's farm – Stouffer's Restaurant in Cleveland, where my parents had taken me for dinner.

Yes, I was back in Cleveland for a visit. Over a year had gone by since my parents had visited me in Paris. Because I was now entitled to the four-week vacation every French employee got in those days (it has since increased to five weeks) I let myself be convinced that it was time to go home again. I had to admit I was pretty excited. Transatlantic air travel, which has since become grindingly familiar, was new to me. I'd originally gone from New York to Paris by boat, but now I returned by plane, overnighting in what was now being called The Big Apple before taking another plane to what was still being called The Mistake by the Lake.

What a thrill it was to be back in New York. Everything looked so fresh and energetic. The cars were big and shiny – all American cars, of course, but I'd grown used to seeing vehicles the size of the Citroen 2CV or the Fiat 500, and in Paris what they called a "belle américaine" was always pointed to and stared at, particularly when it tried to negotiate its chromed volume through the narrow winding streets of the Left Bank. The people seemed to be wearing much brighter colors than in Paris. Even the "man in the gray flannel suit" executives seemed purposeful and upbeat as they strode along. Clearly, this was a place where anything was possible. And I was part of it again. My heart swelled with pride at being American, and my ear again got tuned to the sounds of the language so that I didn't react with surprise whenever I heard English spoken.

Mother, who often came to New York on business, had an account at the Barbizon Plaza Hotel on Central Park South and had called from Cleveland to reserve a room for me there. Not having slept on the plane, I gratefully sank into sleep as soon as I reached the hotel. When I woke up, I discovered to my amazement that something about being in New York (the sounds? the smells? the feel of the place?) had projected me back in time so that I woke up in a panic, convinced I was late for my old job in Rockefeller Plaza. I quickly realized my mistake but got up anyway and went out for breakfast, since I was in a city whose breakfasts are the best and cheapest you can find anywhere.

Once out on the street, another realization swept over me. Although my watch said 11AM, in New York it was six hours earlier. Undaunted, I was able to locate a coffee shop at the bottom of Fifth Avenue that was just opening up. A nice young man served me breakfast, and since I was the only customer at 5AM, we chatted. When it came to the inevitable discussion about the weather, I had to admit that I hadn't been in town. "Where were you?" he asked, and when I said, "Paris" his eyes opened wide.

I finished my breakfast, paid and headed up Fifth Avenue to do some window shopping. As I looked admiringly at the imaginative displays of FAO Schwartz, I heard footsteps and turned to see the coffee shop guy running toward me, waving his arms. Had I forgotten my umbrella or something? "Miss, wait, when can I see you?" What in the world did he mean? Gasping for breath, he blurted it out. "I mean, you live in Paris, right, so I figured maybe we could go out tonight". I turned on my heels without so much as speaking to him, checked out of the hotel and arrived at the airport in plenty of time to catch my plane for Cleveland.

If Cleveland had changed, it wasn't for the better. When I was a girl, downtown was such an exciting place to me. The Statler Hotel was considered the epitome of elegance and the two big movie theatres, the Ohio and the State, further down Euclid Avenue provided the finest in entertainment. Sometimes mother would even take me to a live performance at one of the theatres in Playhouse Square. Now the once-fine buildings looked shabby and neglected, and all of downtown showed alarming signs of decline. In contrast, the outlying regions of the suburbs, which in my day had hardly been more than open fields with an occasional gas station, were built up and thriving. The Stouffer's where we went to dinner wasn't the original downtown one, but a big new one in a bustling recently-built shopping center of which mother was very proud. In her vocabulary, open land as nature made it was "unimproved". Ugly but functional buildings such as stores or parking structures were called "improvements".

I realized with dismay that returning to Cleveland meant playing the game mother's way. In Paris she had been, literally, on foreign ground and although she made demands, she couldn't have her own way all the time. Here it was different. She had an agenda for me, and I was expected to stick to it unquestioningly. Her list of activities included dragging me along to endless business meetings, shopping for things I wasn't interested in buying, and "family obligations" such as visiting great-aunts in nursing homes or putting flowers on graves. The fact that I had friends to see or things I wanted to do by myself was of absolutely no interest to her. It took less than two days for me to stop feeling like a self-sufficient, independent person. I was again enslaved to mother's doctrine of total subservience.

Daddy and I immediately reverted to our system of meeting in bars in order to have real conversations. He questioned me eagerly about events in France, and for the first time I was able to measure the difficulty of his life in Cleveland with mother. I simply hadn't thought about it before. Now that my own life was so much richer, I felt like an escaped prisoner coming back to talk to a former fellow inmate. My conscience was especially bad because I knew that when I was twelve, Daddy actually left home for a while. At the time, I didn't understand why he eventually came back. Later he explained that he ran into me downtown and I looked so sad, he realized it was unfair of him to leave me alone with mother.

Now I had done the same to him. But Daddy was serene. He talked about having discovered Mexico as a new great place to spend his vacation time alone and practice his Spanish, now that Castro had made it impossible for him to return to Havana. He talked about retiring in a few years and being able to travel even more. I refrained from asking whether he intended to take mother along, but I sensed that it was quite possible he wouldn't.

We found we had a new topic to giggle about – Cleveland. Daddy proudly displayed a recent copy of the Cleveland Plain Dealer whose headline article was about Eisenhower visiting Paris. The article described how our president, along with De Gaulle, rode in triumph down the Champs-Elysées – which the paper parenthetically described as "the Euclid Avenue of Paris."

I had a story to match his. Walking downtown a few days earlier, I had been stopped by a policeman who accused me of jaywalking and asked me for ID. From a reflex acquired in Paris, I was carrying my passport so I showed it to him. He had obviously never seen an American passport before. He looked at the front and back cover, then opened it at random to a page that said, "This passport is not valid for travel in Hungary."

"Are you Hungarian?" he asked. The absurdity of it was irresistible. There we were, speaking Cleveland-accented English to one another. Besides, my family was of Hungarian origin.

"Yes," I said.

He apologized profusely for having stopped me, launched into a long description of what the lines in the street meant, then sent me on my way with the hope that I would enjoy my visit to Cleveland.

There were parts of my visit I actually did enjoy – the time I spent with my sorority sisters from college, the Animal Crackers. Beaver, happily married and four months pregnant, braved mother's objections and whisked me away whenever she could. At first we just chattered happily, as if we had never been apart. But the first time we went to a tea room  where we used to go when we were in college, the reality hit me – Sparrow was gone. It didn't seem possible. She was as young as me, and her life was over. How could that be? Beaver showed me a picture of

Sparrow's daughter, the only picture she had, and explained that Robert's family had decided to raise the child in Detroit. For one wild moment I thought of contacting them and trying somehow to make the little girl understand who her mother had been. Beaver knew what I was thinking. "No, Bear, we tried, we really did. But the family made it clear they wanted no contact with any of us."

Briskly changing the subject, she told me about Owl, the intellectual, who was now in upper New York State getting a master's in library science. Apparently she had just met a young man who shared her interest in medieval poetry. As for Bambi and Colt, they both lived in a Cleveland suburb called Chagrin Falls. Both were married to engineers, and both had a child – a boy for Bambi, a girl for Colt – who were now toddlers. The plan was for us to all get together on the occasion of a party – Beaver mentioned what kind of party but the name didn't register – that Bambi was throwing at her house.

She and her husband had bought a recently built, boxy two-story house with aluminum siding which didn't look very different from any of the other new homes in the neighborhood, except that a large bouquet of multi-colored balloons was tied to their mailbox. Inside, the living and dining rooms were festooned with streamers, and there was even a banner that said "Welcome Home Bear" which nearly brought me to tears. For a long time we all hugged and giggled and hugged some more. Most of the girls hadn't changed a bit, except for Colt who had gotten quite plump. That became understandable when I learned she had started a catering business specializing in cake decorating. I too am a person who can't cook without tasting.

The girls all claimed I looked terrific, very sophisticated, very French. Of course I'd been unable to resist wearing my fake Chanel suit, and it had exactly the effect I'd hoped for. They asked all kinds of silly questions, like "Do you dream in French?" and "Have you met Brigitte Bardot?" It was great fun. I spent some time making polite conversation with some of Bambi's neighbors who'd been invited too. Colt was being kept busy running after her little girl, who had decided to try to grab all the streamers. Bambi's little boy was better behaved, but she was busy being a hostess and making sure we all had punch and cookies.

After about an hour she clapped her hands and told us to all sit down because the demonstration was about to begin. I had no idea what she was talking about – this was hardly the setting for a political demonstration. When we were all seated in the living room she began piling funny-looking items in plastic on the coffee table. They were in various shapes and sizes and colors, and each of them had a lid. Bambi was rapturously explaining the uses for each item.

"What is this stuff?" I whispered to Beaver.

"It's called Tupperware, everyone is going crazy about it. Bambi's a representative."

As I listened to Bambi's spiel, and Beaver explained the intricacies of the Tupperware sales system, I felt a chill of estrangement. My sorority sisters and I were clearly on different paths. I wasn't married, I had no children, and I wasn't even interested in a contraption that could keep my leftovers fresh. Should I be? My innards ached with the memory of my abortion. But my child, had it been born, would not have been raised in a setting like this. No suburban three-bedroom house, no two-car garage, no Tupperware. I tried to appear involved, but I had to admit to myself that as happy as I was to see the Animal Crackers again, I was bored. With a pang, I thought of Sparrow. She had committed suicide! Was this what drove her to it?

Toward the end of the party, I was sent deeper into gloom when Bambi pulled something out of a drawer and handed it to me, saying she'd kept it for me. It was a newspaper clipping announcing the birth of twins to Mr. and Mrs. Franklin Edmund Hartford III, formerly of Cleveland Heights, now living in Dallas.

I hardly needed to be reminded of Frank. Even without Bambi's self-styled clipping service, I found memories of him everywhere I turned. The ice cream parlor, the neighborhood library, the street he lived on, not to mention my own house – everything conspired to present me with a continual pageant of my lost love. My old familiar feelings of insecurity were fueled by all the reminders of how unsuitable I was. And mother was certainly no help. Everywhere she dragged me, to meet the boring people she did business with, it was the same story. She would brag about how smart I was, and how I was working in Paris ("Say something in French, Barbara") but she always ended up making it sound like I was really looking for a job in Cleveland. Sometimes people just responded vaguely and politely, but other times they took mother seriously and actually recommended that I meet people they thought might offer me a job. Usually I was able to weasel out of it, but things came to a head the weekend before I was due to return to Paris.

Mother was a commercial real estate broker and analyst. That meant that she didn't deal in residential properties, for which I was immensely grateful. If I'd had to listen to endless descriptions of how her clients liked the kitchen but found the bedrooms too small, I would probably have gone insane. As it was, the mere thought of fifty thousand square feet of unimproved industrial space sent mother into paroxysms of delight, but at least she was doing things on a grand scale. I grudgingly had to admire her for that. In fact, she was only the seventh woman in the United States to become an expert appraiser of industrial property – a pioneer, you might say.

One of mother's biggest clients was a man I knew as Judge Milner. From the stories I'd heard about properties he'd bought and sold, it sounded to me as if at one time or another he'd owned at least half of downtown Cleveland. The Saturday before my flight to Paris, Judge Milner and his wife Grace were giving a garden party. I thought it was normal for mother to be invited, but she made it sound as if Queen Elizabeth had invited her to Buckingham Palace. Daddy had long since established that he never wanted to be involved in events like that, but I had no such defense. After weeks of telling everyone I was looking for a job in Cleveland, mother had convinced herself it was really true. This garden party would be an invaluable opportunity for me to meet some influential people.

The party was held at the Milners' palatial residence in Shaker Heights. Although that suburb was named for a group known for their simplicity, its architecture betrays its honorees' ethic in every possible way. When I was a girl in Cleveland Heights, "living in Shaker" was synonymous with success, just beyond our reach. In recent decades, much to their credit, Shaker Heights has successfully achieved racial integration. But that day at the Milners', the only black people present were servants – lots of them. Maids and butlers moved back and forth from the kitchen to the back yard, a vast expanse of lawn on which ornate wrought iron tables and chairs had been set up. There was a lot to eat and even more to drink. Many of the ladies wore long dresses and picture hats. Mother had on a flowered dress and a small straw hat and she wanted me to wear something similar, but I insisted on wearing my fake Chanel. In Cleveland, that suit was like a security blanket for me.

I was introduced to Grace Milner, who smiled vaguely and nodded as mother deluged her with compliments about the beauty of her home. When mother switched to the inescapable topic of my living in Paris, Mrs. Milner invited us to follow her to a room where, she said, I'd feel right at home. Situated between the entrance hall and the dining room, the room was crammed with silk-covered furniture decorated with fringed pillows. It was, she said, their French room. A color TV, rare in those days, sat on a Louis XV console. The walls were covered with paintings, some oils, some watercolors. Most were the standard postcard views of Paris – Notre Dame, the Opera, booksellers along the Seine, etc. She pointed to a grouping of three gilded frames, each housing the picture of a wistful, big-eyed Paris gamin. Oh my God, those were the *poulbots* that painters like Vali ran up for tourists. If only he could see them now, housed as if they were treasures from the Louvre. I looked for a signature but found none. Maybe they were Vali's. The only signed *poulbots* were from artists who couldn't paint anything better.

Just then Judge Milner entered the room. Thinking my scrutiny of the paintings was discerning approval, he began to compliment himself and his wife on their ability to discover and support young talent. His wife chimed in with the information that I was now living and working in Paris, saving mother the trouble. He stared at me intently, then began questioning me about what kind of work I was doing, how I liked it, how much it paid, what the buying power of my salary was, and what standard of living I could maintain. My answers convinced him that I liked my job and was able to get by, even in an expensive town like Paris.

Mother sputtered, "But Judge, don't you agree she would be better off having a well-paid job right here in Cleveland?"

"Now, Tilda, the girl has a head on her shoulders. Sooner or later she'll get fed up with all that French stuff and come home." Then he turned to me. "Young lady, your mother is a fine woman and you're her only daughter, so don't stay away too long." He winked. "But you don't always have to listen to her. I don't."

The next day, as I began packing for my return to Paris, I discovered my fake Chanel suit wasn't in my closet. I asked mother about it – she said it had some spots on it and needed to be cleaned. "But don't worry," she added, "I've already washed it and it's in the dryer right now." I let out a shriek and rushed down to the basement, but it was already too late. The heat of the dryer had turned the loosely woven fabric of my suit into matted felt, shrinking it to fit a dwarf.

I confronted mother with the damp mess that had once been my favorite outfit. Before I could utter so much as one sentence of complaint, she launched into a diatribe about how everything is wash-and-wear these days and if the French are so darned perfect they should know that, or at least have a label in there saying "dry clean only" and in any case I should be able at this point to take care of my own things instead of making her do everything, because I act like I'm so grown up and all but basically I still have absolutely no sense of responsibility. There was no point in showing her the label that said "*nettoyage à sec seulement*". In fact, there was no point in trying to reason with her at all. I couldn't just let it go, though – I was too upset. So I told her she should have asked me first. That unleashed another torrent of self-justification, which I tried to rebut, thus causing both our voices to rise to the point that Daddy noticed the din.

"For crying out loud, it sounds like a goddamn henhouse around here. Can't a man have some peace and quiet in his own home?"

Mother wheeled to face Daddy and her eyes narrowed. I knew what was going to happen next – she was going to cast an evil spell. When I was a little girl, the first movie I ever saw was "Snow White and the Seven Dwarfs". The wicked witch was so scary, I used to hide under the seat whenever she was on the screen, afraid that if I looked at her she would cast an evil spell on me. I loved the rest of the movie and I saw it endless times, but whenever the stepmother queen prepared to transform herself, bam! I hit the floor.

With mother there was no escape. When she felt cornered, or felt Daddy and I were ganging up on her, she cast the spell. I can't explain it any other way. Mother had been trained as an actress, and she could command a very theatrical presence. Once the spell had been cast, it threw a pall over the whole house. Even if she wasn't in the same room with us, we could feel the tension. During those times, she also had a habit of drawing her breath sharply with a kind of inward hiss. That sinister state of affairs lasted however long mother chose, usually between three days and a week. No matter what we said or did, she alone could break the spell by speaking her magic words. Since I was about to return to France, the hissing continued for only one day before she spoke the words: "Are you ready to be forgiven?" We were, we always were.

Arriving in Paris, I felt a sense of deliverance that is perhaps unusual for an employee about to return to work after a vacation. The city had donned its fall colors, in a parade of seasons that had become deliciously familiar to me now. Frou Frou the cat gravely acknowledged my return, allowing me to scratch his back without pouting about my absence. The concierge had been taking care of him and "his" apartment while I was gone. Hansli was also away and wouldn't return for another week. How good it was to be back. I dared to think, "back home".

Unpacking my suitcase, I looked at all the gadgets I'd brought back from the States that in those days couldn't be found in France. One in particular, a Charles Addams piggy bank – when you put a coin on the black box, a ghostly hand reached out to grab it – struck me as something Claire's brother Alain would enjoy. I thought he'd get a kick out of showing it to his HEC business school friends. Without even waiting to see Claire the next day at the office, I picked up the phone and called the Lagrange family.

Madame Lagrange answered. She sounded happy to hear from me, but I could tell something was wrong. "What is it, Hélène?" I asked. "You sound like you don't feel good."

"Oh, Barbara, I don't know how I should feel. Just after you left, Alain and some of his friends from school enlisted in the Air Force. Now they're being shipped to Algeria. Jean-Paul says I shouldn't worry, it's just an uprising and it'll be over soon. And of course we're glad Alain is doing his patriotic duty. But I can't help being upset. Alain is my only son, and I'm worried. No matter what you call it, whether it's outright war or 'just an uprising', Alain is in danger."

As I was soon to find out, we were all in danger.

# GENERATION GAP

## II

# *Sex and the Silents – the Worst Deal in America*

Any member of the Silent Generation who went swimming as a child has a sense memory of one of the world's most uncomfortable inventions – the wool bathing suit. Men and women alike – and their juvenile counterparts – were expected to cover large areas of their bodies before approaching water in public. Things had improved since the turn of the century; legs were no longer completely covered but the suit still reached mid-thigh. Sleeves had shrunk or were replaced by broad shoulder straps, but the worst part was the fact that the suit was made of wool.

When wet, the tightly woven material became heavy as lead. Not only it hindered movement, it seemed to have a life of its own, often trying to head in a different direction from the body it covered. The worst part, however, occurred when the bather came out of the water and tried to dry off. Then the wool would cling to the bather's flesh like a bed of thorns, still soggy long after skin and hair had dried. While drying, the wool would gradually shrink and become unbearably itchy, particularly if sand had become embedded in it. The discomfort was in inverse proportion to the pleasure of going swimming.

Because of the wool bathing suit, children of the Silent Generation learned that there was a disagreeable price to pay for enjoyment. It was a useful lesson, because as it turned out, fate had a particularly nasty surprise in store for Silents once they reached puberty. In 1948, when the oldest Silents were in their late teens or early twenties, the United States was rocked by the moral equivalent of an atomic bomb. Sex raised its hydra head in the form of the Kinsey Report. Words that had never been spoken, thoughts that had never been expressed, deeds that had never been described were suddenly out in the open. People who were nearing middle age or older did their best to come to grips with it. But youngsters – the Silent Generation –

found themselves presented with a list of tantalizing temptations no young Americans had ever had to deal with before.

Subsequent generations, faced with those same temptations, were at least equipped to deal with the consequences. But therein lies the nasty twist of fate for the Silents. The Pill, the medical breakthrough that absolved sin and provided an open invitation to indulge in sex, only came on the market in 1960. That meant that every single Silent, from the oldest down to the youngest, had to go through puberty and young adulthood being driven crazy by temptation but unable to fulfill their urges without taking the risk of the girl getting pregnant.

In those days, that was a serious risk indeed. Abortions were expensive, socially unacceptable, dangerous and hard to come by. Any "nice" boy who got a girl pregnant felt honor bound to marry her. And marry her he did. Statistics show that the sober, responsible Silent Generation was the earliest-marrying and earliest-babying generation in American history. Men married at an average age of 23, women at 20. They married, essentially, to be able to do all those things the Kinsey Report talked about. They wanted to have fun, but they had to pay the price. Sure, it was a rotten deal, one that no Americans before or since have had to cope with, but they didn't question it. Probably, to this day, most of them still haven't questioned it. They chalked it up to "just our luck". The kind of luck they'd known all their lives.

In the 1950's, life was good for a newly married Silent Generation couple. The husband's job with a large corporation gave them the kind of financial security they had never known as children. There was every reason to expect that security to last – by placing his faith in the success of the corporation, the employee could be sure of a steady series of raises and advancements. It was an exhilarating expectation.

The home occupied by the young couple was another source of satisfaction. It was far more spacious than the cramped quarters of their childhood, and it was reassuringly similar to their neighbors' houses, but best of all, it was a world of their own. A world they alone inhabited, in which they became the "elders" of the new suburbia. They could make their own rules, solving their problems with problem-solving committees of their peers. They answered only to themselves.

Thus it was that in the 1960's, with the advent of the Pill, many Silent Generation members took sexual matters into their own hands. Couples formed by the date-and-mate obligations of the previous decade were now bored with each other. One solution, the key party, was an offspring of their suburban lifestyle. Groups of couples, generally from the same community, gathered for a party. After the requisite time spent in the "conversation pit", drinking and talking, each couple threw a key on the coffee table. The husbands took turns drawing a key from the pile, and then went home with the wife who the key belonged to. A sexual version of the problem-solving committee.

The invention of nylon put an end once and for all to the miseries of the wool bathing suit. If only the sexual malaise of the Silent Generation could have been dealt with as efficiently and agreeably! Failing a ready-made solution, the earliest-marrying generation in American history created another, and much sadder, statistic. Unhappy couples split in record numbers, and divorce rates soared to epidemic proportions.

In retrospect it is easy to find reasons why so many Silents turned to divorce as a solution to their problems. It was a form of revolt against their parents and grandparents, for whom divorce was simply unacceptable. To the dissatisfied inhabitants of the new suburbia, it was all the more acceptable because so many of them were doing it. And it was legal, because they made it legal.

Because of them, the number of states with no-fault divorce laws jumped from zero to forty-five.

The new laws were being made by men – in those days, women in government were rare – and it was men who benefited from them the most. Men were now released from the constraints of an unhappy marriage and were free to make new lives for themselves. Even the obligation to pay alimony and child support didn't weigh too heavily on "company men" with healthy salaries and regular promotions.

For women it was different. Beaver Cleever's family had split up, and even if Mrs. Cleever still had the ranch house in which to raise her 3.3 children, she had to do it alone. Divorced women became a new and uncomfortably large demographic in America. Fewer of them remarried than did their male counterparts. Unlike their mothers who had played an important Rosie-the-Riveter role during World War II, few of them had any chance of finding work outside the home. They were still dependent on their ex-husbands for support, and on each other for moral support. Was this all the reward they got for playing the game and being "company wives"? Was Sylvia Plath right when she said that a woman's place was in the oven? It all seemed unfair.

The certainties of the 1950's, the correctness of the new suburbia, had become eroded by doubt a decade later. Early marriage and corporate discipline had once seemed like a fortress against their elders who questioned their maturity. Now the Silent Generation, characterized as the Lonely Crowd, began to ask themselves how they were doing. The answer, as provided by a welter of how-to books, was hardly reassuring. But how, when they had done everything right, could things have gone so wrong?

For generations, the close-knit family was the core of American life. The Pilgrims in New England, the pioneers heading west, the waves of European immigrants had always stuck together. It was the source of their strength. Now divorce was shattering family bonds, at the same time that corporate policy caused employees to move to a different geographic area, far from their relatives.

The Silents were born into crushing poverty, but the distress was felt nationwide and shared by all. They grew up in an America united by its fight against Nazi fascism. They entered adulthood with the certainty that they were creating a brave new world. Now, as the nation began to unravel, they looked inward and found few answers but endless questions.

# VI

# L'AMOUR TOUJOURS

The Larousse dictionary gives the following definitions for the word *plastique*: 1) The art of sculpting or modeling. 2) The aesthetic effect of any given shape. 3) Synthetic material made essentially of macromolecules which can be molded, generally with heat.

In 1960 the people of Paris began to experience another kind of *plastique* which Larousse then added to the dictionary as: 4) A pentite-based explosive with a putty-like consistency which only explodes with a detonator. The *pains* or loaves of plastique are compact, lightweight, odorless and easy to conceal. When placed in a doorway or windowsill, the explosion of a single *pain de plastique* isn't enough to blow up a building but it does serious damage to anything within a few yards of it, including people.

In 1958 when General de Gaulle first came to power, everyone thought he was in favor of keeping Algeria for the French. But his actions over the next two years seemed unconvincing to *Algérie Française* nationalists, especially the ultra-rightist group known as the OAS. As the conflict in Algeria intensified, OAS activists decided to spread their expressions of discontent to the mainland, particularly Paris. Their action of choice was terrorist bombings using plastique explosives.

When the first bombings occurred, people were outraged. One of the victims was a little girl who lived in a building inhabited by a politician the OAS didn't like. The politician wasn't in the building at the time of the explosion, and anyway he lived on an upper floor. But the little girl, the concierge's daughter, was blinded by shattering glass from her ground floor window under which the plastique had been placed. The papers spoke of nothing else, but far from deterring the OAS it seemed to spur them on. Soon *plastiquages* became a common event, and from then until the end of the Algerian war in 1962 the people of Paris got in the habit of walking in the middle of the street at night.

At the end of the day, concierges would roll out garbage cans for collection, and there were many cases of plastique explosives being placed in the cans. The lids flying off under the impact of the bomb could be a lethal weapon, so it was safer walking as far away from them as possible, in the middle of the street.

I was very surprised to see how calmly the population reacted to these bombings. When I remarked on it to Monsieur Grégoire the upholsterer, he explained patiently that an occasional explosion could hardly be compared to what they went through during the war. I realized with a jolt that the war had ended only fifteen years earlier, so that even people in their twenties like me had memories of the German occupation, and those memories weren't pleasant. With the worsening crisis, people reverted to behavior I assumed was a throwback to World War II. If we opened our apartment windows at night in our usually silent neighborhood, Hansli and I could hear the sound of crackling short-wave radios broadcasting news from the BBC. People obviously mistrusted the French media to give them the big picture. Whenever the French press or radio did transmit bad news, people immediately rushed to the grocery stores and all the staples, like flour and sugar, were bought up in a matter of hours. This was wartime behavior, but we were not at war. What was happening in Algeria was referred to as "les événements" and in fact was always officially called "the events" until 1998, when the French government finally relented and allowed historians to refer to the Algerian War. There was a historic precedent for this – at the end of the 18th century, the fall of the Bastille and the overthrow of the monarchy were also referred to as "the events" until finally, many years later, they became known as the French Revolution.

Given the somewhat chaotic nature of these "events", Hansli and I often refrained from going to the movies or the theatre at night, preferring to stay at home and listen to music on records or the radio. We fully expected this to provoke a new outburst of thumping and banging from our upstairs neighbors, but no such outburst occurred. Finally we figured it out – the Nozets had left and new people had moved in. Whoever they were, they were certainly not averse to music or given to pounding on our door. Although neither of us had laid eyes on them, we could tell from the sounds above us that there were two of them, and the concierge told me they were a young married couple. When we heard their footsteps on the stairs, we tried to catch a glimpse of them. But they were as elusive as the Nozets had been intrusive.

Attracted by the posters announcing the event, I decided to improve my homemaking skills by attending the Salon des Arts Ménagers (Home Arts Show). It was, basically, three shows in one, exhibiting large appliances, small kitchen gadgets and regional food specialties. I began with the last category, wandering happily between stands of smoked hams from Bayonne, blood sausage from Alsace, and *saucisson* from Lyon with intriguing names like "gendarme" and "Jesus". The name of the former was understandable, since it was shaped like a policeman's nightstick. The name of the latter was baffling. There, as with the wine exhibits, people were only given a free taste if they seemed ready to buy. Accustomed to the bargain prices I got at my neighborhood wine cellar, I refrained from involvement with the wine. But I couldn't resist a salami covered with peppercorns, which I sampled and bought. I was also given a small paper cone with a dollop of something delicious that turned out to be chestnut cream. I bought a can of the stuff, and was instructed in the art of making a dessert called Mont Blanc, i.e. a "mountain" of pureed and sweetened chestnuts topped with the "snow" of fresh cream.

I definitely wasn't a customer for any large appliances, but it was fun to see the French breathlessly catching up with everyday conveniences such as washing machines and refrigerators. The refrigerators were much smaller than American ones, probably because most Paris kitchens were much smaller than American kitchens. As for the washing machines, they were designed to wash clothes as well as a country washerwoman. They were capable of heating the water to boiling – a must for the heavy linen sheets most people had on their beds. With five wash cycles and four rinse cycles, the whole process could take up to two hours.

To my surprise, the most fun turned out to be the small kitchen gadgets. There were things I'd never even dreamed of, such as an *anti-monte-lait,* a thing to keep milk from boiling over. Made either of metal or glass, it was a round disc that you put in the pan before heating the milk. When the milk boiled, the disc banged up and down in the pan, making a noise that alerted you to the situation and also preventing spills. Other clever devices included a metal grill to put on the stove to toast bread, which also doubled as a heat diffuser, and a string shopping bag that could be rolled up into its own little bag, attached to the bottom, so you could keep it in your pocket or purse.

But the first prize in creative gizmos went to something known as *le fil à couper le beurre.* It was simply a piece of wire, wound tightly like a spring, with a small wooden dowel attached to each end. When you grasped the pieces of wood and pulled on the wire, it became "a butter-cutting wire", the idea being that butter in those days was often presented in a mound. The wire could also slice soft cheese or paté. The French apparently thought this was the *nec plus ultra* of gadgetry, as reflected in an expression I had often heard. *Il n'a pas inventé le fil à couper le beurre* (he didn't invent the butter-cutting wire) is what they say to express skepticism about a person's creative or intellectual powers.

As I returned from the Home Arts Show, I noticed the truck that was parking in front of our building. It was bright yellow, not so much a truck as a *camionette,* a "truckette" – a cute, compact vehicle that looked like a child's toy with rounded edges. The reason

I noticed it was that it was decorated with a logo I had just seen at the show – a happy-faced sun with the words "Solio, the Sunshine Oil". I started walking upstairs and heard footsteps behind me. The young man who was in the truck was following me. When I stopped on the landing to fish in my purse for my keys, he nodded with a grave smile, said "Bonsoir" and kept on climbing the stairs. Aha! So that was the guy upstairs.

Just as, when you come across a word you've never heard before, you begin to hear it everywhere, suddenly we kept bumping into our new neighbors. Their names were Henri and Marie. She was a legal secretary. He, of course, sold that cooking oil. They seemed friendly, and Hansli and I were anxious to make sure our relationship didn't deteriorate into Nozet-like hostility. So we invited them over for a drink. They didn't seem deterred by the knowledge that Hansli would be practicing every day – they even said they enjoyed it. Marie seemed rather shy and addressed most of her comments to Frou Frou the cat.

The big surprise came when Henri spotted a joke book Daddy had sent us, to amuse me and to help Hansli improve his English. It was one of those books that had photos of famous people, with word balloons making them say funny things. For example, Eisenhower leaning toward President Kennedy and asking, "Does the roof still leak in the Oval Office?" To my amazement, Henri started leafing through the book and laughing at the jokes, which he then undertook to explain to Marie. She was unimpressed by the humor, but I was impressed with his grasp of idiom. Most English-speaking French people I'd met had learned the language in school or on trips to Britain. Henri, I realized, understood American slang. When I asked him if he'd ever been to the States, he just smiled and shook his head.

The next day when I left my office to walk home, there was the little yellow truck. I started to ask Henri how he knew where I worked, but before I opened my mouth I realized I'd happened to mention it in our conversation. Obviously Henri was paying attention. He said lightly that his route home took him past my office, so he might as well offer me a ride. I said I might as well accept it.

That's how it began – ever so casually, ever so uninvolved. Occasionally we would stop in a café for a quick drink on the way home. I found his conversation fascinating for many reasons, not the least of which was that he seemed so interested in me – who I was, where I came from, and what I was doing in France. He was much more accessible than the Lagrange family, whose intellectualism and *vieille France* veneer I found impressive but daunting. I could never be like them, but Henri was, at long last, a French person I could relate to.

One day he invited me to have lunch with him. In those days, the lunch hour in most French offices lasted well over an hour. Bosses would take at least two hours for a business lunch, and in old-fashioned families the custom was for daddy to go home for lunch, joined by his wife (who never worked) and children. Lunch would then be followed by a nap for daddy while the children played quietly before returning to school. The long, elaborate lunch hour was virtually an institution in France. I remember Jean-Paul Lagrange saying plaintively to his wife one day that he had been so busy at the office, he only had time for a one-course lunch.

At first when I started working for Mr. V, I too went home for lunch every day to cook for Hansli and me. I still did it occasionally, but more often than not he stayed at the Conservatory all day. So when Henri proposed that we eat at a restaurant he knew of on the Left Bank, I was happy to accept. I felt no time constraints, and I liked the idea of being away from the neighborhood we lived in. The restaurant was in a street so narrow it seemed to date from the Middle Ages. The inside was similarly ancient, with dark wooden beams on the ceilings and small panes of leaded glass on the windows. The ground floor was crowded and noisy, but the room upstairs was smaller, quieter and more intimate. Here was our first chance to really get to know each other. Over an inexpensive but delicious three-course meal, we indulged in the discovery of shared tastes and opinions. When he drove me back to my office in his little yellow truck, I had the feeling that for a few hours I had replaced my everyday world with a special world only Henri and I shared.

What was my relationship with Henri exactly? Once or twice a week we continued to have lunch, and our conversations were innocent enough. But his intensity told me the innocence was only temporary. He had a way of looking at me – no one had ever looked at me that way before. I tried to define it. It wasn't an invitation or a supplication or a provocation. It was an exploration. He was gravely studying me like a mountaineer about to embark on a perilous climb. I found it very flattering, and incredibly sexy. Every reaction I had, either to the food or our surroundings or a remark he made, was duly noted in the mental notebook he was keeping on me. I began to wonder what his observations would add up to. Was he interested in me as a lunchtime conversation partner, a friend, or something more? I began to fantasize about what he would be like as a lover – and then realized that he could read my thoughts.

When he finally made the first move, I was more than ready. Still he held back, not wanting to go too far too fast. Every time he touched me I was thrilled, but he measured the intensity of his caresses. As a result, every time I thought I couldn't feel anything more thrilling, he went a step further. When he provoked a gasping response from me, he leaned back and looked at me with a smile as if to say, "Did you like that? Do you want more?" If I resisted, he seemed almost pleased. I was learning how to play the game. No doubt about it, I was a novice and he had turned my ignorance into a personal project.

I wasn't sure how I felt about that. He was married, so his interest in me could only be secondary. With Frank I'd been the "wrong sort of person", and I'd learned what it was like not to really count. In fact, I'd never really counted for anyone – unless it was Hansli who counted on me for companionship and regular meals. This was different. Henri was offering me equal partnership in a private game that looked like it could be fun, more fun than I'd ever had. His slow, deliberate approach told me that he intended it to last a while, whatever it was.

Didn't I deserve a break? I remembered the feeling I used to have in college when the pep pills kept me up all night. I was smarter and stronger than all those poor folks who had to stop everything and sleep. I could have it all. Now I felt the same way – I could handle my regular life plus a secret love life. Henri and I were smart, and no one would get hurt. It had been nearly two years since my abortion, and I'd stayed away from men. But I knew instinctively that Henri would be careful. Every cell in my body was aching for sexual fulfillment, urging me to give in to him in order to get what I so desperately wanted.

Our coming together, when it finally happened, was a mutual triumph. It was clear to both of us that whatever else we were meant to do in life, nature had intended us to be lovers. Everything felt right, and absolutely natural. My worries about orgasm were over.

When I first started having sex with Frank, I didn't know there was such a thing as female orgasm. Frank gave me my first clue when he asked me why I didn't make any noise. I was puzzled. What kind of noise should I be making? He didn't know exactly, but he'd read somewhere that a woman's orgasm can be vocal.

He also mumbled something about squeezing that I absolutely could not understand. He meant vaginal squeezing, but he was too embarrassed to say so and anyway I was too bewildered by the concept of female orgasm to pursue the matter with him. He asked me if I liked having sex with him and I told him, with great sincerity, that I did. But these new things he was demanding made me feel inadequate. On top of the guilt I already felt about sinning with Frank, here was a new kind of guilt. I was failing to behave the way he thought I should. Obviously I wasn't a good lover, and I had no idea what to do about it.

The next clue on my search for answers was given to me on the stairway of the American Hotel, the *hotel de passe* where I'd lived before Hansli and I got our apartment. The fifth and sixth floor rooms were rented to people like me because none of the girls or their johns could be expected to perform after climbing that many stairs. As it was, the fourth floor was reserved for the very fit or the very cheap. The second and third floors were more luxurious than the fourth – I had caught glimpses of mirrors and suggestive paintings – but the fanciest rooms of all were on the first floor. There the rooms had oversized beds, satin sheets and mirrors on the ceiling. Caroline, Mimi and Renée – the youngest, prettiest girls – worked those rooms.

And that wasn't all, as I found out one day as I was leaving the hotel on my way to the Pension Maupommé. On the stairs between the first and second floor I ran into the owner, Monsieur Claude, who was on his way up. He inquired after my health, which I told him was excellent, and to be polite I inquired after his. To my surprise, he launched into a long diatribe about the weather and how people must be particularly careful not to catch cold. Why was he being so chatty? As he nattered on, I became aware of another sound I was hearing. We were standing near Caroline's room and its door was closed, meaning she had a customer inside. Was something wrong? I could hear Caroline moaning and shrieking. With a shock, I realized that part of the service she provided was sound effects. That was the noise Frank had talked about!

Diabolically, Monsieur Claude watched my face as it registered puzzlement, then shock, then recognition. His eyes twinkled as he wished me a good day and continued on his way upstairs. I walked out with more questions than answers. Obviously if Caroline was making those noises it was to make her customer happy. But it sounded like she was suffering. Is that what men want, to make women suffer? Are you expected to actually feel pain? If you don't make any noise, are you a bad lover? And what about the squeezing?

I had no more opportunities to continue my search for the mysterious female orgasm until my one-night stand with Philippe. Despite the excitement and mental confusion of the moment, I was determined to make some noise, even though I wasn't suffering. The shrieks I'd heard Caroline make sounded too shrill – the neighbors might hear them. So I opted for a low moan. To my amazement, not only Philippe shuddered with pleasure but I enjoyed it too. Opening my mouth and making sounds gave me a thrilling rush of release.

I had every intention of trying it again the next time Philippe and I got together. For a while, when he never called, one of the things that bothered me the most was my disappointment at not being able to do more orgasm research. The difficulties I encountered after that took my mind off the problem entirely – that is, until I met Henri and started worrying again. When our flirtation led to a full-fledged love affair, I finally discovered the endlessly renewable delights of the female orgasm.

My physical delight was so great, coupled with my relief that I didn't have to worry about orgasm any more, that I didn't focus on things I should have been worried about. Such as, I was having an affair with a married man, and a neighbor at that. I knew his wife Marie, and she knew Hansli and me. What would happen if she found out? And even supposing she didn't, what was in this relationship for me?

Those were questions I didn't bother to ask myself. I was totally absorbed by my trysts with Henri once or twice each week – anticipating them, living them, remembering them. The logistics were complicated too. Now that we were lovers we felt uneasy about being seen together in the little yellow truck. He would call me at my office, using an assumed name (you can't be too careful) to give me the address and time of our next meeting. I would arrange my work schedule, locate the place where I was going and figure out how to get there, then grab a sandwich and head off. I would get to the hotel (usually a place just barely more respectable than the American Hotel) and ask for Henri under whatever name he was using that day. When I knocked on the door of the room I could feel my heart beating faster, and when he opened the door and took me in his arms, the rest of the world just melted away. Nothing else mattered but the feel of him, the taste of him.

Getting involved with Henri was like entering a different universe. In fact, he was a universe of his own, with an outlook and reactions that were totally new to me. He made me see things I'd never seen before – watching the chestnut trees in the spring so I'd know exactly which day they burst into bloom, waiting for the first hot day of summer when people started wearing lightweight clothes that revealed their bodies. He revealed another body to me, my own. He discovered a certain spot on the back of my knee that drove me wild when he touched it, especially under the table in a restaurant or café.

One of the things he enjoyed doing was finding ways to perform private acts in public places without attracting attention. His appetite for this behavior increased when he saw how it excited me. Each of us had a role to play. His job was to be as provocative as possible. Mine was to pretend that nothing was happening, no matter how hard it was for me to keep my composure. Sometimes it was very hard indeed. Once, when we were walking down the Faubourg St. Honoré, surrounded by trendy shops and fashionable people, he leaned over and murmured in my ear, "You know, what you have between your legs is what legionnaires in the desert dream about."

Henri's upbringing had contributed to his originality. He was born in Brittany, the son of a master sergeant in the French army. If he had followed his family's wishes he probably would have led an ordinary *petit-bourgeois* life. But he didn't. His father demanded that he choose a career in the military. Henri adamantly refused. The father declared that if he didn't join the army he would apprentice him to a carpenter.

"The sword or the saw, those were his very words," said Henri bitterly. It seemed to me that his father had a rather florid way with words, but I could certainly understand Henri's resentment. My mother had made me go to college in Cleveland, but she hadn't forced me into an occupation I hated.

Henri's response was to run away from home when he was seventeen. Paris drew him like a magnet, and he naturally gravitated into an area in the northern suburbs where other runaway teens like him could share housing. They pooled their resources, paying for rent and food with the money earned from odd jobs. Before long, Henri got a job at the PX of a nearby American army base. While he unloaded crates and boxes, he picked up American slang. By the time De Gaulle expelled the U.S. bases from France, Henri had acquired enough proficiency to be hired by an import-export company as a bilingual file clerk. From there he worked his way up to a sales position (the official term was "commercial representative") with a company that made something the French call *rollmops*. Along the way he met Marie and they got married. She didn't like the smell of the rollmops, which are pickled herring individually wrapped around pickles. So she arranged for Henri to commercially represent Solio Oil, "sunshine in a bottle", in six of the twenty *arrondissements* of Paris.

By that time he knew Paris inside and out. He enjoyed showing me unusual and surprising sites, such as a country churchyard in the heart of Paris, or a cemetery in Montmartre that is only opened once a year, on All Saint's Day, because there are no living relatives of the people buried there. Once, opening an anonymous *porte-cochère* on a busy street, we found ourselves in a courtyard that was as large as a London square, with a fountain in the middle and steps leading to each of the houses surrounding it. At one time Chopin had lived in one house and George Sand in another, after their love affair was over and they were no longer on speaking terms.

Another thing I learned from Henri was how the French have institutionalized infidelity. The mistress and the lover are stock characters in every bedroom comedy ("Good grief, it's my husband!") but they are also accepted in everyday life. I think it's because in the 19th century it was common for a woman to marry the man her family chose for financial reasons – it was known as a *mariage de raison* – but often neither spouse found happiness in the marriage. As a sort of consolation prize for being reasonable, society turned a blind eye to philandering. In fact, it even created interesting ways to make infidelity convenient and nonintrusive. The consecrated time for this activity was "le cinq à sept", i.e. from five to seven. That was a time period when one's schedule was vague enough to provide a variety of excuses. Men were held up at the office or stuck in traffic. Women were late coming home from the hairdresser or shopping for a hard-to-find item. What they were doing, in fact, was meeting in one of the innumerable hotels that rented rooms by the hour. Some of these places were quite upscale, with underground garages that provided confidentiality and room service that served fine food and wine. Other places were kinkier, with peepholes from one room to another or esoteric accessories.

The language itself provided another form of accommodation. The French are almost obsessively private by nature, and this is reflected in the way they express themselves. If they refer to a person the word is feminine (*une personne*) and they can then talk of the person as "she" regardless of the person's sex. If you are introduced to someone, it is perfectly acceptable not to be given that person's name. The indefinite pronoun *on* is often used to avoid describing the number of people being discussed or their gender. No wonder French is the language of diplomacy. You can get by with murder while still seeming to be forthright.

Henri and I had to be careful about the way we expressed ourselves because of the form of address. When we were in bed together we used the familiar form *tu*, but when Marie or Hansli was around we had to be sure to say *vous* to each other. So it was a relief when Marie found a larger, less expensive apartment in the 15th *arrondissement* and they moved there. The 15th, on the other side of town, was an area I never set foot in. Henri and I developed a complicated series of excuses we could use if we were ever seen together. Mercifully we never had to use them.

Hansli probably could have figured out that I was having an affair if he'd been paying attention, but by that time he wasn't. He'd spent the past year working hard at the Conservatory and branching into activities that his professor, the great French cellist André Navarra, called *faire du métier*, i.e. being a pro. Maestro Navarra felt that before an artist could start giving recitals and taking himself seriously, he had to be fully trained as a professional musician.  That meant doing all sorts of odd jobs such as backup in a recording studio or working in a pit orchestra.

Once Hansli announced with glee that he had a paid gig in Limoges, replacing a friend in the orchestra for a Sunday matinee performance of "Rigoletto".  He said it would be fun and I could come along, which I was glad to do because Limoges is famous for its porcelain.  We took the train Saturday morning and headed straight for a restaurant we'd found in the Michelin guidebook.  As was often the case in those days, the food was incredibly good and copious, and inexpensive to boot.  It's a good thing Hansli was able to enjoy the meal, because that was the only enjoyment he got out of that weekend.  When he went to the theatre and was given the score, he discovered to his horror that the friend he was replacing was first cello and "Rigoletto" is full of cello solos.  He spent the rest of his time in his hotel room practicing, while I went shopping.  The performance went well and he got through his solos without a hitch.  But it was a shock to both of us to hear "Rigoletto" sung in French.  Instead of "*La donna è mobile*" they were singing "*Femme est volage.*"

Both Hansli and I were unrepentant language snobs.  We rejoiced in our knowledge of French, English, German and Italian.  Hansli learned Italian before I did, because he sometimes studied in Italy during the summer.  He taught me some phrases, and I learned more from a book he had in German called "Italienisch in 13 Wochen" (Italian in 13 Weeks).  My big chance to work on my Italian came in the summer of 1961, when Hansli attended a two-month master class that Maestro Navarra was giving in Siena.

I knew quite a lot about the city before I even went there, thanks to the articles written for "The New Yorker" by a man named Arturo Vivante.  Through his writings, I had learned that Siena was unique, even among the individualistic city-states of Italy.  It had once rivaled Florence as a Renaissance power, and still maintained a healthy animosity for anything Florentine. It was ruled, as it always had been, by the Chigi family, an aristocratic clan of bankers with close ties to the papacy. Despite this, the actual city government was staunchly Communist, and had somehow managed to remain in power even under Mussolini. This was a city to be reckoned with.

Siena turned out to be everything I expected and more. Its self-contained, magical environment was so special, I felt like I was inside one of those transparent paperweights that contain a whole cityscape – except that if you turned it upside down there would be confetti instead of snowflakes. Unlike most cities, whose streets are criss-crossed in a rectangular grid, Siena is circular. At its center is the piazza, a huge circle surrounded by Renaissance buildings. The main street branches out from the piazza and circles around it in ever-widening rings, like a snail shell. With the exception of a magnificent church made of black and white marble, all the other buildings are in earth tones ranging from ochre to… burnt Siena.

I thoroughly enjoyed being on vacation in Siena. Hansli was staying in student housing with the other musicians but he found me an affordable room in an upscale hotel called the Golden Cannon. I could sleep as late as I wanted every morning, and then go to a café for a deliciously decadent Italian breakfast – a frothy cappuccino and a cream-filled pastry known as a *bombolone*. I often lingered there, listening to the conversations to see how much I could understand. I didn't feel like an eavesdropper, as most of the people spoke emphatically from one table to another or to the *padrone* behind the counter.

Another thing that helped me understand was their hand gestures. Italians, when they speak, love to gesticulate. There's an old joke about it. Q: How do you gag an Italian? A: By tying up his hands. Sometimes, at a distance, I could follow an argument just by watching the hand gestures. On television, the people who read the news were filmed from the chest up, but you could tell they were gesticulating while they spoke because their shoulders kept bobbing up and down. They spoke relatively slowly and distinctly because in those days, when television was new, each region of Italy spoke a different dialect. People had to get used to the "standardized Italian" of national TV, which then became the norm. Now everyone speaks the same language, and the local dialects are losing ground.

I spent hours in the hotel lobby or in cafés watching quiz shows, game shows or the adventures of an adorable mouse called Topo Gigio. Soon this paid off by giving me the courage to start speaking Italian. I needn't have worried. My hesitant attempts to communicate were invariably met with the delighted exclamation "*Ma lei parla italiano!*" (But you speak Italian!) even when I'd replaced the words I didn't know with a French or English word with an "a" at the end.

Everything Arturo Vivante had said about Siena was true. There were still anti-Florentine graffiti on the walls. The symbol of the aristocratic Chigi family was carved into many public buildings, alongside posters urging people to vote Communist. I had read about Count Chigi, the last of his line. Vivante explained why he had no children. He had married a woman who was highborn but not Sienese. After a few months of marriage, the Countess found that she was bored with life in Siena. She flounced off, leaving her husband a note saying that if he wanted to see her he would find her in Florence. The Count had rarely if ever left his home city. He got on a train, but as the wheels turned they made a noise that sounded to him as if they were saying "Torna, torna" (go back, go back). He got off the train at the next stop and went back to Siena, never to leave again.

I was fortunate enough to meet Count Chigi. Two of the cellists who were studying at the Accademia Chigiana, a French girl named Huguette and a French Canadian boy named Pierre, decided to get married while they were in Siena. Since their families were far away, the Count took them under his wing. He fussed over the wedding preparations as if Pierre and Huguette were his own children. He was a striking figure – tall, slim and impeccably dressed. The elegance of his dark, perfectly tailored suits was always set off by a silk handkerchief that blossomed from his breast pocket. His aquiline features looked severe but his expression was kind. His generosity toward the citizens of Siena was legendary, and he made no exception for the young married couple. Pierre was given gold cufflinks and Huguette a pearl necklace.

Siena is divided into thirteen *contrade* or districts. Each *contrada* has its own symbol and its own flag, and each is fiercely independent. People even told me that marriage between citizens of different districts could sometimes be a problem. The rivalry between districts reaches fever pitch during the period preceding an amazing horse race called the *Palio* in which each *contrada* enters a horse. Although there are now several Palios each year, in those days there was only one. Luckily for me, it took place in August, while I was there. The weather had turned hot, so hot that it caused a water shortage. Every day between 10AM and 6PM the city turned the water off. This was apparently a common occurrence and everyone was prepared for it. Large fifty-gallon plastic buckets that elsewhere would be used as trashcans were filled with water to get everyone through the day.

The days before the race were filled with feverish preparations. People hung out *contrada* flags and tried on their costumes. The piazza, which was usually lined with cafés, was cleared to make room for the race. That included the café that was our usual hangout, the Fonte Gaia. All the tables and chairs had been removed from its terrace. I couldn't understand how a horserace could be held in a place where we usually sat drinking Cinzano before dinner, but Hansli and his friends explained to me what was happening.

The Palio is a tradition that dates from the Middle Ages, and everything about it is medieval. The racetrack, if you can call it that, is created by putting padding on the piazza's buildings to minimize the impact if horses and riders slam into them as they go around curves. Many spectators are packed into an oval enclosure in the center of the piazza. Others buy tickets to watch the race from the windows of one of the buildings. Because the music students were regular patrons of the Fonte Gaia, we were allowed to view the proceedings from the upper floor of the café, free of charge.

The Palio is the most dishonest horserace in the world. Every jockey in the race has been bribed by some people to win and by others to lose. So whoever actually wins the race is in trouble. But a horse doesn't need a jockey in order to win. Sometimes jockeys choose to be thrown from their horse when they're ahead, considering the risk of injury from the fall to be preferable to facing a lynch mob.

On the morning of the big day, each horse was draped with the colors of its *contrada* and led into the church (every district has its own) to be blessed. My hotel was in the "giraffe" district, and I was able to get into the church to watch the blessing. The pews had been removed to make room for the crowd, not to mention the horse who docilely clip-clopped his way to the altar where the priest sprinkled him with holy water. The people leading the horse were dressed in medieval costumes, and I was amazed to see how completely authentic they looked. I hadn't realized it until I saw them in period clothing, but many inhabitants of Siena had faces that came straight out of paintings by Michaelangelo or Da Vinci.

After lunch we all hurried to take our places on the upper floor of the café. It had a small balcony, which afforded us a wonderful view. People were packed like sardines into the fenced-off center of the piazza, and there wasn't a window or a balcony that wasn't jammed with people. Some onlookers had even climbed onto the crenellated clock tower. Before we could see anything we heard cheering, and then the parade began. It was traditional to precede the race with a procession that included drummers and flag-bearers from each *contrada*. Halfway around the piazza the parade stopped, and to the flourish of a drum roll the flags were tossed and waved in intricate patterns. This happened thirteen times, and each district seemed to outdo the others. The drumming grew in intensity as the flags were tossed higher and higher in a dizzying display.

The parade culminated with the appearance of a float carrying a statue enclosed in a painted structure. This was the Palio, the embodiment of the race. Was it a man or a woman? It was so covered with flowers and multi-colored pennants, I couldn't tell. After it had passed, the piazza was cleared. The race was about to begin.

I've seen pictures of horsemen in, I think, Mongolia playing a form of polo with a sheep's head for a ball. That was the kind of wild cavalcade the Palio was. The jockeys rode bareback and there were no rules. Around and around they galloped, trying to force each other into the padded walls of the buildings. Everyone was yelling, but someone somewhere must have been counting, because eventually a shot was fired and that was the end of the race. Instantly, the piazza was flooded with a sea of *carabinieri*, the Italian police in their white summer uniforms. They seemed to appear out of nowhere. Their job was to surround the winning jockey and keep him from getting killed. The winning horse, meanwhile, was covered with wreaths of flowers, some of which he ate. They also poured Asti Spumante into his water bucket.

Italians love to joke about their police. Q: Why do *carabinieri* always go out in twos? A: Because one knows how to read and the other knows how to write. For the French, the police are no laughing matter. Parisians have often told me they prefer to settle disputes among themselves, because if the police get involved, both parties might end up getting in trouble. City cops are bad enough, constantly checking everyone's papers and insisting that "rules are rules". But the national security police, the CRS, are far worse. They have a reputation for being ruthless and even deadly.

Returning to Paris after the comic-opera setting of Siena was a shock. The weather was gloomy and it was *la rentrée*, a time not only for school children to return to school but also for their parents to get a cold shower. The French report their earnings in the spring but are sent their tax bill at the end of August, just as they're returning from vacation. They also come home to find that the price of everything has increased, and the calendar for social unrest begins at *la rentrée*. The autumn of 1961 was particularly difficult because of the Algerian situation, which had gotten worse and worse.

When the army first went into Algeria, the idea was to put down an uprising and allow the French to keep their colony. Everyone except Algerian nationalists could agree about that. But once De Gaulle started talking about "self-determination" it became clear that his real aim was to lead the Algerians to independence. Most of the French people in Algeria, both *pieds noirs* and army officers, united in an attempt to prevent that from happening. In contrast, people in mainland France became more divided. Not everyone wanted to support the French army's actions any more. A group of artists and intellectuals, headed by Jean-Paul Sartre and Simone de Beauvoir, signed a manifesto proclaiming that they respected people who refused to bear arms against the Algerian people and supported those who helped the Algerian cause.

From that time on, the Métropole was riven with demonstrations and counter-demonstrations, strikes and *plastiquages*, and all sorts of subversive activities. After a lull during the summer holidays, the *rentrée* of 1961 was particularly brutal. The CRS had orders to use their *matraques* (riot sticks) at will, and rumor had it that a large number of Algerian demonstrators had been clubbed to death and thrown into the Seine.

One evening Hansli and I went to a movie on the Champs-Elysées. When the film was over we walked out to discover that the center of the avenue was filled with tanks, lined up one behind the other from the Etoile all the way down. The soldiers peering out from the tanks' turrets didn't look particularly hostile, but it was still scary.

Another evening when we were at home listening to music on the radio, the prime minister interrupted the broadcast to inform everyone that renegade paratroopers from the French army in Algeria were about to fly into Paris. He urged everyone to rush to Orly Airport to intercept them and convince them not to attack us. That turned out to be a false alarm, but people everywhere were jumpy, including at the office. Germaine the receptionist nervously scrutinized visitors and incoming mail. Louise the Communist file clerk was often seen carrying a sheaf of anti-war pamphlets, although she didn't try to distribute any to us. Raoul the driver constantly gave us his personal interpretation of the latest news from the war front. This didn't help Claire's morale, as she was worried about her brother Alain.

Claire's parents often invited me for dinner. I tried to cheer them up by telling them about my adventures in Siena, but the conversation inevitably turned to Alain. He wrote to them frequently, and his morale seemed to be good. His mail was rarely censored, which Jean-Paul attributed to the fact that Alain was the son of a journalist and had learned how to say things without actually coming out and saying them. Certainly Alain's letters hinted that the things he was seeing and doing had changed his way of thinking. He seemed less didactic and more compassionate. His values were different.

Hélène proudly showed me an object she had placed in a clear plastic display case. It was lovely but I didn't know what it was. Claire explained that it was a *rose des sables*, a "sand rose", that Alain had sent them from Algeria. This mineralogical marvel, with its sand-colored petals that indeed looked like a rose, was formed by the slow evaporation of gypsum in certain areas of the Sahara that had formerly been marshes. Alain had sent them a lyrical description of the sand rose, contrasting the lengthy and humble process needed for its creation with the ephemeral beauty of the finished result. He seemed to be saying that however long his military service lasted, the outcome – like the sand rose – would make it all worthwhile. I know we were all thinking the same thing. "Please God, let the war be over soon and let him come home safe."

When the crisp autumn weather brought the chestnut vendors out on the streets again, I realized I was beginning my fifth year in Paris. That called for some kind of celebration. As if she'd read my mind, Ursi called to say she and Fritz were having a party, kind of a miniature Bavarian Oktoberfest in Pigalle. I was happy to accept her invitation. My involvement with Henri had caused me to turn down numerous opportunities to visit my friends on the Rue Fromentin, and it was nice to get caught up with them again.

Christiane, the rather prim girl from Geneva, had just gotten engaged to Djibril, an equally serious young man from Senegal who was studying to be a doctor. She told me her parents seemed very upset that she was marrying an African, and didn't want to hear about them moving to Switzerland after their marriage.

Christiane hoped her parents would get over it in time. If they didn't, she and Djibril would go on living in Paris, where he had been offered an internship.

Rolf, on the other hand, was heading back to Berlin to complete his doctoral thesis in history. His Paris days were nearly over. As for Pauli, he seemed as happy-go-lucky as ever. I noticed that his French had greatly improved, and he had actually landed a job of sorts as Paris correspondent for a weekly Swiss magazine. It was surprising to see Vali at the party without one or several Bluebell Girls in attendance. I kidded him about it and he told me, with a fake grimace, that they were all on strike to protest the war. He asked me if I was married yet and I told him I was having trouble choosing between my many suitors. We agreed that life is like that.

Everyone had brought food, and Fritz had managed to get a keg of real Bavarian beer up all those stairs. With good things to eat and drink, and lots of good conversation and music, the time flew by. Then Djibril looked at his watch, shook his head, and told Christiane they barely had time to walk home before curfew. Oh dear, was this a curfew night? I had forgotten to check – usually I was never out that late. No one else was worried, as they either lived in the building itself or at least nearby. But I was far from my apartment on the Rue Laugier. As there was no room in Ursi and Fritz's tiny flat for me to stay overnight, they volunteered the information that Vali would have room for me in his studio. He and I looked at each other and grimaced. I was no Bluebell Girl and he was no Henri, but life is like that.

It had been a long time since I'd seen Vali's paintings, and I was struck by the power of his recent work. The landscapes had a touch of *fauve* wildness to them, and the portraits were as fascinating as Soutine's without the insanity.

"I'm no expert," I said, "but I think this is good stuff."

He grunted with pleasure and grinned. "It's hard work. I have to lift weights every day – for my muscles," he added, flexing his biceps.

Why did he always have to be so annoying? He had a way of looking at people, particularly women, as if he was judging horse-flesh. I hated that superior, probing look. He was staring at me that way now, and I was particularly annoyed because I knew I was failing the test. My legs were too short, my hips were too wide and no one, including myself, had ever found me to be beautiful. There were parts of me, secret parts, that Henri had taught me to appreciate, but that was certainly no business of Vali's. If only I could be with Henri now, instead of this woman-izing show-off.

"OK, where do I sleep?" I asked curtly.

He was only slightly surprised by my hostility. I think he knew how I felt about him.

"OK, la Miss. You can sleep on this couch I use for my models."

I hated it when he called me "la Miss" which he pronounced, as the French do, to rhyme with "geese". It was a way of identifying me by my nationality, rather than who I was as a person. What could you expect from someone for whom people were mere objects?

I turned my back on him and took off my sweater and skirt, thankful that I was wearing a slip to cover my bra and panties. At least it was warm in his studio, so the blanket he put over me was all I needed. My plan was to pretend to doze so I wouldn't have

to talk to him any more, but before I knew it I had fallen sound
asleep.

The lovely autumn didn't last long that year. Winter came early,
bringing temperatures that were so low they broke records
that had been set in the 1940's. We were much better off than
Parisians had been during the war. Fuel was expensive but there
was no shortage of it, so being indoors was not a problem. I
could still walk to work if I dressed warmly, but this created unexpected problems with Henri. We continued to get together in
hotel rooms, and the sex was still great. But we also liked to have
lunch together when we could, and there was a café where we
had become regulars. With the cold winter weather that café
became a problem, not for Henri but for me – because of their
restroom.

One of the curses I carry through life is that I'm a public lavatory
klutz. Even in a nicely appointed facility, I always land on the
stall where the door won't close properly or lock. The automatic
features, the water faucet and particularly the hand dryer, never
turn on for me no matter how much I wave my hands around –
or else they turn on when I've walked away in frustration, as if to
taunt me. So you can imagine how much trouble I had with that
most problematic of French toilets, *le trou turc*, the Turkish hole.
It isn't even a toilet at all but rather, as its name implies, a hole
in the ground surrounded by a slab of porcelain which has cor-
rugated footpads. I wish they'd drawn the feet so you could see
which way you're supposed to be. I've never been able to figure
out if you're supposed to crouch with your back to the wall, as if
you were actually sitting on a toilet, or face the wall so you squirt
closer to the hole.

In cold weather the Turkish hole was doubly challenging because
of the additional clothing I was wearing. My favorite winter garment was a heavy loden cloak with a hood, which I topped off

with a long woolen scarf. Lifting all that cloth to keep it out of the wet, while juggling a purse (there were rarely any hooks in those places) plus squatting to do my business was simply more than I could handle. Not to mention the part where you pull the chain to flush. Often – and in our favorite café specifically – the water came rushing out in a flood that rose above the footpads. So you had to be ready to leave, with all your garments and possessions nicely arranged, before opening the door of the stall, reaching over to pull the chain, then running for your life.

Henri was greatly amused by my difficulties, not only with Turkish holes but other aspects of French life that the French take for granted, such as tipping the usher at the movies or allowing dogs in restaurants while infants are frowned upon. He also helped me with the hardest pronunciations – those of English words incorporated into French usage. I never knew if they were pronounced the English way or the French way. Sometimes it was one, sometimes the other. He told me about a brand of cigarettes called High Life. "You'll never guess how that's pronounced – eesh leef!"

It was from Henri that I first learned about a new singing group called The Beatles who no one in France, including myself, had ever heard of. He knew the lyrics to "All My Loving" and I was charmed by the thought that "while I'm away I'll be home every day, and I'll keep all my loving for you." The tune was nice too, and as I hummed it to myself I was promising Henri to keep all my loving for him. I only wished it was reciprocal.

Pretty soon I began hearing Beatles music all over town, thanks to the invention of the transistor radio. Older people complained that the silence of parks and beaches was now broken by what they called "yé yé" music, but even they were tempted by the new gizmos because of the news bulletins that were broadcast every hour. Hélène Lagrange carried a transistor with her everywhere, anxiously listening to news of the "events" in Algeria. I got all the news I needed just by reading the headlines displayed by the newspaper kiosks as I walked to work and back. The morning papers carried news of the previous night's events, while the evening papers focused on what had happened earlier that day.

On the morning of February 9, 1962 there were huge headlines concerning a "tragedy at the subway station Charonne." I didn't buy a paper, figuring Germaine or Raoul could give me the details. When I got to the office, Raoul wasn't there but Germaine told me more than I had bargained for. The evening before, there had been a big anti-war demonstration. The demonstrators were marching peacefully along the Boulevard Voltaire, from the Place de la République to the Bastille, shouting slogans and waving banners.

Suddenly, out of nowhere, the CRS police charged them, shooting tear gas and hitting everyone with their clubs to disperse them. Panic-stricken, some of the demonstrators ran down the stairs of the Charonne metro station, hoping to escape from the police.

But the iron gate had been drawn shut and locked so that no one could enter the station. The first people who ran down the stairs were followed by waves of others, and before anyone realized what was happening, eight people had been crushed to death and dozens injured.

Louise the file clerk, who was renowned for her punctuality, hadn't shown up for work yet. We agreed it was more than likely that she was in that demonstration. She had no telephone, so Raoul had gone to her home to see if she was all right. Just then Germaine's switchboard lit up. When she answered her face went white and all she could say was "No... no..." She hung up and tears streamed from her eyes. Louise was among those killed.

Dying for a political ideal was more than I could fathom. Where I came from, politics meant badges and balloons and choosing between an elephant and a donkey. How could anybody believe in something to the point of risking their life? How could people's beliefs be such a threat that the government shrugged off their death?

The authorities stated that the demonstrators had attacked the CRS police who were acting in self-defense. But given the circumstances, nobody believed it and a few days later the country was paralyzed by a general strike. No matter whose side you were on, everyone agreed on one thing. The "events" had gone on too long, and people were fed up.

Was that what finally tipped the balance? Three months later, in May, Algerian representatives of the National Liberation Front who had been in exile in Geneva, Switzerland crossed the border to meet with General de Gaulle's representatives in the spa town of Evian. Within a matter of days they had signed the "Evian agreements" that put an end to hostilities. Algeria was given its freedom. The war that wasn't a war was over.

There again I was puzzled. When I was a child, the end of World War II, first in Europe (VE Day) and then in Japan (VJ Day) was met with confetti, ticker tape parades and wild celebrations. Here was a terrible conflict that had dragged on longer than World War II, and when it ended – nothing. No parades, no celebrations. I realized that no matter how much of a spin De Gaulle tried to put on it, France had lost a precious colony. There was nothing to celebrate except that families like the Lagranges sighed with relief at the thought that their boys would now be coming home. Those who had been pro-Algerian kept a low profile, not wanting to incur the anger (and possible revenge) of their former pro-*Algérie française* adversaries. But it comforted me to think that perhaps feisty little Louise hadn't died in vain.

In early June, Claire invited me to come over to her house after work. Her parents were going to a dinner party that evening, and the idea was that she and I would use the family's record player to practice a new dance called the twist. Alain wasn't home yet but he was due to be shipped out in a week. As soon as he got back we planned to have a big party, a "surboum", and teach him all the new dance steps.

We were busy gyrating when the phone rang. Claire's face went white, just like Germaine's had, and she said the same thing, "No… no…" My heart froze with dread as she hung up, trembling. "What? How?"

"A helicopter accident. His last mission. Caught in a freak sandstorm."

I don't know how long we sat there, hugging and sobbing. We knew it was only a matter of time until Jean-Paul and Hélène got home, and Claire would have to tell them. When at last they opened the door, laughing and joking, they froze at the sight of us in tears. Jean-Paul seemed unable to process the news. "It can't be. The war is over. He was coming home. Our only son."

Hélène let out a blood-curdling shriek and sank to the floor like a felled tree. I watched helplessly as a woman I had always considered to be the epitome of elegance and wit rolled on the floor moaning. I knew that even if the earth had opened up and swallowed her, it would not have been enough to cover the depth of her sorrow.

# VII

# COME WEEZ ME TO ZE CASBAH

One of the many nice things about working for Samy Valentin was the free concerts. Since he was in the music business, Mr. V always had an ample supply of tickets which he often distributed to his staff. Claire and I attended a Beatles concert that was held in a stadium. We were able to see the Fab Four but the crowd was screaming so loudly we couldn't hear a thing.

I much preferred the events held at the Olympia Music Hall, a venerable theatre that was the Olympus of entertainment. All the biggest stars in the world performed there, not just French singers like Jacques Brel and Charles Trenet but international celebrities as well. When I saw Marlene Dietrich she must have been in her sixties at least, but she closed her show with a can-can number in which she kicked as high as the chorus line. Josephine Baker was equally up in years, but she still looked and sounded great.

The most unforgettable concert I ever saw at the Olympia was the one given by Edith Piaf in 1963. Even when I was living in New York, the sound of her voice epitomized for me the very essence of France. And her name had special meaning for me too – *piaf* means sparrow. They called her *la môme Piaf*, the Sparrow Kid! She was in ill health and very frail, so much so that the audience watched in hushed fascination as she walked from the wings to the microphone in the middle of the stage. A tiny figure wearing her signature black dress, it seemed to take an eternity for her to shuffle that far. But when she reached the mike and grabbed hold of it, it was as if she had suddenly plugged herself into a source of energy. There came that fabulous voice, belting out one famous song after another.

She sang a selection of old favorites, including "La Vie en Rose". Then she was joined by a handsome young man named Theo with whom she sang some love duets. Her life had been marked by a series of passionate love affairs, and Theo was destined to be her last amour. Her final number, which she sang alone, was calculated to bring down the house – and it did. It was "Je Ne Regrette Rien" (I Have No Regrets), a song that was a perfect incarnation not only of her life but of the way people were feeling in post-war France. "No, I have nothing to regret," she sang. "Good or bad, right or wrong, I don't care any more."

The war was over and the wounds were healing, but the pain was still there. A year after Alain's death, a memorial service was held for him in the village church near Mamie's farm. He had never been given a proper burial because the helicopter crash had blown everything to smithereens. The only thing they found that was specifically his was a signet ring that Hélène was now wearing. I remembered that ring. Once, when Alain and I were playing hide-and-seek in the barn, the glint of the ring had allowed me to spot him in a bale of hay.

I would never visit Mamie's farm again. Mamie herself, much weakened after suffering a stroke, was now living in a rest home. Giving in to the pressure of a cement manufacturer who wanted the riverfront property, the family had decided to sell the estate. They intended to buy a house in a new gated community not too far from Paris that offered golf, tennis and swimming.

France was becoming modernized. Television sets, refrigerators and stereos were now affordable enough to be found in most households. Mom-and-pop grocery stores were giving way to a new invention, *le supermarché*. And the fashion industry had changed too. Women who wanted stylish clothes no longer had to have them made by a tailor. Many major fashion designers created a new ready-to-wear line, *le prêt-à-porter*, that could be found in department stores. Reasonably priced knock-offs of the latest designs appeared in shops, along with shoes and accessories. Paris had always been the fashion capital for the rich and famous, but now designers like Courrèges and Saint-Laurent were making clothes that were accessible to everyone. Post-war France was redefining itself as the leading source of luxury and indulgence in a world that was increasingly riven by the Cold War.

The best expression of the rivalry and animosity between the United States and the USSR was the space race. Viewing that race from Western Europe, with the U.S. on one side and the Russians on the other, was something like being the net in a global ping-pong match. We were in the middle of the action, but it was completely over our heads. As a result, people in France tended not to take sides but rather to cheer on whoever was ahead. When Yuri Gagarin became the first man to go into space, he was brought to Paris and feted like a native son. But the French didn't play favorites. During his presidency, Kennedy's image was as popular as a movie star. After his assassination, he became a household saint.

International politics in the year before JFK's death was an exhilarating sport. Would the wily Russian peasant outwit the handsome knight? Tune in tomorrow for the next exciting episode of Kruschev vs. Kennedy. The other members of the cast were equally fascinating. De Gaulle regularly appeared in public holding hands with his former enemy, German chancellor Adenauer, and the two men, Le Vieux and Der Alte, dreamed of creating a new Europe. Meanwhile in Rome, a modest humanitarian who loved the arts reached out to the whole world in a loving embrace. For a while, John XXIII was everyone's Pope, and the ecumenical world he longed for seemed within our reach.

I attended a concert at the Salle Pleyel conducted by the great Russian Armenian composer Aram Katchaturian, whose music I had always adored. It was a thrill to see him in person, a powerful bear of a man who delighted in pleasing his audience. He led us through his haunting violin concerto and the stirring melodies of his "Spartacus" ballet suite to thunderous applause. The public demanded an encore and he delivered – his famous "Saber Dance" brought the house down.

At that concert I also had the opportunity of seeing some Russian soldiers close up. They were tall and lanky, mostly blond. They chewed gum and walked with the arrogant swagger of men from a superpower visiting a less powerful country. They looked… just like Americans!

It was time for me to go home for a visit, but I had a strange sense of foreboding – not about being in Cleveland, but about the travel. Henri, who was envious of me making the trip, would have given anything to get on the plane instead of me. I was accustomed to flying and had no fear of it, but I couldn't shake a feeling of doom. I took the plane anyway (here Daddy would ask, "So, did you live?") and got to Cleveland in one piece, where-upon I decided I had no talent as a fortune-teller. But the sense of foreboding persisted, so it wasn't about the travel. Maybe I just didn't want to be in Cleveland.

Mother had calmed down about finding me a better job, mostly because I'd given her something to boast about. Just for fun, one day when I was bored at the office, I'd begun to write English lyrics for some of Mr. V's nonsense songs. It was something that came easily to me, after all those skits I'd written in college. Claire saw what I was doing and brought it to Mr. V's attention. I was surprised by his positive reaction, and even more surprised at how seriously he took my scribblings. It turned out there were far-off places like Turkey and South Korea that bought the rights to his music, and they paid more if there were English lyrics. Ceremoniously, Mr. V enrolled me in the French Guild of Songwriters who would col-lect royalties on the performance of my work. I couldn't imagine it ever adding up to much, but it made mother proud as punch.

Daddy was pleased too, of course, but he was less impressed than mother because he knew how easy it was for me to do that kind of work. He and I had been playing with words since I was a child. I was very proud when I first managed to solve a weekly New York Times crossword puzzle, but Daddy wasn't content until I could knock off the big Sunday puzzles – and in ink. Pencils were for wimps. The weird vocabulary of crosswords delighted us. "Did you know," Daddy would ask, "that a baby merganser is a smew?" Then we'd start making silly rhymes. "Merganser is the answer but smew is too."

One Saturday when the weather was beautiful, Daddy suggested we go out for lunch and then for a drive. Mother begged off – she had a big appraisal to finish. Daddy and I felt light-headed at the prospect of spending the afternoon together alone. Mother whipped out her camera and insisted on taking pictures of us before we left. We struck silly poses, standing in front of Daddy's beloved Buick convertible. Then we faced the big question of where we would eat lunch.

When Mother was involved we always went to respectable restaurants with linen on the tables and headwaiters. Left to our own devices, we usually succumbed to our love for greasy spoons, places covered in white tile where you sat at a counter on wobbly stools. That day, however, Daddy declared that he felt like having a pastrami sandwich, meaning that we headed for Bernie's Delicatessen.

Deli was Daddy's favorite kind of food bar none. He always said that Jewish food reconciled him with being Jewish. He adored the chocolate phosphates, which we called "Jew beer", and the Kosher dills which reminded him of the pickle barrel in his mother's grocery store. Apparently "Mrs. Glass's Fancy Groceries", owned and operated by my Grandma, sold the best pickles and the best herring on the whole East Side of Cleveland. Daddy was

Grandma's youngest child and she loved to spoil him. Whenever she baked a pie or a cake, she made a small one with an H on it just for Daddy. He told me how she made strudel, starting with a tiny ball of dough in the middle of a large round table. She rolled the dough thinner and thinner until it was almost transparent and covered the whole table.

I never knew her. She died before I was born, one of the many victims of the Cleveland Clinic disaster on May 15, 1929. Some X-ray film caught fire in the basement of the clinic and the poisonous fumes, moving through the ventilation system, caused most of the patients to suffocate. Grandma had just undergone minor surgery and Daddy was on his way to the clinic to bring her flowers. When he got there, he had to identify her body instead.

Daddy adored his mother and he couldn't get over her death. He was obsessed by things he had never told her or done for her. It even gave him nightmares. As we sat in Bernie's Delicatessen eating our sandwiches, he again told me something he had said several times before. "Don't do anything you'll regret later, and don't wait until it's too late to do something for someone." We were talking about mother, and he urged me to be patient with her. "She means well. It isn't her fault, really, that she's so annoying. If you had a fight with her and then she died, you'd always feel guilty."

"As it is," I said, "I feel guilty about letting you eat that pastrami sandwich. The doctor said you should stay away from that stuff."

Daddy shrugged off the doctor's recommendations, saying he felt fine and anyway what's the point of living if you can't even enjoy your food. He took a deep breath and patted his tummy to show me how flat it was. I had to agree – he looked great. Even at age 62, he was still Handsome Herbie, as his poker pals called him. He looked at the table next to us, where two old men were daintily nibbling gefilte fish. "See those old guys?" he asked in a low voice. "I never want to be a decrepit old coot like them."

After lunch we drove out to Amish country. We both loved the prim houses with their crossed curtains and the boxy black horse-drawn carriages. Perhaps because of the severity of our surroundings, we were in a reflective mood. Daddy wanted to talk about where I was in my life, what I had done and where I thought I was going. I felt flustered, almost like when he caught me making out with Frank. I didn't have much to show for myself and I couldn't really tell where I was going. I saw no point in telling him about my affair with Henri – how could he possibly approve?

We talked a little about Hansli, who was about to graduate from the Conservatory and begin his professional career. Daddy pointed out that although our friendship could continue, his new activities would deprive me of his companionship. What Daddy was concerned about was whether the life I had chosen for myself in Paris was enough to make me happy. Without hesitation I told him it was. Finding a rich, handsome husband would be the icing on the cake, but the cake was delicious anyway.

"That's my girl," he said with a grin. "You'll have your cake and eat it too, with or without icing."

The next day, Sunday, mother suggested we have a picnic to celebrate her finishing the appraisal. We packed up some sandwiches and headed for our favorite park, about half an hour out of Cleveland Heights on the road to Brecksville. When we got there, Daddy parked the car and I set off to find a perfect table. Before I got very far, mother called me back. "Your father doesn't feel well. I think we should go home."

Daddy looked like he was in pain but he put on a brave face. The terrible thing was, if he didn't drive us we were stranded. Neither mother nor I had a driver's license. Cell phones didn't exist in those days, and there wasn't a public phone in the park. As long as I live I'll never forget how Daddy drove us back, holding the wheel with his left hand and holding his left arm with his right hand to control the pain. When we got to the house he insisted on parking his beloved car in the garage, while mother called the doctor.

Pete Jankowski was the Cleveland Transit System's company doctor, and he was also one of the guys Daddy played poker with. Although it was Sunday, he came within minutes of mother's call. He examined Daddy and said calmly, "Listen, Herb, you've had a heart attack. Not a big one, but you should go to the hospital anyway so they can check you out, run an EKG, that kind of thing."

Daddy protested, saying Pete could do all that the next day when they were at the office. Pete said no, he had a really busy Monday and wouldn't have time to run Daddy's tests. I could tell they were playing poker, each trying to bluff the other one out. Pete won, and mother and I went in the ambulance that took Daddy to the hospital.

They ran the tests and said he was fine for now but should remain in observation. They also put an oxygen tent over him, a clear plastic affair through which Daddy smiled wanly at us. I was supposed to be having dinner with Bambi that evening but I didn't want to leave the hospital. I went into the hall where there was a phone booth, to tell Bambi what had happened and to cancel our dinner. When I went back to the room mother was standing outside the door.

"Something's happened," she said. "They won't let us in the room."

"The hell with that," I thought, and pushed the door open. Daddy looked like Christ being taken down from the cross, his limp body being held by strong arms. They had tried to revive him but failed. He was dead.

I wanted to think it had happened too quickly, without warning, but I knew it wasn't true. I had known all along that something terrible was going to happen. Maybe mother knew it too, when she sent Daddy and me out together. At the funeral, Daddy's friends from the office told me that on Friday, his last day at work, he spent the afternoon talking to each of his co-workers – as if to say goodbye. So he knew too. And what good did that do? Could any of us have kept it from happening? What was the use of my premonition, if I still let him eat that pastrami sandwich? No amount of forewarning could make the loss any easier. When Sparrow died I learned what it meant to lose someone you love – it's forever. Now my Daddy was gone. It wasn't right. It wasn't fair.

They did an autopsy, and the doctors told us that if he hadn't died of a heart attack he would soon have had a paralyzing stroke. He would have lived the rest of his life in a wheelchair. I remembered Daddy whispering to me that he didn't want to be "a decrepit old coot", and I felt a little better.

Mr. V sent a telegram of condolences, adding that it was all right for me to take some extra time before returning to Paris. This fit right in with mother's plan for the two of us to go to Bermuda. It seemed to me like an absurd idea, even though mother said it would make us feel better. I wanted to stay in Cleveland and grieve. But I remembered Daddy urging me to be patient with mother, so I gave in. She sold the Buick to a man who opened the garage where Daddy had left it and drove it away. The next thing I knew, we were packing swimsuits and cocktail dresses, and off we flew to Bermuda.

Technically we were out of the country, as the tiny island belonged to Great Britain.  It was charming to see black traffic cops wearing British "Bobby" helmets and Bermuda shorts.

We were staying in a vast, sprawling and utterly characterless place called the Tropics Gloriana overlooking the harbor in Hamilton.  It turned out that most of the hotel staff – the maitre d', the barman, the concierge, etc. – were French, all recent graduates of a hotel school in Nice.  They had jumped at this assignment, which sounded like they were being sent to a tropical paradise.  In actual fact, Bermuda is both miniscule, meaning there aren't many places to go, and isolated, meaning it's far from the West Indies where the action is.  The French were all bored and homesick.

They were delighted when they learned – thanks to mother, of course – that I lived and worked in Paris.  I was able to fill them in on the new movies I'd seen, the new books coming out, the latest gossip about Brigitte Bardot.  In exchange they pretended not to notice when mother shamelessly stole silver spoons for her coffee service in Cleveland.  The spoons were engraved with the hotel's initials, TG, which also stood for Tilda Glass.  Mercifully the demitasse cups and saucers bore the hotel's name written in full.

We spent five days and four nights "doing" Bermuda – boat trips around the island, jitney rides to places of interest, cocktail hour by the swimming pool and as decent a dinner as the French cook could muster from local ingredients.  I was extremely polite, and both mother and I forced ourselves to be cheerful, but our relationship was strained.  Finally on our last day, as we were window-shopping in downtown Hamilton, she grabbed me by the arm.  It was surprising – usually she never touched me at all.

"You act like such a stranger.  We're supposed to be close.  Talk to me!"

"What do you mean? What do you want me to talk about?"

"Talk about us – what's wrong."

Unexpected as it was, I knew this was an opportunity Daddy wouldn't want me to pass up. I took a deep breath and launched in. It seemed appropriate to begin at the beginning, so I started telling her about my first memory of our life on 107th Street when she and Daddy were fighting in the bathroom. She immediately interrupted me.

"That was all your fault."

"But mother," I protested, "I'm talking about when I was really little, maybe two years old."

"Oh yes, that was your fault. You wouldn't do what I told you. Your father blamed me and then we'd fight and it ruined our relationship."

Although my head was spinning, I managed to spot a Meissen plate like the ones mother liked to collect in the window of an antique shop. I steered her into the shop, and by the time she had haggled over the price and successfully concluded the purchase, we were able to revert to amiable chit-chat. So much for our heart-to-heart talk. So much for our "feel good" trip to Bermuda.

What a relief it was, getting back to Paris. Once I was away from mother and from Cleveland, it was easier to imagine that nothing had happened. I was accustomed to being away from Daddy, and there were no constant reminders of his death. There were still pangs when, for instance, I'd remember a funny Italian expression I'd forgotten to mention, and realize that I wouldn't have another chance to tell him. Sometimes I would wake up in tears after dreaming about him. But it didn't really hit me until the following spring. My birthday is in April and every year Daddy would return from his vacation with a present for me. Since he started vacationing in Mexico, a country known for its Taxco craftsmen, the present was always a beautiful piece of jewelry.

Now, for my 28th birthday – and for all the birthdays to follow – there would be no present from Daddy. I was gloomy as I trudged up the stairs to Mr. V's office. It was my birthday, but I didn't feel like celebrating. Halfway through the morning, Mr. V's voice came over the intercom, asking me to come to his office. He invited me to sit down and then reached over his desk to hand me something. It was a small square box. With an embarrassed smile, he urged me to open it. Inside was a lovely gold ring.

"Don't ask me why I'm doing this," he hastened to say. "I was shopping for jewelry with Lulu when I saw this ring and a little voice said to me, 'Buy it for Barbara, it'll make her happy."

He had no idea it was my birthday, and of course he couldn't know whose "little voice" it was. I explained it to him, and he was deeply moved to think that Daddy had chosen him to be my surrogate father. For me, it was proof of something I had sensed confusedly but hadn't been able to express – that Daddy wasn't really gone. He was still there, and he would never leave.

With my birthday came another realization – I wasn't getting any younger. Where I came from, a girl like me who was still single at almost thirty was likely to remain an old maid all her life. In principle, I was really interested in getting married. In actual fact, I had no idea what to do about it. My only thought was to marry Henri – provided, of course, he got a divorce from Marie. There were times when that seemed possible. They often had fights. From what he told me, it sounded like she was a very difficult person. I felt sure he'd be much happier with me, and I told him so. He agreed, swearing to me that he was leaving her. But it never happened – there were always complications he said I couldn't understand.

Finally, in early 1964, he told me about a complication he hoped I would understand. For his work, he was being given a promotion and a new territory to cover. That territory was Algiers. As in, Algeria? Yes, the war was over now and there were great opportunities for the expansion of Solio into a new market. And would he be taking Marie along? Well, yes, she was excited about it. She hoped it would give them a fresh start, and he didn't have the heart to let her down. All I could think about was that he did have the heart to let me down, and Algiers was very far away.

Before he left, he treated me to a weekend getaway in a manor house in Normandy. The rural setting – old half-timbered buildings set among apple orchards – was beautiful. I glimpsed it briefly as we made a short tour of the region, just long enough to buy some food. Henri loved to do what he called "saucissoner", i.e. nibble on slices of sausage washed down with wine. That sustained us through a heroic bout of lovemaking, all the more intense because we didn't know when we'd see each other again. He kept insisting on the fragility of his relationship with Marie, and he promised to stay in touch. On Sunday we returned to Paris and on Monday he left for Algiers.

His departure would have been impossibly difficult for me if it hadn't been for Hansli. Following his graduation from the Conservatory Hansli had been engaged for a series of concerts in Switzerland and Germany. But now he was about to give his first recital in Paris. The programs had to be printed and invitations sent out. For a whole week we had the excitement of seeing his name in big letters on all the *colonnes Morisse,* those thick columns with domed roofs that carry posters announcing cultural events.

The recital was well attended and Hansli played beautifully. His program, a balanced combination of German classics and French moderns, went without a hitch. He had a new accompanist, a French girl named Monique with whom he'd already been on tour. Ursi, Fritz and I were bursting with pride as we rushed backstage to congratulate them. We had to wait our turn, and as we watched them we noticed that Hansli had his free arm around Monique's waist.

"I guess our little cousin has grown up," chuckled Ursi.

Yes indeed. He had grown a mustache and taken to smoking cigars. The skinny teenager had turned into a sleek adult, ready to take on the world. I would have to find someone else to feel motherly – or cousinly – about.

Sure enough, shortly afterward he began dropping hints that since he was working with Monique, it would be very convenient if she could share the apartment. The idea of moving out didn't bother me. I had already found a studio I liked in the same neighborhood. And to my surprise, I discovered that I actually enjoyed having a place of my own. No one to cook for, no one to clean up after. No one to share my life either, but that was another problem.

I drifted into a casual affair with a fellow named Jacques, a musician and songwriter who I met through the office. Neither of us felt strongly about the other, although it took care of what he called "our sanitary needs". But often, in his arms, I would find myself near tears when the memory of Henri invaded me.

At the office, Mr. V had me spending more and more time writing English lyrics, which he said were selling well. This was proved to me in June when I got a statement from the Songwriters Guild with a nice fat check attached – the equivalent of about six months' salary. I opened a savings account and began to inquire about the price of a plane ticket to Algiers.

All this time Henri and I had been exchanging letters. I was happy to hear how much he loved his new job. I was thrilled to know how much he missed me. Most important of all, each letter brought fresh evidence of his impending breakup with Marie. Finally it happened – he wrote to say that she had returned to her mother's house in Arles, and could I come to be with him?

When I started making arrangements – without revealing my real reason for making the trip – a lot of people told me I was crazy. Algiers was still considered to be a dangerous place, even though the war was over. That didn't bother me – all I could think of was how much I missed Henri. I felt like I couldn't live without him.

Claire, who had been such a good friend in time of need, again came to my rescue. She introduced me to a family acquaintance named Omar, an Algerian graduate of the elite ENA (National School of Administration) in Paris. Three years prior, Omar had met Claire's brother Alain on a field trip to Moscow that was reserved for France's brightest students. The two young men struck up a friendship, and on returning to Paris Alain introduced his new friend to the rest of his family. When I met Omar, I remembered having seen him at Alain's funeral.

Omar's life changed abruptly with the granting of Algerian independence. He had been following the path of other ENA graduates, occupying a promising position with the regional government of a southern French province, when he was suddenly forced to choose between what had become two different countries. Shortly before I met him, he had decided to give up his French nationality in order to rally to his newly liberated homeland. This was his last trip to Paris before taking a position in his home town of Algiers as one of the youngest members of the Algerian government.

When Claire told me about him, I expected someone solemn, perhaps even dour. Omar was quite the contrary. Compact and athletic, with twinkling eyes and a winning smile, he was always ready to crack a joke. We hit it off immediately, and after laughingly comparing Algeria to the Wild West, he promised the Lagrange family that he'd look after me.

Omar was shrewd and perceptive. When no one could over-hear him, he asked me what my real motivation was for going to Algiers. Without going into detail, I told him it was to be with Henri. It seemed a good idea to put them in touch, so I gave him Henri's address and phone number. I also wrote Henri, telling him to expect a call from Omar who was leaving for Algiers the next day.

Not sure how long I'd be away, I asked Mr. V for a temporary leave of absence without pay. I had enough money in my savings account to tide me over a few months. He reluctantly agreed, but handed me some sheet music and asked me to continue send-ing him lyrics in English. I paid two months' rent in advance, bought my plane ticket, wired Henri to meet my flight – and I was off!

The Algiers airport was a low, rambling building that might have been mistaken for a warehouse if it hadn't carried the sign "Aéroport d'Alger". A few small planes were parked here and there on the airfield. Our plane stopped several yards away from the airport building. I had just started walking across the tarmac when I saw Henri heading toward me. As we rushed into each other's arms, I felt like I was in a remake of "Casablanca" with a happy ending.

Passport control and customs were mere formalities, and Henri whisked me out of the airport to his car. I was so happy to see my lover, I had eyes only for him. Much later I learned that had I been paying attention, I would have spotted Omar standing discreetly behind a pillar, making sure I hadn't been stranded. When he saw us happily reunited, he left unnoticed.

As we drove toward the city, Henri explained how Algiers is built on a hill that overlooks a half-moon shaped bay. After a few miles of dusty roads lined with nondescript industrial buildings, we rounded a corner and I could see it – *Alger la blanche*, the white city. Unlike other, prouder port cities that rise from the ocean to dominate it, Algiers descends gracefully into the water like a woman letting her hair down before sinking into her lover's arms.

The city spreads out above the bay in a fan shape. To the east is the oldest, most authentically Moorish sector which includes the famous Casbah. The center of town, principally built by the French, contains administrative buildings and a university along with shops, cafés and restaurants. Those were areas I would get to know later. The day of my arrival, Henri steered us to the west, up winding streets to a residential area known as Hydra which was where he lived. During the colonial era, Hydra had been reserved for wealthy Europeans, mostly French. Now, two years after Independence, only a few influential Algerians had managed to find homes there. Departing Frenchmen had left their residences to people like Henri who had come to work there, or to the *coopérants* – literally, the "cooperators", people who showed up from various parts of the world to help build the new country.

Henri had a spacious, airy flat in a modern apartment building. As we went in, I was struck by the fact that for once he wasn't opening the door of an anonymous hotel room. This was where he really lived. Everything in the apartment belonged to him, carried his smell, was part of his world. And now, at last, so was I.

For the first few days we did little else than make up for the many months we'd been physically apart. As a welcoming gift, Henri had bought me a red caftan with brocaded stripes, edged with gold trim. It was a long robe with a deep V-neck, which he encouraged me to wear around the house with nothing on underneath. It looked very sexy, and gave me a delicious feeling of being a vamp. Henri said I looked like an oriental princess in a sultan's harem.

The exoticism of the setting overwhelmed me. A dusty light came through the louvered blinds that shut out the heat of the day. I could hear street vendors hawking their wares in melodious singsong voices. When we went outside, we could see a series of villas with terraced gardens stretching down to the glittering bay below. At night, Henri took me to a place known as the Officers' Club. It was a holdover from colonial days, complete with a carved wooden bar with gleaming brass rails, ceiling fans, and waiters in white jackets with gold buttons. As we sat under a lattice dripping with bougainvillea, drinking cocktails so complicated I couldn't guess their contents, Henri explained in a low voice that now that the war was over this had become the meeting place of people involved in the oil business. I noticed that most of them seemed to be European, not Arab, and everyone was speaking French.

The first taste I got of what the newly liberated nation was really like came when Henri took me into the center of town to have lunch with Omar. In the time between Omar's return to Algiers and my arrival there, they had gotten acquainted and even become good friends. The restaurant where they liked to meet for lunch was halfway between Omar's office at the Palais du Gouvernement and Henri's office on the Rue Michelet. The two of them were a mirror image of the restaurant's clientele – half Algerian, half European, mostly businessmen. The food was similarly bilateral, with the main dish, the *plat du jour*, generally a staple of French cuisine while the first course and dessert were Algerian.

My favorite dish there was an appetizer called a *brik* – a triangle of flaky filo dough with an exquisitely seasoned egg cooked inside. A similar dish, called a *bourek*, contained chopped meat or tuna. At dessert time the filo dough made another appearance, this time as baklava filled with chopped nuts and drizzled with honey, usually served with the wonderful mint tea that is a staple in North Africa. Waiters take pride in the way they serve the tea, pouring it from a great height into the circle of cups or glasses on a tray without ever spilling a drop. The cup has no handles, but Omar taught me how to hold it with two fingers – the index finger underneath the cup, the thumb on the rim – so as not to burn myself. The boys joked about the *hamd'ullah* (literally, thanks be to God) – the famous burp to express gratitude at the end of the meal.

"This is a businessmen's restaurant," said Omar. "If no one here is burping, it must mean that business is terrible!"

It turned out that Henri's father, the army officer, had once been stationed in Algeria and Henri had childhood memories of Algiers. Those memories often coincided with Omar's own childhood, and we began to have fantasies that they had perhaps known each other as little boys, since they were the same age. They took me to a park – le parc de Galand – just off the Rue Michelet on the slope of a hill called the Telemly. Both boys remembered having pony rides in the park, and they recalled with great fondness a parrot named Jako who was always there in his cage, endlessly saying *"cacaouhète à coco, cacaouhète à Jako"* (a peanut for the parrot, a peanut for Jako). There was no longer any trace of the cage, much less the parrot, and since Independence the pony rides had been stopped.

Many such vestiges of the colonial era were now disappearing. Theaters and cinemas were closed, as were department stores and many smaller shops. I had been warned that consumer goods I took for granted in Paris would be unavailable in Algiers, but the only items I felt were indispensable were the cleaning and lubricating fluids for my contact lenses. It was easy to pack extra supplies of them, and for the rest – I was ready for adventure.

My "bodyguards" Henri and Omar were in complete agreement when it came to keeping my adventurousness under control. In Paris Henri had never been domineering, but here in Algiers everything was different. Many women were veiled, and all were expected to defer to the men. Any woman who displayed too much independence was at risk of being arrested and carded by the police as a prostitute. There were other dangers too. The French had left behind a lot of booby traps and unexploded plastic bombs which occasionally went off. Murders, whether motivated by politics or vengeance, were not uncommon. Still, the general feeling among the population was one of joy and relief. After a decade of war that had claimed the lives of one out of every seven Algerians, leaving no family untouched, even an uneasy peace was a blessing.

Henri and Omar assured me I had nothing to worry about – they had planned out my daily schedule. On days when he had to work, Henri dropped me off at a beach Omar had located, not too far from the center of town, where I would be safe. It had been very popular in colonial days, but now it was virtually deserted. No girls or women swam there, although veiled mothers sat on the sand watching their children play in the water. Some boys and men came for a swim and generally left fairly quickly, perhaps to go back to work. I only swam there myself when Henri or Omar was with me.

The principal feature of the beach was a wooden shack which served as both a restaurant and a bar, run by an affable middle-aged man named Jamal. From his eagerness to please me I deduced he was a friend of Omar's. Near the shack was a lanai made of reeds with tables and chairs underneath. I liked to sit there to work on lyrics for Mr. V, or just to daydream, or to chat with Jamal. Like many other Algerians I met, he assumed I was French and asked if I came from Paris. If I said yes, people invariably asked what neighborhood I came from and if I knew their relative so-and-so who had a grocery store or worked in a garage there. At first, their questions put me on the defensive. They didn't seem to detect a foreign accent in my French. But if they thought I was French, why were they being so friendly? Hadn't they just fought a long and bitter war against the French?

I asked Jamal, and his response astounded me. "The French are our brothers," he said. "War between brothers is the cruelest war there is, but now it's over. We can be brothers again." I didn't have the heart to tell him that in my opinion, very few French felt the same sense of brotherhood.

The lunches that Jamal managed to produce on little more than a charcoal brazier and a gas ring never failed to amaze me. Skewered meat or fresh fish was grilled and served with salad or fresh vegetables, followed by fruit or pastry – simple fare, simply presented but absolutely delicious. When Jamal found out that I was American he insisted on serving me my national beverage, Coca Cola, with my lunch. Like the French, he laughingly called it *le Beaujolais du Texas*. I asked him if he had any limes to put in the Coke and he didn't, but the next day he presented me with an entire bagful of them, and from then on there were always limes for me.

When Henri didn't have to work we spent the day together. Sometimes we just stayed in Hydra, wandering no farther than the *ravin de la femme sauvage,* a wild tangle of underbrush that tumbled all the way down the hill. I tried to find out why it was known as the "wild woman's ravine" but no one could tell me. Sometimes we went to the beach together, or he took me driving around the city. My favorite place to visit, off limits if I was alone, was the Casbah.

I loved it for many reasons. Even when I was a child it was the symbol of romantic escape. In the old movie "Algiers", Charles Boyer murmured "Come weez me to ze Casbah." In grade school we used to add, "And we will go on ze roof and spit on ze people." Later, in Paris, I learned that "Algiers" was actually the remake of a famous French movie called "Pepe le Moko" in which Jean Gabin, not Charles Boyer, played the role of the doomed gangster trapped in the Casbah.

Visiting it in real life was not a disappointment – it was even more mysterious than it appeared in the movies. Most of the streets were stairways or alleyways lined with arched, iron-studded wooden doors. Above the doors the upper floors of the buildings jutted out, sometimes so far that their windows nearly touched those of the building across the street. The streets twisted and turned to the point that I could never tell exactly where I was. There were a few main streets, and those were lined with shops of every description. Street vendors were everywhere, hawking their wares.

I was able to resist the temptation of the ornate fabrics, often containing gold thread, that were hung out in swaths to attract passers-by. But despite the hot weather, I found the multi-colored hand-spun wools irresistible, and I bought a few skeins to make myself a poncho. Henri and I both fell in love with the Tunisian birdcages made of white-painted wire – magical dwellings with a square base surmounted by a bulbous dome. We bought one, not to keep birds but as the first act of setting up housekeeping together.

Henri also bought me my first hand of Fatma, a small gold hand on a gold chain. In Arabic it's called a *khamsa*, which means "five", for the five fingers of the hand. Its purpose is to ward off the evil eye, and it is particularly lucky if someone else offers it to you as a gift. That was the start of my *khamsa* collection, which has since grown to include hands of all sizes, some in base metals, some in gold, some with pearls or precious stones, some very plain, some very ornate, some given by friends, some I bought myself. I love them all.

I didn't know what to get for Henri, but the Casbah provided an unusual opportunity. Before Henri left Paris, we went shopping for clothes for him to wear in Algiers. In a store called Old England he tried on a jacket and trousers made of white seersucker with a thin blue stripe, imported from the USA. They looked great on him but they were very expensive. He decided he could afford the trousers but not the jacket. Then one morning in the Casbah, in a tiny alley, I spotted a shop selling all sorts of bric-a-brac. In the midst of it, on a hanger, was the jacket – the exact same material, in Henri's size, for a fraction of the price. He had the trousers on already, and when he put on the jacket it was a perfect match. We met Omar for lunch that day and he said it was *mektoub*, fate, that had allowed Henri to complete his outfit. The boys wondered about the fate of the tourist who had brought the jacket to Algiers, and jokingly looked for dagger holes in the garment. We decided he'd lost it in a card game.

Henri loved anything American, so he was delighted when Omar told us that near El Biar, just outside of town, there was a U.S. Expo being held that weekend. It wasn't on my list of "things to do in Algeria" but their enthusiasm won me over and I agreed to go with them. The expo was held on a dusty open field that otherwise served as a fairground. People milled in and out of tents that held exhibits about agriculture, American history, and the principles of democracy. The women were mostly interested in demonstrations of new-fangled cooking gadgets, while the men gazed dreamily at a mock-up of the space capsule that John Glenn had used to orbit earth.

To one side of the fairground was an area that had been fenced off to form a corral. In it were over a dozen Texas longhorn steers. The poor beasts were grouped forlornly at the far end of the corral, oblivious to the shouts and exhortations of the people looking at them. Like the others, we hung over the top rail of the fence, calling to the cattle.

"Know what's the matter?" said Omar. "They're homesick!"

Henri immediately agreed, insisting that I had to "talk American" to them to see if they'd react. The idea seemed absurd but appealing. I gave a few tentative hoots and hollers, and their ears pricked up. My mind raced as I searched for the right phrases to interest Texas longhorns. What was it they always said in Westerns? "C'mon, li'l dogie," that was it. I shouted it out, and the first steer started to amble towards me. I repeated the phrase several times, and each time I added more of a twang.

"C'mawn li'l dawgie, git along," I drawled. The steers loved it. Soon they were all clustered together in front of me, and I was able to reach over the fence to pat their muzzles or scratch their ears. I addressed them with every trite Western phrase I could think of, making my voice as nasal as possible. As the steers lowed in response, I realized how different my voice sounded from what they'd been hearing since they arrived in Algeria – mostly Arabic with a smattering of French. I also realized that at this U.S. Expo I appeared to be the only American person present.

Henri and Omar were busy pointing out to whoever would listen that although I spoke French, I was an authentic Yankee who had a special power over Texas longhorns. The onlookers nodded dutifully and looked impressed.

From then on, Omar rarely missed an opportunity to kid me about my nationality. Once we were sitting on the terrace of a café when he was accosted by an itinerant carpet seller. Algiers was full of such fellows, schlepping their wares on their backs. I felt sorry for them but basically they were a nuisance. Omar spoke briefly in Arabic to the man who nodded emphatically, and I assumed we'd gotten rid of him. I was wrong. The man rushed over to my side of the table, kneeled down in front of me and proceeded to spread out all his carpets, while babbling in Arabic interspersed with as much French as he could muster. It was clear he wouldn't leave until I bought something, and I was relieved when I was able to limit my purchase to a tiny prayer rug.

As he rolled up his wares and moved away, I turned accusingly to Omar. "What was that about?"

He chuckled wickedly. "Oh, I just told him I didn't want to buy anything but that you were an American tourist who loved carpets." I had to laugh despite myself.

On the other hand, Henri's almost worshipful attitude toward Americans was beginning to annoy me. Perhaps because of his youthful experience working for the PX, he seemed to think that the "American way" meant a success story for everyone. Like many Frenchmen who had never actually worked in the U.S., he assumed that Americans had an enviable lifestyle plus the *avantages sociaux* French workers had, such as a government financed pension plan, health care, many weeks of paid vacation, and a long list of religious holidays. As far as I could tell, the French were incapable of imagining what life would be like without those advantages. Not only they took them for granted, they couldn't conceive that a country as progressive as the U.S. didn't have system that was as good or better than theirs.

My attempts to explain this to Henri didn't seem to sink in, and he blithely continued to dream about having the best of both worlds. He was fond of saying that he "liked to keep his options open". I knew that meant that he didn't like having to make decisions. I also knew that some options can't be kept open forever.

Reality hit during the third week of Ramadan, the month-long Moslem holiday that obliges its followers to fast from sunup to sundown. Omar had invited us to join him for dinner at a beach resort he called "Bordj el kifan", known to the French as *Fort de l'eau* (the Water Fort). Omar drove me there and Henri was to join us later after he was through with work. The main feature of the place wasn't a fort but rather a long, very wide sidewalk bordered with tables and lined with barbecues on which delicious-smelling skewers of beef, lamb and merguez sausage were slowly cooking. Interspersed with the barbecues were large vats of oil used for making potato chips. The sun hadn't quite set but cooks were already busy lowering paper-thin slices of potato into the bubbling oil. Omar explained that I was a foreign visitor and I was immediately handed a plate of the crispiest, most delectable chips I had ever eaten. A few minutes later it was officially sundown and everyone was digging in when Henri showed up, looking stricken.

Omar clapped him jovially on the back. "What's the matter, my brother? Did you lose your winning lottery ticket?"

"It isn't funny, Omar." Henri avoided looking at me. "Marie is coming back to Algiers tomorrow."

The rest of the evening was spent trying to figure out what to do. We didn't know what Marie had in mind – she had simply sent a telegram announcing her arrival time. Was she attempting a reconciliation or moving back for good? In either case, it was clear I couldn't be part of her welcoming committee. I had to move out of Hydra the next morning. I had seen a beautiful old hotel, the St. Georges, but Henri said it was too close to Hydra. He suggested the Hotel Aletti, another Algiers landmark near the center of town.

Omar settled the matter. He ordered Henri to deliver me and my luggage to his office the next morning. I would be staying with him and his family.

My last night in Hydra was far from romantic. Henri was too perturbed to be amorous. He wandered around the apartment, obsessively removing any trace of my presence while I packed my belongings. We decided I should take the Tunisian birdcage with me to Omar's. "We'll have a home for it one day, you'll see," Henri said earnestly.

The precariousness of my situation had finally begun to dawn on me. When Henri dropped me off at Omar's office, promising to call me soon, I felt panicked. Here I was in an unfamiliar place with nothing to do except to wait and see if Marie felt like going back to her husband. I couldn't bother Omar who had a lot of work to do, and lunch was out of the question because of Ramadan, so I set off aimlessly on foot.

In front of the Government Palace where Omar worked was a large esplanade called the Forum. Since it was on a hill, it consisted of broad steps and terraces, on one of which was a World War I memorial statue showing grief-stricken women mourning fallen soldiers. I remembered having seen the Forum in French newsreels that pre-dated Independence. De Gaulle had spoken to the *pieds noirs* there in 1958, giving his famous "Je vous ai compris" speech in which he assured the colonial population that he understood their problem. Two years later, when he had shown no signs of actually addressing their problem, there were bloody riots at the Place du Forum. But now it was quiet and uneventful – the crowds that had once swarmed there were gone, and the occasional passers-by gave no clue to the locale's tumultuous past.

I climbed higher and higher, until I reached a street that began to slope down in the opposite direction. My eyes must have been more moist than usual, because as I crossed the street I suddenly realized that one of my contact lenses had popped out. Now that was a real problem. I figured the likelihood of replacing it in Algiers was close to zero. I had to find it, so I crouched down in the middle of the street and began searching.

Almost immediately I was surrounded by street urchins who appeared out of nowhere, eager to help. "What did you lose, lady? Money? Jewelry?"

When I explained that I was looking for a contact lens they seemed baffled, but bravely dove to their knees and began handing me every tiny scrap they found. The closest they got were pieces of a broken Coke bottle. The way they were swarming over the street, my poor little lens was probably getting squashed. I had given up hope when one of them stuck out his hand and asked, "Is this it?"

It was. It actually was.

"You're lucky, lady," said one of the kids.

Despite my gloom, I had to agree. I emptied my purse and pockets of all my loose change, and while the kids squabbled over it

I walked down the street telling myself to cheer up. This had to be a good omen.

After a few more hours of wandering I started to head back to Omar's office. It was a hot day and as I passed by a café I realized that I was dying of thirst. I entered the café, stood at the counter and ordered a lemonade. The bartender, a burly middle-aged man, looked at me severely.

"You must resist. Sundown will be here before you know it."

"You don't understand. I'm not Muslim." I suddenly realized that my days at the beach had turned me the color of the other inhabitants of Algiers.

The bartender laughed. "At this time of day, nobody's Muslim."

"No, really," I insisted. "I'm not Algerian, I'm not Muslim, and I'd like a glass of lemonade, please." I was really thirsty and really annoyed. When he crossed his arms across his chest and refused to move, I decided to up the ante. I fished around in my purse and pulled out my passport. "You see? This is me. I'm American."

He glowered and shook his head, but poured me a glass of lemonade. As he handed it to me, he muttered, "I've seen people resort to a lot of low tricks to break Ramadan. But a fake American passport? That's the worst!"

As I walked to Omar's office, I began to worry about what it would be like living with his family. Perhaps they wouldn't welcome a Jewish American visitor. How would I fit in? Omar was waiting for me, eager to get home. During Ramadan everyone leaves work early so they can be ready to eat the minute the sun goes down.

Omar's parents' house was located at the top of the Telemly hill, on a steeply stair-stepped street called the Rue des Sept Merveilles – the Street of the Seven Wonders. The moment I stepped in I was greeted effusively by the whole family who seemed delighted to have the opportunity of welcoming me. In fact, I immediately felt as if I'd been adopted, a feeling they encouraged by telling me to call Omar's father Baba and his mother Yema, the way my "sisters and brothers" did.

Omar was the oldest of seven children, five boys and two girls. Amina, the oldest girl, was eighteen and her sister Yasmina was sixteen. After Omar came Ahmed and Lakhdar, then the two girls, and then fourteen-year-old Namir. Ali, the baby, was ten. I couldn't resist calling them the Seven Wonders, and their parents beamed their approval.

The meal began with steaming bowls of *chorba*, the traditional soup used to break the day-long fast. With its big chunks of meat and vegetables, it would have been enough for me, but of course they were hungrier than that. Next came grilled meat, roasted potatoes and a salad called *salade algérienne* because its colors – green peppers, white onions and red tomatoes – were those of the Algerian flag. Meals at Omar's house always ended with trays of dates, figs and Oriental pastries. But during Ramadan they also made a special treat called *zlabia*, pretzel-like twists of sweet dough that were deep-fried and then soaked in a mixture of honey and rose water. I found them irresistible and I'm afraid to say I couldn't stop eating them. Far from making me feel embarrassed, the family was delighted. Not only did I like their food, but it gave them something to kid me about.

I was in a household of people who loved to kid each other and argue about everything and anything. They were spectacularly well equipped to do so, since everyone was trilingual. They spoke Arabic and French, but because Yema's family came from the mountains of Kabylia, they also spoke Berber. Quiet, mild-mannered Baba had worked as a government bureaucrat under the French, but now he was retired. The family loved to kid him about the fact that he spoke Berber with an accent.

Yema, whose intelligence shone from her strong-featured face, was perfectly fluent in all three languages – but she was illiterate. Omar was fond of saying, "If my mother could read and write, she'd be prime minister." The more I got to know her, the more I agreed with him.

The sisters were different from each other, both in character and physically. Amina was short, slight and shy. Her younger sister Yasmina was chubby and ebullient. Ahmed, a car mechanic, was the family jokester and Lakhdar was a gifted athlete, a star player on the local soccer team. Young Namir was quiet and bookish, and Ali – like any little boy his age – loved to get into mischief. Strangely Lakhdar, with his brown hair and freckles, looked a lot like my cousin Alfred. When I remarked on it, Omar explained that a lot of people on their Kabyle side of the family looked like that. The Berbers were named for their barbarian ances-tors who had swept down to North Africa from Europe. Many of them were light-haired and some were even blue-eyed. During the Arab invasion the Berbers were forced to retreat to the Atlas Mountains where they still lived.

The family told me how Yema's mother had traveled all the way to Algiers, alone and on foot, in the 1920's. She had with her a goat to provide milk and a double-bitted axe to protect herself with. There was some discussion about whether or not she had actually used the axe, but everyone agreed how dangerous the journey was. Like all Kabyle women, grandma wore her wealth in the form of silver jewelry, some of which Yema showed me. It was incrusted with coral and decorated with green, yellow and blue enamel. Some of the pieces hanging from the necklaces were actually French coins, which in those days were made of silver.

The conversation then turned to grandma's sister and her family, who I didn't know, and I began to realize how tired I was. I hadn't slept much on my last night in Hydra. The family wished me good night and I went up to my room, which was small but pleasant with a window opening onto the garden in the courtyard. That night, it was easy to fall asleep.

When I woke up the next morning, Omar and Ahmed had already gone to work. I found Yema, Amina and Yasmina on the roof making couscous. The roof was a flat terrace surrounded by a low wall, from which you could see a wonderful view of the city below and the bay beyond. After admiring it for a while, I turned to look at what the women were doing. They were on their hands and knees, taking the semolina that is the basis for couscous and rubbing it through large round sieves. It was called "rolling the couscous", a process that called for rubbing the semolina through a series of sieves with ever-tighter wire mesh that caused the grains to get smaller and smaller. I had always assumed that the semolina was simply manufactured to the correct size but they assured me that the lightest, fluffiest couscous had to be hand-rolled. It reminded me of Jewish families competing for the best matzoh balls.

They invited me to try my hand at rolling the couscous, and I readily agreed. I had grabbed some figs off the tree in the garden on my way upstairs, and I felt ready to try anything. At first it didn't seem all that difficult. I imitated their movements, leaning forward with my whole body to help push the grains through the sieve. It was easy, and even fun. But after twenty minutes or so my back, thighs and arms had all begun to ache and I had to stop. The women had been at it for over an hour – obviously, they were in much better shape than I was.

When we all went down to the kitchen they made me some "summer couscous", not the traditional recipe but steamed semolina served with buttermilk and white grapes. It was wonderful. At dinner that night, the couscous was served with the usual accompaniment of boiled chicken and vegetables with grilled lamb chops and merguez sausage. Nobody mentioned my couscous-rolling activities, but once we started eating Yasmina asked everyone how they thought the dinner tasted. With a twinkle in his eye, Ahmed pretended to taste the semolina very carefully and then made his pronouncement. "It tastes like… like… American couscous!"

The next night, just before dinner, I finally got a call from Henri setting a date for us to meet for a drink the next day. I was overjoyed to see him but being in a public place, we had to avoid any outward signs of affection. Still, we sat next to each other on the *banquette* of the café and he was able to give me some of his secret caresses. I was hoping for concrete news but he was evasive. He seemed more anxious to talk about us than about Marie. "Our love is so special, we must do everything to preserve it."

"Everything" meant, of course, that I shouldn't leave Algiers. That was no problem – I was having a wonderful time on the Street of the Seven Wonders, and I didn't get the feeling that I was wearing out my welcome. I still had enough money to get by, and Mr. V kept sending me work to keep me busy. But what was really happening? I was again engulfed by those old familiar feelings of inadequacy. I was second best, not quite good enough. Would I ever be number one?

I decided the only way to deal with the problem was to not think about it. As I became more involved with the family's daily life, the days were filled with new and interesting activities. I began doing the marketing with Yema and the girls, and it was fun to haggle over the price of everything. They taught me to put henna on my hands and dark kohl around my eyes, both for beauty and to protect against infection. I accompanied them to the tomb of a saint, Sidi Abderrahmane, where to my surprise they didn't pray but sat around chatting with other women.

In a culture where females are not treated as equals, I was surprised to discover how women bond together simply by virtue of their gender. Whenever I went to a gathering attended only by women, I was instantly accepted as a member of the sisterhood. The saint whose tomb we visited was reputed to grant women's wishes, and everyone spoke openly of their desire to find a good husband or get pregnant or make a rival disappear. We giggled like schoolgirls as we swapped stories about men and their foibles. Amina had a suitor who occasionally came to the house, and we speculated about when he would propose. There were no such prospects for Yasmina – everyone kidded her about how difficult and picky she was. No one was good enough for her.

They had pried out of Omar what my situation was with Henri, and they even met him once when he came to the house to pick me up. Far from disapproving of my having a relationship with a married man, they only seemed interested in debating whether he would make me happy or not. Marriage, I learned, was an impermanent institution in Algeria. A dissatisfied husband could simply confront his wife in a public place and say "I repudiate you" three times, and that was it.

In those days, less than half the women in Algiers (outside the Casbah, a stronghold of traditionalism) were veiled. Of those who were, the young ones usually wore high heels and short skirts that you could glimpse through the folds of the veil when they walked. The long white outer garment, called a *haik*, was placed on the head and then draped around the body, sort of like a Roman toga. This was completed by a small lace-trimmed veil that was placed on the bridge of the nose and then tied behind the head. Although they refused to wear it themselves, the girls had a *haik* at the house and one day for fun I tried it on. I thought I might wear it outside to see if I could "pass". I was still mastering the art of draping it properly when Omar came home. When he saw what I was doing he was furious.

"How can you do this, even for fun? Don't you realize what this represents? In this country, traditionalists are the enemies of progress. For Algeria to thrive, we have to give equal opportunity to everyone, and not hide behind the veils of obscurantism!"

Like everyone else in the family, I responded meekly to Omar's outburst. Since his father's retirement and his return from Paris, he was the one who ruled the roost. Not only was he the best educated, he had actually experienced the real world outside Algeria so obviously he knew things the others didn't. They all recognized that, and willingly respected him as head of the family.

But there were nuances. One thing Omar had managed to escape by living and studying in France was the horror of the war in the years between 1957 and 1962. When Ahmed thought about the war, he lost his jocular manner. No one in their immediate family had died, but uncles and cousins had fallen victim to terrible atrocities – as had so many others, including close friends. All over the city were centers for the orphans of *chouhadas*, or martyrs, and most of the streets with French names were being re-named after heroes of the Revolution.

The war was over but definitely not forgotten. I realized that first-hand one morning when I woke up to find the neighborhood abuzz with excitement. At the bottom of the hill, the main street was filled with French tanks, and soldiers in French uniforms were swarming over the stairs. "Oh my God," shrieked a neighbor. "They're back! It's started all over again!"

Omar quickly phoned his office and reassured us. It wasn't really the French army, it was movie extras and props. The Italian director Gillo Pontecorvo was shooting his film "The Battle of Algiers". Since I spoke French and Italian, they let me hang around the shoot for a few days. As always on movie sets, the actors spent most of their time sitting and waiting for the lighting, props and extras to be in place. I was particularly impressed by one of the actors, a Frenchman named Jean Martin, who was extremely kind and gentle. He spoke passionately of the great victory the Algerians had achieved by winning their independence. When the film came out, it was banned in France and it was several years before I actually saw it. When I did, I discovered what a great actor Jean Martin was. It was he who played the icy-eyed French colonel who marches his troops into Algiers, scaring everyone to death.

One of the neighborhoods where the film was shooting was at the base of a cliff. Looking up, I could see what appeared to be a Catholic basilica overlooking the bay. I asked about it at dinner and the family told me it was a venerable old church called Notre Dame d'Afrique, Our Lady of Africa. Omar assured me I would enjoy visiting it, and the girls offered to go with me. Baba said that it was too far for three girls to go alone and we would have to take a male family member with us. The only one available was ten-year-old Ali, but he stood up tall and assured everyone he would protect us.

The most remarkable things about the church were its vast dome and the large number of votives hanging from the ceiling. In the 19th century this had obviously been a church devoted to the sea and those who sailed on it, whether merchantmen or fishermen. Those who wished to give thanks to Our Lady of Africa offered models of their boats which hung in profusion above our heads. As we studied this charming sight, we were approached by a wizened old sacristan who spoke to us in French. He was at pains to show us a row of candles which, he explained, were used to accompany our prayers to heaven.

"I know you're not Catholic," he said, "but I think in your religion you also like to light candles, don't you?"

We mumbled an affirmative answer. Yasmina and I were having trouble keeping a straight face. He handed us a candle, urging us to take it home and light it. "Tell your mother it will bring blessings from Our Lady of Africa."

We went home and gave Yema the candle and the message. She nodded and said, "He's right. We're all children of the same God."

I knew she meant it. The family had never exhibited the slightest trace of anti-Semitism. *Au contraire,* they seemed to feel that we were all Semites together, with Abraham as a common ancestor. Politically, they were nervous about the state of Israel who they viewed as a potential threat to Arab interests. But in those days, Algerians were even more nervous about a would-be ally – Egypt – who they feared was trying to take control of their country.

The first president of Algeria, Ben Bella, had just been removed from office and placed under house arrest because he was too chummy with Egypt. Ben Bella was a charismatic, hedonistic leader who liked to show up unannounced to play soccer with the kids in the vacant lot of a poor neighborhood. The people loved him, but they also loved to enumerate his foibles. Once, I was told, the Egyptians offered him a battleship and he accepted. When the ship sailed into the Bay of Algiers, he had a contingent of sailors do exercises on the deck for everyone to see. But when they tried to turn the ship around and sail away on maneuvers, it keeled over and sank. "What else can you expect from Egyptians," the people said. "Ben Bella should have known."

The new president was a tall, very thin and ascetic man named Houari Boumedienne. He was as sober as Ben Bella was jolly. Even I could feel the change. Luxury items left over from colonial days, like perfume and cosmetics, disappeared from stores. There was less celebration of revolutionary victory and more strengthening of Islamic values.

But life on the Street of the Seven Wonders went on as usual. I got into the habit of going to the market and helping with the cooking and cleaning whenever I could. My reward came in the evening after dinner when Omar, the girls and I, sometimes accompanied by Ahmed or Lakhdar, went for a walk. In the dark, the smell of the night-blooming jasmine was overpowering. We walked silently, our ears pricked, listening. If someone heard music we followed the sound. Then a discussion ensued between the girls, who argued until they agreed on the identity of the musicians. Their favorite was an ud player, singer and composer named Boujema el Ankis. But there were others they liked too.

Once a group of musicians had met with their approval, then it was up to Omar to guide us to where the wedding or other festivity was taking place. He walked right up to the door, knocked, and when they opened he motioned to me. "We are here with a foreign visitor. Can we come in?"

The answer was always yes. Foreigners were honored guests at any occasion. But being a woman, I was always sent to the room where women were celebrating, separate from the men. The women seemed to enjoy teaching me how to do a "you-you", a high glottal shriek used to express approval or encouragement. I even tried to learn a few dance steps. Although, as a Westerner, I disapproved of their sexist segregation, I had to admit it was fun to wiggle my hips without worrying what some man thought I looked like.

My real concern, of course, was Henri – and Marie. The longer she and I were both in Algiers, the more he worried about her running into me, and the more I worried about him actually getting a divorce. Every time we got together, it was in places that were farther and farther from the center of town. He tried to characterize our secret meetings as "excursions", opportunities for him to show me new places, but I had that familiar old feeling of being back in the arboretum with Frank where no one would see us.

One day he picked me up at the house and announced brightly that he was taking me someplace special. He knew I loved oysters, and enjoyed my surprise when he told me that was what we'd be having for lunch. We headed out of town to a place on the coast called Sidi Ferruch where, he explained, the French had created a *vivier*, an oyster farm. It took nearly an hour to get there and at first glance it didn't look like much – just a series of narrow wooden piers sticking out into the water. But when we walked on one of the piers he showed me the removable baskets in the water, filled with oysters, and the ropes to which mussels were attached. "There's our lunch," he exclaimed.

The *vivier* was now run by Algerians but they still catered mostly to Europeans. They even sold wine and we indulged in a bottle of Mascara, a full-bodied Algerian varietal that was popular in France too. We were the only customers there, and we felt like we were in one of those nostalgic films where the love story ends badly. But Henri was undaunted. After our meal we walked along the beach and he kept kissing me and saying things like, "When I kiss you I see stars." It was very nice.

We had started to drive back and were perhaps a mile away from Sidi Ferruch when there was a huge explosion and the sky lit up behind us. The restaurant and the warehouses of the *vivier* had blown up. He stopped the car and we just sat there, shaken. If we had stayed there five minutes longer we would have blown up too.

When we were calm enough to discuss what to do next, we debated whether to turn around and go back to Sidi Ferruch. Henri wisely suggested that we should continue driving toward Algiers and look for a place to call for help. Soon after we set off, we were reassured to see a string of emergency vehicles passing us in the other direction.

By the time we got back to the Street of the Seven Wonders, the news had been announced on the radio. They said that an old plastic bomb left behind by the French had exploded. The moment I walked in the house, Yema sent up prayers of thanks to God while the others pestered me with questions. Several people had been killed, and they were afraid we were among the victims. I tried to reassure them.

"I'm sure it sounded worse on the radio than it really was."

As I said the words, I found myself thinking of Daddy. In the early 1950's when he was on vacation in Havana, we heard some frightening news on the radio. Fidel Castro's rebels attacked the Government Palace and there was a lot of gunfire. The radio said that an American tourist in the hotel across the street – the hotel Daddy was staying in – had been killed accidentally when he stood too close to the window of his room.

We were in paroxysms of anxiety until we finally heard from Daddy that he was all right. When he got home, he told me the story. He had been at the beach, and then took a bus back to his hotel. When he got off the bus, he immediately knew something was wrong. Usually the square was full of people, talking animatedly and drinking coffee sold by ambulatory vendors with coffee urns on their backs. But that day the square was empty and silent. He went to his hotel room and waited to see what would happen. When he began to hear gunfire, he took the mattress from his bed and placed it over the window to protect him from stray bullets. Then he sat at the far end of the room until the battle was over. He too tried to downplay the drama of the event by saying, "I'm sure it sounded worse on the radio than it really was."

As sad as it was to be reminded of Daddy, I felt a certain smugness at following in his adventurous footsteps. And my trip to Algeria afforded me an opportunity to live out one of our fantasies as well. Long before the "Indiana Jones" films came out, Daddy and I used to dream about being archeologists. We didn't want to be in perilous jungle-type settings with snakes and bugs, but rather in a more urban location, digging up layers of ancient artifacts. Omar told me about such a place, a coastal town called Tipaza to the east of Algiers.

Omar loved to pore over maps, studying the location of the towns dotted along the Mediterranean coast. He had a theory – "my own crackpot theory", he would say – about the Phoenician traders of ancient times. They had small boats with which they left Lebanon and sailed around the Mediterranean buying and selling goods. Omar claimed to have figured out how long their supplies lasted, and then he calculated how far they could sail before needing to put in to shore for more. With a flourish, he pointed on the map to the evenly-distanced towns along the coast. "You see? Every time they needed fresh supplies, a town grew up!"

Tipaza was one such place. It had been colonized by the Romans who developed a thriving metropolis from the Phoenician port. After promising me for weeks, Omar finally found time to take me there. At first I was disappointed by the sight of a modern fishing village next to which a vacation village was being built.

Then we drove past a bluff to another inlet, and that's where ancient Tipaza was. It was in ruins, but it was still identifiable as a city. There were main streets rutted by chariot wheels, decorated with what had once been statuary and fountains. There were smaller streets lined with the foundations of houses, and here and there rose the proud columns of a temple.

What amazed me the most was that we were free to roam through the ruins. No one was there to guard the place and nothing was cordoned off or even marked with a "No Trespassing" sign. Omar, who had been there before, took me to see the ruins of a Roman villa. When we were standing in what had been the atrium, he told me to bend down and push away the sand on the ground. I did so, revealing a beautiful mosaic floor.

I looked at him questioningly. "We know it's there," he said, "but we don't have the funds to deal with it yet. So we just let the sand cover it."

Near one of the fountains, he told me I might find pottery shards if I dug for them. I had hardly begun digging when I found a curved piece that looked like part of a handle. I dug some more and found other pieces, some of which I could fit together. It was like a dream come true, especially when I found another curved piece that fit with the first, completing the handle.

Probably in an attempt to distract me before I wreaked complete havoc with the site, Omar pointed to a hilly area at the edge of the ancient city. Roads had been dug into the hill, and a series of arched doorways seemed to lead to caves or troglodyte dwellings. "That's the necropolis," he announced.

"It looks like a Club Med for the dead," I joked.

In a way, that's exactly what it was. The dead had their own city next to that of the living. We walked up the hill, which afforded an excellent view of the ruins. I took pictures, and Omar clowned around giving orations in fake Latin.

At the edge of the ruins an open field stretched out from the base of the hill. I looked down at it and thought, as I had so often before since coming to Algeria, about the strange attraction of the place. The sky and the ocean seemed bluer than anywhere else, the green seemed greener and the earth was a dark red as if drenched by the blood of endless battles. Albert Camus had written about his visceral attraction to this land – not a geographical or political concept but an actual physical attachment, like an umbilical cord linking you to the earth. To my surprise, I felt exactly the same way. I loved the gentle landscape of the Ohio countryside, and France was thrilling, but I wouldn't have laid down my life for either place. Here I could totally understand how people would be willing to die for their land.

In the field below, Omar had found something and was motioning to me to come. As I approached, he kneeled down and sent a strange projectile flying my way. Two or three others whooshed by before I reached him.

"What on earth is that?"

He chuckled, pulled up a plant and handed it to me. It was a vine with small green fruit that looked like pickles. The stems of the fruit were coiled like springs, and when you touched them they sent the fruit zooming as if by jet propulsion.

"I don't know the botanical name of this plant," he said. "I call them flying cucumbers."

We immediately engaged in a flying cucumber battle that had us ranging over the field looking for fresh munitions. When we reached the area nearest the hill, we stopped short at the sight of some Roman tombs. They were stone sarcophagi that had either been sunk into the ground or been covered by succeeding layers of dirt over the centuries. Most still had their lids on but some were open – and empty. One, particularly moving, was a twin sarcophagus shaped for two bodies lying side by side.

Omar motioned to an open one-person tomb and reached out for my camera. "Lie down here and I'll take a picture."

I shrugged my shoulders and stepped into the tomb to see how it felt before lying down. It couldn't have been more than three feet deep, and lengthwise it seemed to be exactly my size. That was touching – someone like me had been laid to rest here, perhaps thousands of years earlier.

I expected the experience to be somewhat creepy. I certainly didn't expect it to be something that would mark me for life, but it was. As I lay down I began to hear a buzzing – or perhaps it was a whirring, and I felt it rather than heard it – of all the life forces that had preceded me in that place.

A feeling swept over me – an epiphany, really – that the elements that composed my body had been borrowed, or recycled, from the organic matter that surrounded me. With that came the realization that sooner or later, those elements would be decomposed and reused in a different way. It was inevitable, but lying there in that ancient tomb, it wasn't frightening. Below ground level, looking up at the flowers and grass, I felt warm and comfortable. This was our world's environment and I was a part of it – part of a whole to which I belonged as absolutely as anyone who had preceded me, or anyone who would follow me. I was one with the earth, from which I came and to which I would return. There was nothing to be afraid of.

As we drove back to Algiers, Omar stopped the car when he saw a *fellagh*, a farmer, trudging along the road. He asked the man if we could give him a ride and the emaciated, weather-beaten fellow gratefully accepted. They spoke in Arabic, so it wasn't until we had dropped the man off at the next town about ten miles down the road that I could find out what they were talking about. Before Independence, the man had worked on a farm owned by a Frenchman. Now the farm was owned by the government, but the man's life hadn't improved. Quite the contrary. The man's wife was sick and there was no medical service as there had been before. The only way he could get medicine for her was to walk a dozen miles to the nearest town. His supervisor was a cruel man who refused to pay him for the time he needed to get to a pharmacy.

Omar shook his head. "It wasn't supposed to be that way," he said grimly.

That night after dinner, Omar and I went up on the roof to look at the stars. I could tell he was in a reflective mood, like me. We sat back to back like bookends, looking up at the heavens. After a while I asked what he was thinking about.

"I'm dreaming of a time," he said, "when the stars will shine on all humankind."

"But they already do," I protested.

"Yes, but the time I dream of is when people actually realize that."

I knew that his work wasn't going the way he wanted it to. Political interests and corruption were eroding the ideals on which the country was founded. Plus, their human resources were meager. Omar was one of only two Algerian graduates of the ENA, and there were fewer than half a dozen former students of Polytechnique in the government. Unlike the British who didn't fraternize with their colonial subjects but gave them Oxford educations, the French tendency was to mix with the natives but not educate them.

Omar brusquely changed the subject and began talking to me about Henri. Surprisingly, for someone who had been trained as a diplomat, what he had to say was very unflattering.

"You must be careful of Henri. He is *Shaitan* – Satan, the devil."

"Why do you say that? What do you mean?"

"He's a manipulator. He uses people."

I tried to get him to say more, but at first he refused. Finally, grudgingly, he told me he had recently found out that Marie's uncle was one of the founders of the Solio Oil Company. It was because he married her that Henri got his job.

So that was the "complication I couldn't understand"! No wonder he didn't get a divorce – he would lose his job. Had he been looking to me to get him another, better one? Had he ever been truthful with me, except about sex? Or was he even lying about that? No, certain things didn't lie, no matter how deceitful he was. But I felt like a fool.

A few days later I went to the post office known as *la Grande Poste* to mail some lyrics to Mr. V. It was a glorious building with ornate domes, built by the French in Moorish style, perhaps to celebrate the triumph of colonialism. I didn't mind standing in line. It gave me an opportunity to admire the carved wooden grillwork and inlaid mosaics.

As I turned to leave, I found myself nose to nose with Marie. I had prepared a hundred scenarios for when that might happen, but they all failed me at the sight of Marie, smiling at me, holding out her hand over her pregnant belly.

"What a surprise," I managed to gasp.

She didn't seem to suspect anything. She chattered away about what a small world it was and how I really must come to visit them. I told her I was sorry but my stay in Algiers was nearly over and I was about to return to Paris. As I said the words, I realized how true they were. It was over, and I was leaving.

It wasn't hard getting a return reservation. I was in the middle of thanking Omar's family, leaving them the Tunisian birdcage as a farewell present, when the phone rang. It was Henri, speaking in a low, urgent voice.

"Barbara, I've got to see you."

"I'll see you in hell, Henri. Thanks for the memories." I hung up.

Omar made jokes as he took me to the airport but it was hard saying goodbye. How could I ever thank him for his friendship and hospitality?

"Don't worry," he said, "I'll probably wash up on your doorstep before long. Those of us in the government who refuse to take bribes are getting death threats. You'll have a chance to return the favor."

"My door will always be open to you, my brother."

On the plane, I had a window seat but in order to reach it I had to ask a man sitting in the aisle seat to stand up. I said "excuse me" in Arabic and when he didn't react right away I repeated it in French.

"Oh, pardon, mademoiselle," he said, rising to let me by. It turned out he was a Kabyle who spoke Berber and French but no Arabic. He assumed I was an Arabic-speaking Algerian who also spoke French. He also assumed that this was my first trip to Paris, and he was at pains to explain what a dangerous place Paris could be for a nice Algerian girl.

I smiled, leaned back in my seat, and told the man not to worry. I intended to be very, very careful.

# GENERATION GAP

## III

## *The Enablers*

"Better things for better living through chemistry" was more than a postwar advertising slogan. It was a religious credo. Nylon and orlon delivered us from discomfort. Drip-dry clothing delivered us from ironing. Plastic delivered us from breakage. DDT delivered us from infestation. Penicillin delivered us from disease.

Everyone bowed down in worship of the ever-expanding periodic table of the elements, thankfully and expectantly. Confidence in new scientific discoveries was total. People craved the reassurance of indoor asbestos and outdoor DDT. They sat in lawn chairs to watch nuclear testing.

The first whistle-blower, Rachel Carson, only published her findings in 1960 and it took decades for her warnings to be taken seriously. In the years following World War II, there seemed to be no human problem that chemistry couldn't solve.

Among the most beloved of these new substances were the new drugs – wonder drugs, miracle cures, magic bullets, eagerly embraced by physicians and patients alike, oblivious that there might be a downside. Who knew that penicillin allergy could kill? Who knew that amphetamines created addiction? For the Silent Generation in their young adulthood, the word "drug" had only positive connotations.

Alphamethylphenethylamine was discovered at the end of the 19th century but it wasn't until World War II that amphetamines, as they came to be known, were widely used. As a stimulant, amphetamines had considerable advantages over cocaine, which had been used by the military in World War I. Amphetamines were easier to get hold of than cocaine and were cheaper too. Not only the American troops, but also the British and German armies were routinely given amphetamines to counteract fatigue, heighten endurance and raise the men's spirits. The Japanese gave them to wartime factory workers with the slogan: "Get rid of drowsiness and cheer the spirits up." Some men's spirits were so successfully raised that they continued their use of amphetamines or other, stronger stimulants after the war was over. Many others turned to alcohol to compensate for the loss of the drug they had unwittingly become dependant on.

Confident of the qualities of amphetamines, and blissfully unaware of their addictive properties, the post-war medical profession went on to discover other miracles their pet drug could perform. The market for amphetamines virtually exploded when it was announced that they could be used as diet pills. Suddenly, women became disproportionate drug users – they received twice as many prescriptions for amphetamines as men.

Probably the most famous of these drug users is Kitty Dukakis, wife of the former Massachusetts governor and presidential candidate Michael Dukakis. In her autobiographical book "Now You Know" she confesses to a twenty-six year addiction to diet pills. At the time her addiction began when she was a teenager – a time when amphetamines were not considered to be habit-forming "hard" drugs like heroine, morphine or cocaine – her behavior seemed normal.

Unfortunately for Kitty, her dependence on diet pills led her to another addiction – alcoholism. We now know that the euphoria created by amphetamine use is followed by intense depression and fatigue. Alcohol is only one way of counteracting such feelings. Mood enhancers and anti-depressants are another. Studies show that by the late 1960's about two-thirds of all psychoactive prescription drug users and more than four-fifths of stimulant users were women. The overwhelming majority of them were members of the Silent Generation.

The Silents, with their "gray flannel mentality", lacked the imagination to use drugs for fun. Coming as they did from the Great Depression, they were all about basic survival instincts – having a roof over their heads, enough food to fill their stomachs, a steady job that provided enough income to cover their expenses. Even their use of amphetamines was linked to serious motives. Male Silents, whose elders had been given drugs as soldiers, used them to work harder and get farther. Female Silents were deadly serious about losing weight and achieving their physical ideal. Nobody was having any fun, but everyone was becoming not only addicted, but also inured to the idea that drugs were an acceptable part of modern life. If drugs were chemicals, they had to be good. The general public had no idea that it could possibly be otherwise, and they had no inclination to look for a downside.

Americans in the 1950's tended to view their everyday lives as the springboard toward a glorious future – a "Jetsons" world of gadgets, robots and space travel for all. For the Silent Generation in particular, the future had to be better than the past. The bad old days were filled with hardship and deprivation – nothing to be nostalgic about. Whereas the future, as incarnated by the younger generation, was sure to be glorious. Thus they invested all their hopes in their children, who they felt sure would share their values and carry their ideals to fruition.

Many members of that younger generation, the Baby Boomers, did share their parents' materialistic vision. But by the 1960's many of them had become rebels, beatniks, flower children. Inspired by a handful of revolutionary Silents like Bob Dylan, Alan Ginsburg and Abbie Hoffman, they flaunted their nonconformist lifestyle which included fanciful clothing, unconventional behavior, unfettered sexuality and, of course, recreational drug use.

The Silent Generation was shocked and outraged. They found the rebels' behavior to be an incomprehensible reaction to the hard work and careful upbringing they had invested in them. Having no gift for self-awareness, they were unable to see themselves as drug users and bitterly condemned their children. The generational rift was best expressed by the Silents' reaction to the tragic events at Kent State University, near Cleveland, when the National Guard fired on a group of students protesting the Vietnam War. Newspapers published the high school yearbook photos of the young men and women who were killed. But when reporters went to Kent, Ohio to ask townspeople for their reactions, they were told that those photos were a lie. "They had long hair, they were dirty, they took drugs. They should have killed more of them."

Such intense acrimony was a reflection of the depth of their resentment. They had done everything right, paid the price, played by the rules. They were entitled to expect the best. How dare these kids flaunt their ideals? It was unpardonable. It wrecked their vision of the future.

For the children of the Great Depression who grew up during World War II, the best decades of their lives turned out to be the 50's and early 60's when everything seemed possible and the future looked bright. As the world around them changed and things speeded up, the Silents were outstripped by the pace and baffled by the disappearance of their value system. They had thought that a "Jetsons" future would be their legacy, and that the world would be grateful to them for it. Instead of which, the world turned their backs on them. The Boomers became the arbiters of all things. No trends were set when it was the Silents who went from "thirtysomething" to their forties, fifties and sixties.

They matched the world's indifference with their own. It was not within their canon of "nice" to protest. And even if they were given no leadership roles, even if their children were often a disappointment and the future looked far from promising, they themselves were not so badly off. Wasn't that what they had always strived for?

Just because the Silents were, precisely, silent is no reason for them to continue to be ignored by history. As Arthur Miller said in "Death of a Salesman", referring to the emblematic Willy Loman, "Attention must be paid to such a man." Silents were not the heroes of the generation that preceded them, nor the rebels of the generation that followed them. They were neither particularly good nor particularly bad. But they were pivotal. Since at this point it is highly unlikely that any Silents will create a generational self-examination, it will fall to others to study them and the effect they had on their country. Because of them or despite them, they were the turning point.

At the beginning of the twentieth century, the United States was a nation of healthy, enthusiastic, sexually naïve innocents. The Great Depression broke the nation's spirit and its children, the Silent Generation, set the nation on a course toward instant gratification and chemical dependency from which it may never recover.

# VIII

# Come Together, Right Now, Over Me

In the early decades of the 20ᵗʰ century, the French and Americans were in love with each other's music. When New Orleans jazz came to France at the end of the First World War, it created a sensation. Great French composers like Maurice Ravel and Darius Milhaud began to incorporate *le jazz nègre* into their work. Meanwhile the work of impressionist composers such as Debussy and Ravel was universally considered the *nec plus ultra* of serious music. Many American composers came worshipfully to France to study, not the least of whom was George Gershwin. Legend has it that when Gershwin asked Ravel if he could study with him, Ravel asked him how much money he was making with his composing. Gershwin had a hefty income from his successful Broadway musicals and Hollywood film scores and when he told Ravel the amount, Ravel replied, "You should be giving me lessons."

Even with the inclusion of jazz, French music – both classical and popular – kept its distinctive flavor. Torch songs such as "La Vie en Rose" were known and loved worldwide. Accordion music like "Under the Bridges of Paris" made everyone nostalgic for France.

But the arrival of rock music in the 1960's changed French popular music forever. The new singers took names like Johnny Hallyday, Dick Rivers and Eddy Mitchell. It was hard to distinguish *le yéyé* from other rock music except for the language, and even that wasn't much of a stretch. Anyone who knew the hit song "Black is Black" could follow along when Johnny Hallyday sang "Noir c'est noir, Il n'y a plus d'espoir."

Mr. V began to publish French rock music and he had a recording studio where some of the newcomers were given a chance at success. Occasionally, just for fun, I was allowed to sing back-up on some of the recordings. Most of the new lyrics sounded more like "doo-wop" than French, and no longer needed translating into English.  But my main occupation at Valentin Productions had become far more interesting to me.

Over the years I had dealt with endless contracts for music rights. After mastering the legal terminology in English I became so familiar with it in French that Claire and Mr. V stopped looking over my shoulder to make sure I'd written it correctly.  Gradually I came to a point where I was making suggestions about how to improve the wording to our company's advantage.  It came to me naturally, and I enjoyed it.

The meaning of my aptitude never occurred to me.  Mr. V's suggestion that I go to law school took me completely by surprise.  I had absolutely no ambition, no notion of having anything even vaguely resembling a career.  My first goal had been to get away from Cleveland, and my second goal was to fend for myself in Paris – getting by, earning a living, making ends meet.  Having achieved that, I felt pretty self-satisfied.  Why should I aim for anything more?

I tried reasoning the way the French would.  Question: Who was I, how would I define myself?  Answer: An American woman (not girl anymore, now that I was past 30) living in Paris.  Profession: bilingual secretary.  I'd always hated being defined as a secretary. It meant snapping to it when someone said those awful words, "Take a letter."  It meant trying to read my notes when I'd taken dictation too fast.  It meant fussing with carbon paper and onion-skin copies that were hard to correct, and sometimes typing the whole thing over if there were too many mistakes.  That certainly didn't define who I was, although it was the way I spent a lot of my time.

Reasoning that way, it made a lot of sense for me to try something else.  Going to law school didn't necessarily mean becoming a lawyer, but having a degree from the Sorbonne would definitely qualify me for something more than typing and taking dictation. And attending a university in France cost virtually nothing. Still, I hesitated. It had been over a decade since I graduated from college. Would I succeed in graduate school – and at the Sorbonne, yet? If I could only succeed at the price of incredibly hard work, would I hate it more than I hated being a secretary?

Faced with my hesitation, Mr. V sweetened the pot. In early April the annual meeting of the International Music Publishers Association was being held in New York. If I agreed to enroll in the fall term of the Faculté de Droit, he would send me to New York as Valentin Productions' representative at the IMPA meeting. That was an offer I couldn't refuse. I filled out the enrollment forms, sent for my college transcript, and started planning my trip to New York.

As soon as I wrote mother about it, she replied that she would come to New York to be with me. I couldn't really blame her. Our birthdays were only a day apart, and they occurred during the IMPA meeting, so it would be a perfect chance to celebrate. Also, with my professional obligations, I figured she couldn't drag me off to Cleveland. What I didn't tell her was that I planned to spend an extra week in New York after the meeting, seeing friends and just plain having a good time.

I had never wanted to think of myself as a businesswoman, but I needed a briefcase to carry the various documents I was taking to the meeting. When I went to purchase one, the salesman helped me choose a model that would be appropriate for a young *femme d'affaires*. Me, the would-be writer, the language buff, the bilingual secretary. Being a businesswoman in France wasn't so bad. I knew that in the States, women who wanted to rival with men professionally felt they had to be as hard-edged and aggressive as men, and that was something I didn't want to do. In France it was different. Women in business were as few in number as in the U.S., but it was acceptable for them to use their femininity as a weapon instead of trying to hide it. Without compromising herself in any way, a woman could charm a male adversary into closing a deal – and both parties had a wonderful time in the process. Vive la différence!

Along with the briefcase, I packed a small selection of feminine but businesslike clothes. It was 1967, and the length of women's hemlines was big news. A year and a half earlier, when I returned from Algiers, Mary Quant's mini skirt had invaded Paris. At first the Carnaby Street look was considered "far out", but gradually it influenced clothes worldwide. A French designer named André Courrèges created clothing that was even farther out, with geometric lines and a space age look. As men's hair grew longer, women's skirts got shorter. Glamour girls wore skirts that seemed to barely cover their pubis. I wasn't that daring, but I did wear dresses that stopped well above the knee. Matching gloves and hats were still *de rigueur,* but mercifully they didn't take up a lot of room in my suitcase.

Arriving in New York, I felt very focused. Traveling for business reasons was new to me, but it gave me a sense of purpose I enjoyed. After so much aimless wandering, I liked the idea of knowing what I was doing and what was expected of me. It was scary to think I had the responsibility of representing Valentin Productions, but as soon as I showed up for the registration process I began to relax. Although I knew no one and no one knew me, the company I worked for was well known. People who were working the room quickly came over to check me out.

It was amusing to see how they operated. They would look at my nametag and engage me in some sort of mindless conversation ("Wow! You're French!"). While we were talking, they would be looking over my shoulder to see who they should be talking to next. If no one important was in sight, our chitchat continued for a few minutes. I hadn't expected Mr. V's sweet old tunes to garner much attention, but just then French pop music was suddenly in favor. A song by Claude François called "Comme d'habitude" had been adapted into English by someone far more talented than me, namely Paul Anka. The result was the smash hit "My Way".

I gained assurance as I dutifully collected business cards to give to Mr. V. He would see that I had done a good job of mingling, and showing the colors of Valentin Productions. I even identified some new leads for sales of our product line. To my surprise, I found that the part of the annual meeting I enjoyed the most was the series of symposiums about author's rights and the collecting of royalties. Seen from an international perspective, I found the legal intricacies fascinating. The idea of going to law school in order to work in the field of entertainment law made more and more sense. In fact, it added up to the prospect of a real career, not just a job, and a new definition of who I was.

Mother, of course, had swooped into New York the moment I arrived with a full program of activities for us. Most of them were no surprise – celebrating our birthdays, shopping, going to see some shows. What did surprise me was my encounter with Rilla Romaine.

At the end of World War I, Rilla had come to New York as a young girl, having completed a tenth grade education in a convent school in Cleveland. Her burning desire was to be an actress. For a year she worked her way through classes at the American Academy of Dramatic Arts, where one of her classmates was Spencer Tracy. Then, at last, in 1924 her dream came true. She was accepted as a member of a struggling theatrical company. Originally created in Provincetown, Rhode Island by a group of artists including Eugene O'Neill, the company later moved to New York under the name Provincetown Playhouse. Although

Rilla had small parts, her name was on the playbill of numerous productions, including the world premiere of "The Emperor Jones". Rilla Romaine was the stage name of Tilda Ritter Glass, my mother.

In a Greenwich Village bookstore, mother found the collected plays of Eugene O'Neill. She pointed to the names of the plays she had acted in. We went to Macdougal Street and she showed me the building where the Playhouse was located. For once, I really wanted to talk to my mother. There were so many things I wanted to find out.

First of all, her stage name. It was so perfect for the 1920's. How had she chosen it? Mother explained that when she was a girl in the convent school, she was under surveillance by German nuns and one of them always got her name wrong. "Rilda Titter, ver iss your sewink" she would ask. Mother decided to use Rilda plus a last name that began with "r" like her real name. The director James Light changed Rilda to Rilla and tacked on Romaine.

Mother went on to talk about the early days of the Provincetown Playhouse – how they struggled to make ends meet, praying for good reviews of each new production. Actors were expected to help in other ways, sewing costumes and painting scenery. She rattled off a list of names of people she worked with who, for me, belonged to a cultural pantheon. Other playwrights besides O'Neill included Edna St. Vincent Millay, who I worshipped. I knew many of the sonnets from "Fatal Interview" by heart, and here I was discovering that my mother had actually known the poet herself. Millay's sister Norma participated in numerous productions. The actor Walter Abel, who later worked in Hollywood films, was a key player. Best of all, mother had actually helped Paul Robeson learn his lines for "The Emperor Jones".

We were sitting in a Greenwich Village coffee house, one of the few places in those days that came anywhere near a French café. Their espresso was served with a slice of lemon rind on the side, instead of a piece of dark chocolate like in France, but it was still real espresso. Mother was drinking tea. I looked at her with new eyes. She was someone who had worked with some of America's greatest artists.

"They must have been amazing people," I remarked.

"No, they were terrible."

"What?"

"They were all degenerate. Eugene O'Neill and his friend James Light were total alcoholics. They drank all the time, night and day. If they were too broke to buy whiskey, they'd drink anything. I actually saw them drink turpentine."

She shuddered.

"What about Millay?"

"Oh, she drank too. But the worst part about her was, she was a loose woman. She had all kinds of love affairs, sometimes several at one time."

Mother shifted uneasily in her chair. I was grasping at straws.

"But surely, Paul Robeson wasn't like that."

She frowned at me. "Don't you know about him? He became a Communist and went to live in Russia."

"So if these people were all such monsters, how did you get by?"

Mother proceeded to talk to me about her convent upbringing, strict to be sure and yet comforting. She had entered the school as an outsider, clutching her Jewish prayer book, but by the time she was ready to leave she asked if she could convert to Catholicism. The nuns wisely advised her to wait until she'd been in New York for a while. Then she left New York – and the Provincetown Playhouse – to return to Cleveland because her brother, my Uncle Isaac, needed her to help him with his business. That was where she met my father and he asked her to marry him – ironically, because she was a nice Jewish girl his mother would approve of. So much for conversion. But she assured me that the convent had prepared her for life's vicissitudes, and given her words to live by, such as "Invictus".

Invictus? I knew that meant "undefeated" in Latin. Was that her motto? She explained that it was the title of a poem that she had learned in school and never forgotten. To prove her assertion, she began reciting it.

"Out of the night that covers me,
Black as the pit from pole to pole,
I thank whatever God may be,
For my unconquerable soul.

"In the fell clutch of circumstance,
I have not cried nor winced aloud,
Under the bludgeoning of chance,
My head is bloody but unbowed."

As she spoke, using the impeccable diction she had learned as an actress, her voice gradually rose. The people sitting around us turned to listen. There were often poetry readings in the coffee house, so this impromptu performance was no surprise.

"Beyond this place of wrath and tears
Looms but the horror of the shade,
And yet the menace of the years
Finds and shall find me unafraid.

"It matters not how straight the gate,
How charged with punishments the scroll,
I am the captain of my fate,
I am the master of my soul."

With the last words she couldn't help striking her chest in a dramatic pose. The people around her applauded. She acknowledged them graciously.

That night I found it hard to sleep as I wrestled with this new vision of my mother. I had to feel sorry for the little orphan girl who found solace in corny Victorian poetry taught to her by German nuns. I had to admire Rilla for successfully making a niche for herself in the difficult field of acting. Come to think of it, she had gone on from there to become a success as a commercial real estate broker and appraiser, one of the first women in her profession. No question about it, she was quite a dame – someone I could be proud of.

But at the same time, her rigid narrow-mindedness appalled me. How could Rilla be surrounded by geniuses and not have some of it rub off on her? Thinking back to my own childhood, I remembered mother as being very respectful of the arts and doing her best to expose me to culture, but always at arm's length. The only thing she created herself was tension in our household, and in that she was very creative indeed. Is that what had happened to a girl who dreamed of being an actress?

Was it really her fault? Instead of a warm and loving home environment, she had grown up in the dormitory of a convent school where the beds were separated by hanging sheets. There, fear and loneliness were probably her closest companions.

When she met Daddy, she was probably recovering from the shock and disappointment of her exposure to Greenwich Village bohemians. I remember her mentioning that when he courted her, Daddy wrote poetry. So she obviously had a romanticized vision of him. But after their marriage, what happened? Did mother's encounter with the physical realities of lovemaking revolt her as much as her association with the Provincetown Playhouse? Once she got to Greenwich Village, straight out of convent school, some drunken actor probably made a pass at her – if not worse – that only deepened her fear, and created a revulsion that would be hard to overcome. Heaven only knows what transpired between her and Daddy, but it was obviously not a success. As far back as I could remember, my parents had slept in twin beds. Aside from perfunctory pecks on the cheek, no one kissed or embraced in our house. Mother never hugged or caressed either Daddy or me, whereas Daddy and I tended to be effusive. And then there was "Shangri La", Daddy's mistress. If one of my parents was sexually dysfunctional, it would have to be mother.

Having new insights into my family background didn't make me feel any better. All I wanted to do was to put it behind me and get on with my own life. The IMPA meeting was over and I had plans for the week I would spend in New York before returning to Paris.

The next morning, I went to mother's hotel to help her check out and perhaps accompany her to the airport as she returned to Cleveland. I found her downstairs with her luggage, busily discussing something at the concierge's desk. When she saw me, she smiled and announced that she was arranging for me to be on the same flight with her.

I resolved to stay calm, but the more I tried to reason with her, the more stubborn she became. As her voice became shriller, she rose to her feet to face me down. "You're so selfish and self-centered," she yelled, as everyone in the hotel lobby stared at us.

I knew what she was up to. Given the circumstances, casting her evil spell wouldn't work. What was needed here was a noisier form of expression, a public display like the one a decade earlier with poor Sparrow at the Wade Park Manor. Its purpose was to embarrass me and shame me into submission.

But this time it didn't work. The moment she stood up, what I focused on was the fact that I was taller than she was. Taller, stronger and younger. The more she yelled, the more she shrank. The realization swept over me that the balance of power between us had inexorably shifted, and never again would she be able to control me. When she stopped to catch her breath, I wished her a good trip and walked out of the hotel.

My destination was Chloe's loft. Chloe was a performance artist I had met in Paris through my friend Claire. Besides working for Mr. V, Claire sometimes did volunteer public relations work for visiting performers. One day she told me, "I'm doing you a favor, you'll thank me all your life. I've asked someone to stay at your apartment for a few days."

Claire was right, too. Knowing Chloe was a gift. She slept on the sofa bed in my living room and every morning when I got up there she'd be, intently performing a series of slow, strange movements. She explained that it was a Chinese discipline called *tai chi*, the purpose of which was to strengthen the mind while strengthening the body.

What impressed me the most was her concentration. She was so focused on her inner self, nothing else seemed to exist. When she finished her exercises and returned to an awareness of her surroundings, she seemed refreshed and empowered. I felt jealous of her ability to find desirable things within herself. Nothing like that was happening to me. Everything came to me from the outside in, not the inside out. I had the feeling that Chloe held the key to another approach to life. When she learned I was coming to New York and invited me to stay with her, I jumped at the chance.

In the taxi on the way to Chloe's loft, I reflected on how New York had changed in the years I'd been away. People were now reluctant to walk in the streets for fear of being "mugged', an expression that hadn't existed a decade earlier. Central Park was completely off limits, even by day. The taxi I was in, like most New York taxis, was now fortified with a bulletproof barrier between the driver and his passengers.

As the city became more hostile, its promoters worked to improve its image. I used to refer to the city as "Gotham". Did that sound too dark, too Gothic? Now it was known as the Big Apple, whatever that was supposed to mean.

The biggest change I noticed was the apparent disappearance of institutionalized anti-Semitism. Billboards all over the city trumpeted the slogan "You don't have to be Jewish to love Levy's". Radio and TV comedians unashamedly used jokes that had been previously reserved for Jews only. A large number of Yiddish words like *schlep* and *shtik* and *spiel* had crept into general usage, and when I pointed this out to a Gentile who was using them, he just shrugged his shoulders. Being Jewish was suddenly ok.

That absolutely floored me. I knew enough American history to realize that the early waves of Irish and Italian immigrants had been despised and shunned, just as Jews were when I was growing up. Now Jews, like the Irish and Italians, seemed to have joined the ranks of lovable ethnics with quaint customs and fabulous music.

It was hard to fathom how the assimilation had taken place. While I was away, was there a breakthrough I hadn't heard about? The French were usually pretty good about covering U.S. domestic events, not to mention the American news I got from reading the Herald Tribune, but I never saw a report to the effect that country clubs were no longer restricted.

Was it just a matter of time?  As in, wait long enough and everybody will be accepted.  That certainly didn't seem to be the case where civil rights were concerned.  American Negroes were now increasingly referred to as Blacks, which was progress to be sure, but the time line for their wholehearted acceptance into white society seemed to stretch into infinity.

I was all too familiar with the atrocious images of black demonstrators being attacked by police dogs, or clubbed, or hosed down with water.  The French lost no opportunity to show coverage like that, as if to deflect heat from their own behavior toward the Algerians.  When I tried to compare the two, they often answered, "Oh no, you don't understand.  That's completely different."

As the taxi drove down Broadway, headed for the East Village, we passed a movie theater specializing in foreign art films.  It reminded me of something that had happened to me near there with my friend Jordan, a story I sometimes told in France when trying to explain the complexity of race relations in America.

Jordan was a friend from Cleveland – he and I attended art school together on Saturdays.  His parents were both octoroons, people passing for white who had an eighth Negro blood.  His older brother, like his parents, had light skin and straight dark hair that made them look Mediterranean. But when Jordan came along the two eighths blended into a resolute and very apparent one-fourth. Jordan's skin wasn't that much darker, but his features were Negroid and his hair was kinky. As a little boy, when his brother had friends come over, he was told to hide. He thought it was a game.

When Jordan was old enough to drive, he asked me to go to the movies with him. My parents wouldn't let me. They said they had no personal objections, but what would the neighbors think?

Finally, after I moved to New York, I was able to go out with Jordan when he came for a visit. We went to see a Russian ballet film, "Romeo and Juliet" performed by the Bolshoi. As we walked down Broadway after the movie, he told me about the problems he was experiencing. Having been raised in a white environment, he had difficulty relating to blacks. But if he dated white women and they got involved, he lived in fear of the day they might have a fight and she would call him a nigger.

Just then we saw a large black car parked at the curb. Inside were a very black man and a very blonde white woman, and they were kissing. Jordan and I stared at them in shock. That was certainly something you'd never see in Cleveland. Then we looked at each other, realizing the absurdity of our reaction, and laughed until tears streamed down our faces.

Once the taxi reached Chloe's neighborhood, I started to pay attention to my surroundings which seemed to be the kind of industrial area my mother loved to appraise. There were no shops, no amenities, just a stretch of anonymous-looking brick factory buildings. The taxi delivered me to one of them. Chloe's loft was on the fourth floor, and as I walked up the stairs I began to hear the high, ethereal notes of an other-worldly music. The door was unlocked, so I pushed it open and tiptoed in.

Chloe was there, bending over a long board held up with saw-horses that contained several rows of crystal glasses filled or half-filled with water. A tall fellow stood opposite her, and both of them were moving their hands over the glasses, touching the rims to make beautiful sounds. Each glass produced a different note, and with their four hands they created amazing harmo-nies. In another corner of the loft, a group of performers were rehearsing a dance pantomime that seemed unrelated to the music but sometimes responded to it.

Everyone was so intent on their own activities that my arrival went unnoticed. I looked around for a place to sit, but the loft was a rehearsal space and there were no chairs. I went to a corner of the room to grapple with the task of sitting on the floor, not easy in my short, tight skirt. Sitting cross-legged was out of the question, but I managed to kneel without snagging my stockings. The wooden floor was well polished and very smooth. Looking at the high ceiling criss-crossed with pipes and the tall windows, it was easy to imagine the space being used for its original purpose, as a turn-of-the century factory filled with women in Gibson girl shirtwaists working at sewing machines.

I noticed that everyone in the room was dressed in blue denim. Chloe and another girl were wearing baggy overalls with bibs; the others wore jeans. The water glass guy also wore a jeans jacket, and his light brown curly hair was teased into a huge pyramid-shaped Afro. It occurred to me that the world was becoming a very democratic place in which everyone had taken to clothing themselves in blue cotton. In France, workers wore *bleus de tra-vail* – jackets, pants and overalls made of fabric dyed a deep royal blue. In China everyone wore cotton clothes, often blue, and here everyone was in jeans.

As I mused about a new, blue world the music stopped and Chloe looked up. Seeing me, she skipped gracefully across the room as

I struggled to my feet to hug her. She introduced me to Brian, the water glass guy, and we went into the kitchen so as not to disturb the others. Hunched over glasses of tea, we caught up with each other's news. Chloe was apologetic – she had planned to be with me during the five days I had left in New York, but something had come up. She needed to take part in a happening in upstate New York, and would be leaving the next day.

I told her, sincerely, that I didn't really mind. I had attended a happening in Paris (in French, "un happening") and it was a liberating, exhilarating experience. The performers used the entire theatre space, both stage and seats, to improvise a series of events into which the audience was drawn as both viewers and participants. For me, it erased the traditional lines (audience here in numbered seats, performers there to be viewed through opera glasses) that from then on made "normal" theatre attendance less than satisfying for me. Chloe's upcoming happening sounded wonderful. It would be held on the huge lot of a car dealership, and the cars would be lined up on all four sides of the lot facing in with their headlights on to create the "happening space". My only regret was that I couldn't attend it myself.

As Brian the water glass guy was assuring me that there would be plenty for me to do during my remaining days in New York, and that I was welcome to hang out with him and his friends, Chloe's kitchen began to fill up with other people. Takao, a set designer, arrived with a basket full of vegetables and a set of Japanese knives. Two girls named Dawn and Fawn brought a huge steaming bowl of brown rice. It turned out they all lived in the same building. While Takao deftly chopped the vegetables, Chloe cubed some tofu and fired up her wok. The moment the stir-fry was ready, the pantomime dancers stopped rehearsing and we all crowded around the table to eat.

I was reminded of the clannish behavior of some New York apartment dwellers. In the building I used to live in, we sometimes had parties to which we invited guests from outside, but most evenings we hung out with people from our own building. My apartment had been very different from Chloe's loft. It was located further uptown, in a more fashionable area, but it was a tiny "studio" – a euphemism for an enlarged closet with barely enough room for a bed, a table and two chairs. The narrow hall leading to the bathroom contained the "kitchenette" and a miniscule closet. Most of my neighbors lived in similarly cramped quarters, and in order not to feel too claustrophobic we opened our doors and spilled into the halls to have floor parties.

The summer after I graduated from college and moved to New York was hellishly hot and humid. Once, sitting at my table, I suddenly found myself lying on the floor because I had sweated so much I slid off my chair. At night my neighbors and I would drag our mattresses out to the fire escape in the hope of catching a breath of fresh air. I had never drunk gin and tonic before, but I was told it was the ideal drink for cooling off. Every night there was a floor party, and we took turns buying the gin and the tonic. We sat or stood in the hall, or wandered from one "studio" to another. What made my apartment an attractive gathering place was a tiny black-and-white television set I had managed to buy wholesale. No one else on my floor had one. We would set it on the windowsill, with its "rabbit ears" antenna trained toward the fire escape, so that everyone could enjoy Ed Sullivan or Milton Berle as we slugged down glass after glass of gin and tonic.

I usually passed out before the evening was over. When the TV programs ended around midnight, they would show the flag and play the Star Spangled Banner. Sometimes that woke me up, or sometimes it was the crackling static sound of the "snow" that filled the screen after programming had stopped. I would turn off the set and try to get some more sleep before my alarm rang and it was time to go back to work. One day blurred into another, and my only real focus was on getting to France.

In Chloe's loft no alcohol was served, but after we'd eaten Brian produced a small bag of dried leaves and began to "roll a joint". That was part of the new drug vocabulary that I had set myself the task of learning during this trip. The American language was much more volatile than French, and every time I came back to the States I had to learn new words and expressions. The new drug culture seemed to have spawned a huge vocabulary, which I had only begun to master. As the joint was passed around and we each "took a hit", I silently enumerated the various words I knew for what we were smoking – it was marijuana, of course, but was also referred to as pot, weed, Mary Jane, and grass. Was "shit" also a word for marijuana or did it refer to hashish? I wasn't quite sure.

In the pleasant evening haze, we began to sing. It was something that always happened when Chloe was around. Even when we were together in Paris we spent a lot of time singing. Song was as important to her as speech and movement, and her love for it was contagious. She had a gift for making everyone feel that they too could sing – and sing we did, although no one could approach the range and texture of Chloe's extraordinary instrument.

The songs she composed could only be performed by her, but she had a seemingly endless collection of folk songs that we could all sing together. Most of them were part songs or rounds, which made you focus on the beat or on the correct moment for you to chime in, rather than the actual quality of your voice. There were perky songs like "Marguerite, come feed your fat pig". Others were slower and more lyrical.

To my surprise, we began to sing "Gabriel John". It was a fairly complicated part song that Sparrow had learned from her Welsh grandmother, and that I had taught to Chloe in Paris. Apparently she had taught it to her friends.

> Under this stone lies Gabriel John
> Who died in the year one thousand and one.
> Cover his head with purple stone
> 'Tis all one, 'tis all one, with purple stone 'tis all one.
> Pity the fate of Gabriel John
> If you will, you can or leave it alone, 'tis all one.

The three melodic threads came together on the word "one". It was beautiful, and I shouldn't have started crying but I did. Poor Sparrow! She should have been here with me, singing "Gabriel John" and hanging out with this wonderful group of people. This was what we dreamed of, a nurturing place where we could be creative, be ourselves, be challenged.

Why couldn't I have saved her? Why couldn't I bring her back?

I excused myself and went to bed. Perhaps because of the "pot", I fell asleep immediately.

When I woke up, Chloe had almost finished her tai chi routine. We were both famished, so we walked to an East Village coffee shop where we feasted on three-egg breakfasts with all the trimmings for less than two dollars apiece. Next to the coffee shop, as we walked out, I spotted a store called "American Rags". Their window was draped with red, white and blue bunting and filled with all kinds of jeans – straight leg, bell bottoms, overalls, cut-offs, faded, embroidered, you name it. I was dazzled by the display and couldn't take my eyes off it.

Chloe encouraged me to go in, saying she had often shopped there herself. I hesitated because most of the jeans in the window looked like they'd been made for people half my width and girth – nothing larger than a size 6. Girls that size looked adorable in jeans, but what about big old me? I took a deep breath and followed Chloe inside.

The racks were bulging with blue denim. I didn't know where to start, or if I should start at all. A young man stepped forward to help me and I asked him if there were any jeans my size. He assured me there were, and after giving me an appraising once-over he proceeded to pull hangers off the racks. I chose a few pairs and retreated apprehensively into a dressing room, resolved to do battle with the tight-looking pants. But when I took off my skirt and stepped into the first pair, they slid up over my hips with no resistance. I did have to suck in my tummy to button and zip them, but their support felt like a friendly reminder of the girdles I used to wear.

The big surprise came when I looked in the mirror. I expected to see nothing but bulging hips, but instead the jeans emphasized the length of my legs, even erasing that fatty pad on my inside thighs. I stepped out of the dressing room, and Chloe smiled with approval.

"Wow, you look great!"

Better yet, I felt great. It was amazing how different the jeans made me feel. I crouched down, stood up and spun around, wiggling my tush. I was free!

Was this appropriate behavior for a woman in her thirties? I felt sure that none of my college friends in Cleveland were wearing jeans. As I was pondering this, I became aware of a Bob Dylan song playing in the background. I had often listened to his albums in Paris and knew the words, including the refrain of this one. "I was so much older then, I'm younger than that now." Dylan was right. Age was a state of mind, and if you were smart you could decide for yourself what generation you wanted to belong to.

My panty hose lay in a heap on the dressing room floor. How I had always hated them. They snagged, they ran, they burned my thighs. Now, instead of being encased in unfriendly nylon, my legs rejoiced in the soft touch of denim. I never wanted to take my jeans off. I paid for them and left with my skirt and panty hose in a bag.

Back at the loft, Chloe and I said goodbye. She was leaving for her happening, and I had a lunch date uptown with Hansli whose brief stay in New York coincided with mine. Brian the water glass guy had left me a note inviting me to meet him near Washington Square at 4PM to take part in an anti-war protest. I hugged Chloe and headed for the subway.

It was only when I was a block away from the restaurant, a French bistro called "Chez Nous", that I realized I was still in jeans. That could be a problem. Knowing Hansli, I figured the restaurant was one of those chic, intimate places he loved where you got to know the owners and quickly became a favorite. What would they think of my hippie attire? On the other hand, in France, jeans were hard to find, terribly expensive and therefore "in".

Sure enough, "Chez Nous" was tiny and cute as a button. Hansli was at the best table, enjoying a pre-lunch apéritif. When he looked questioningly at my jeans, I told him with a smirk that I was making a fashion statement and we nodded the matter closed. After ordering our meal, we settled into some serious catching-up. We had lived together so long that we felt it entirely appropriate to stay apprised of the slightest details in each other's lives.

I told him about my experiences at the IMPA meeting, and about my encounter with Rilla Romaine. I tried to make it sound as positive as possible, because Hansli was quite fond of my mother and was disturbed by the strife between us. I saw no reason to try to win him over to my viewpoint. *Au contraire,* I was faintly jealous of his ability to get along with her.

He gave me recent news of Ursi. I knew she had patched things up with her family sufficiently for them to accept Fritz as her husband. They had moved from Paris to Zurich, and we did our best to stay in touch but our correspondence was spotty. Ursi had told me she was expecting a baby and I was happy that this was a pregnancy she wouldn't have to "voluntarily terminate." Somewhat diffidently, Hansli told me she had given birth to a baby boy. An announcement would be waiting for me in the mail on my return to Paris.

Hansli's career seemed to be moving forward nicely. He had just spent a month "with Lenny" in Tanglewood and was about to sign with a booking agent in New York. Then he and Monique were going to do a recital tour in Canada. I kidded him that they seemed to be "making beautiful music together". He nodded and said that when he next returned to Switzerland, he would be posting the bans for their wedding.

Hansli was getting married and Schatzli was going to law school. As we raised our glasses to drink a toast to our futures, Hansli suddenly burst into giggles. He had forgotten to give me an update on Camille, the daughter of Madame Maupommé of the *pension de famille.* I knew that she had married Kenzo, the composer, and moved to Japan but I hadn't stayed in touch with her. Now Hansli informed me gleefully that she had opened a guesthouse in Kyoto and re-named herself Camille de France.

"A la santé de Camille de France," we exclaimed, clinking glasses.

We had been conversing in French, and I knew we were both experiencing the same thing – a kind of heightened awareness due to the fact that we were speaking a language not being spoken by the others around us. We could hear ourselves speaking, and we paid attention to choosing our words carefully and pronouncing them perfectly. It wasn't to be secretive – the owners of the restaurant were French – but it increased our pleasure in savoring the language by contrasting it with our surroundings. Since Hansli's English was now virtually flawless, we did the same thing in France when given the opportunity, but in reverse – using American slang when everyone around us was French. It enhanced our sense of being different.

I had always felt different, even before I left home, and it wasn't something I particularly enjoyed. I would have loved to find a place where I fit in perfectly and was accepted, but I sensed increasingly that that wouldn't happen. The more I traveled and found new things to delight me, the more I felt different. It made me think of Vali, the artist from the Rue Fromentin, the self-described "eternal exile". As a boy, he had walked westward a thousand miles across Europe, looking for a place where he would be allowed to survive. Finally, in Switzerland, a kind person had adopted him and nurtured his artistic talent, but Vali always knew he wasn't really Swiss. He was fond of saying that he felt at home everywhere but nowhere was home.

I mentioned this to Hansli, expecting to have to remind him who Vali was, but instead he thanked me for reminding him of a message he received from Ursi. From his pocket he produced a postcard she sent him, asking him to give it to me if he saw me in

New York. It was an invitation to an exhibit of Swiss artists, one of whom was Vali.

As I slipped the card into my purse, Hansli told me how much he disagreed with Vali. The glass was half full, not half empty. Along with the Swiss passport that was his birthright, Hansli would acquire French nationality when he married Monique, plus German nationality if he accepted a teaching post that had been offered to him in Hamburg. The Americans had given him an unlimited visa, and even my mother had extended an invitation for him to live in Cleveland where he was due to audition for George Szell. For Hansli, everywhere was home.

We raised our glasses again. "To home."

I wanted to split the lunch bill with Hansli but he insisted on paying for it. He kept looking at my jeans and asking if I was getting by financially. It dawned on me that to his way of thinking our roles were now reversed. I was the student and he was the one who would look after me. Before leaving the restaurant, I gave him a big hug.

As agreed, Brian the water glass guy was waiting for me under the statue of Garibaldi, to one side of Washington Square. About a hundred people had gathered at the foot of Fifth Avenue to march for peace. At the head of the procession, a wide banner saying "Stop the War" was carried by four or five people. Behind the banner marched a striking group – a man carrying a doll wrapped in bloody swaddling clothes and a woman with a sign saying "I am Mary – my baby was napalmed in Vietnam". The bloody baby Jesus had been used as a symbol of protest since the previous Christmas, when Cardinal Spellman prayed for an American victory in Vietnam.

As the procession lurched forward, Brian handed me a stick with a poster tacked to it, saying "No More Bombs". Other marchers were carrying signs like mine, or flags, or anti-war props such as a crucifix-shaped airplane with the head of a shark. Some people wore caricatural masks. There were two people on stilts, wearing long dresses and masks of weeping women. Brian said they were Dawn and Fawn.

Someone I couldn't see had a drum and was pounding the rhythm of our march. We shouted slogans – "Ho Ho Ho Chi Min" and "Hey Hey LBJ". I felt exhilarated. There had been peace marches in Paris but I never dared take part in one because demonstrations were monitored by the police. They kept records on everyone, and I was afraid they might classify me as a radical. They could easily refuse to renew my residence papers and work permit. Here I was an American citizen with an inalienable right to demonstrate, and it was thrilling to be able to exercise that right.

I strongly disagreed with the U.S. decision to become involved in Vietnam. Living in France, I was aware of how cruelly the French felt their defeat in Indo-China, particularly the disastrous battle of Dien Bien Phu. Even a decade later they seemed bewildered that their superior military force had lost the war. When the U.S. began sending "military advisors" to the area, American "hawks" disregarded the French defeat. They argued that if we didn't get involved, the Far East would succumb to communism. They compared the situation to Mussolini's invasion of Ethiopia. If we had stopped him then, they said, there wouldn't have been a second world war.

When people talked to me like that, I tried to argue that the French had been a colonial power in Indo-China for centuries. They knew the people and their culture, they were intimately familiar with the land, their military strength was far greater – and yet they were defeated. How could we possibly expect to do better?

Regardless of the outcome, it seemed to me that a bad peace was always better than a good war, but what did I know? My generation had no first-hand experience of war. We had fallen between the cracks. Although some of my classmates' older brothers had died in the Korean War, we were too young to be involved. World War II certainly seemed like a war worth fighting. If I had been born in Europe rather than America I might have been killed, or at least gone through the kind of harrowing experiences European Jews my age told me about. The closest I'd come to wartime myself was in postwar Algeria, so I was certainly no expert. But I was happy to march for the principle of peace, and it felt great to be able to express my views freely.

There were policemen lining Fifth Avenue and they glared at us, but they didn't try to stop our march. Brian said that once Dawn and Fawn were detained and charged with "illegal wearing of masks". The ACLU intervened on their behalf and the ridiculous charges were dropped. All around me I felt the determination and exhilaration of the marchers who would not have been deterred even if the police had attacked us. We were all in this together, and we would make a difference. Peace and freedom would prevail. It was the American way.

After the march, about a dozen of us gathered at Chloe's loft. Some celebratory joints were rolled and passed around. Every time I smoked pot I hoped to achieve the sensation of "getting high" like the others. But it never happened. I couldn't figure out why. I got sleepy, I got the munchies, but I didn't get high. Brian offered the opinion that I was probably someone who reacted better to uppers than downers.

I didn't understand, so he proceeded to explain how a person's system might react better to being revved up rather than slowed down. Downers were the most popular among young people, who were already full of energy but anxious to "space out" on pot or even seek an altered reality with LSD or peyote. Some people, he said, got hooked on both – taking downers at night but needing to counteract them the next morning with uppers. If I didn't react to downers, it was probably because my system was craving uppers. Did I have a history of speed dependency?

How could I? I'd never taken any drugs... Except, of course, when I was in college and I took those "pep pills" the doctor gave me. Did they count?

"They were amphetamines, right?"

"I guess so. They were little blue triangular pills."

Brian nodded and asked me how many I took and how often. I told him about my junior and senior years in college, when Sparrow and I pulled all-nighters just for the fun of it. The pills had been prescribed to help us study for exams, but we didn't need to study that hard. The attraction, for us, was the delicious sensation of being awake when the others were asleep. It made us feel smarter and stronger than everyone else. We seemed to get our best ideas at sunrise. If our supply of pep pills was low, we used coffee and over-the-counter No-Doze to get us through the night. I never thought of it as any kind of addiction. It was something I enjoyed doing, not just because of the energy it gave me. The nicest thing was that when I took those pills, I didn't care any more if I fit in or not, if I had a boyfriend or not, if I was overweight or not. All those anxieties just melted away.

There was no "drug culture" then – no words, no vocabulary, no understanding. How were we to know that a decade later, people who did what we did would be called "speed freaks"?

I felt upset, almost outraged. Sparrow and I were nice girls from good families. Speed freaks were druggies, people who

got arrested and hauled off to jail for possession of illegal substances. We were given prescriptions by our family doctors and
we used them as prescribed – more or less. They were supposed
to make us study harder, and instead they abetted our creative
projects, but what harm was there in that?

We were completely different from people who experimented
with drugs as a "fun thing" and chose the ones that gave them
the biggest high. We were just trying to get our work done and
get through college. And yet, there it was, no getting around
it. Sparrow and I had been speed freaks. We were hooked on
uppers.

When we crashed, we crashed hard – all the harder because we
didn't even realize what was happening to us. If your family doctor gives you triangular blue pills to make you study better, you
obviously stop taking them when you've finished your studies.
The expression "cold turkey" was also missing from our vocabulary. Words denote awareness, and we had neither. We had
stumbled blindly into drug addiction and no one was there to
help us identify it or overcome it.

The isolation I felt when I moved to New York, the depression,
the lethargy – those were all symptoms of my withdrawal, a condition I didn't even know I had. I didn't know why my "get up
and go" had gotten up and gone, but I accepted it unquestioningly. How had I managed to cope with it? The realization
hit me like a punch in the stomach. I drank myself into oblivion every night with gin and tonic. Oh my God, after being a
drug addict I became an alcoholic. Me, a nice Jewish girl from
Cleveland.

I grimly pondered the harsh definitions of my identity. Jewish?
It didn't matter if I felt Jewish or not, or whether or not other
Jews accepted me as such. The real determinant, as I'd learned

from my years in Europe, was that Hitler would have considered me to be Jewish. So that definition stuck.

Nice? I was a speed freak who turned into a lush. Maybe not so nice after all. A girl? Well, not any more. With a wry smile, I acknowledged the fact that my girlhood was over. But I would always be "from Cleveland".

I remembered a New Yorker cartoon showing a man at a cocktail party, wearing an open shirt and gold chains, saying "I come from Cleveland but that's not where I'm coming from now."

That wasn't me. I had no illusions about being from New York or Paris or anywhere other than Cleveland Heights. The important thing, I realized, was not where I came from but where I was going. The next evening I was flying back to Paris, where I had a home and a job and friends – an enviable situation. I would be going to law school in the fall, and there was a good chance I might actually make something of myself, no matter what a shady past I had. I decided to convince myself that learning to accept my imperfections was a sign of maturity.

Besides, it could have been a lot worse. As I understood it, drug addictions – when identified – were hard to shake. Some people never got over them. But my addiction wasn't identified, by me or anyone else. I had no idea that the depressed, discombobulated state I found myself in after college was in any way related to the amphetamines I'd suddenly stopped taking at graduation. It was, in a way, fortunate that I was unwittingly able to substitute alcohol dependence for speed.

Had I stayed in New York, where hard liquor was inexpensive and plentiful, my excessive drinking would probably have turned into a major problem. But there again I was lucky. I found myself in Paris, broke and unable to afford even miniature bottles of gin or whiskey. I had, on occasion, tried to compensate with cheap wine. I shuddered at the memory of how sick it made me, and how Hansli had been there to clean up after me. Not a thought I wanted to dwell on. How fortunate, indeed, that that episode was behind me and I had managed to get through it in one piece.

Suddenly it hit me. I was a speed freak who'd recovered – <u>and Sparrow hadn't recovered</u>. Finally, I was able to comprehend. For years I had obsessed about her reasons for taking that fatal dose of aspirin. Was it post-partem depression? Boredom? Alienation? All of those were reasons that, in normal circumstances, would have pushed her to the brink, but knowing Sparrow, I felt sure she would have pulled back before committing that final desperate act. Now I understood. These were not normal circumstances. She was in withdrawal like I was, and any negative feelings were magnified while weakening her ability to fight them off.

I felt like I was drowning in waves of helplessness and frustration. If only I had understood sooner. If only someone, anyone, had understood in time to save her. A beautiful young life was thrown away. The legacy left to her daughter was the stigma of an unjustifiable suicide. But it wasn't her fault! She had wanted to live. Moments after swallowing the pills, she had tried to reverse her mistake. But the chemically-induced demons that must have been torturing her for months won the battle and killed her.

How ironic to think that I had always envied her. Petite, adorable, talented, socially acceptable, she seemed to embody everything that was right – in contrast to me, embodying everything that was wrong. It was hard to fathom how the society that had borne her aloft had also caused her destruction, while somehow sparing me. My own personal history with drug abuse no longer interested me. I had survived, it was behind me, and that was that. But Sparrow was an open wound I knew I would carry in my heart forever. I would never be able to forgive and never want to forget.

After a restless night, I woke up feeling listless and despondent. Even the prospect of my imminent flight to Paris wasn't enough to cheer me up. But it did oblige me to sort out my belongings, putting everything I didn't need on the plane into my suitcase. I would wear my jeans, of course. I dumped out the contents of my purse to make room for take-on items.

Out fluttered the postcard Hansli had given me, sent to him by Ursi. It was an invitation to an exhibit of Swiss artists, one of whom was Vali. I looked at the dates. The show had been running for several weeks but was still open. I would have time to visit it before catching my plane.

The show was called "Un Certain Regard – Three Contemporary Swiss Artists". The East Village gallery was located in a converted garage with skylights that showed the pictures to advantage. Vali's work covered one wall. It was such a perfect expression of the man, I felt he was in the room. His lines, like him, were acerbic and telling. The inanimate objects he drew, particularly the intricate, old-fashioned Parisian lampposts, almost seemed human. They contrasted with a series of full-length portraits I hadn't seen before, of tall, leggy women in stiff poses. His Bluebell Girls! The way he painted them, they seemed less alive, less interesting than the lampposts.

I chuckled to myself. What a wicked fellow, that Vali. I remembered how critical of him I once was, precisely because he was critical of others. I was too unsure of myself then, too inexperienced to understand that beyond his sarcasm was pain. His paintings showed it clearly. The girls were lovely, beautifully proportioned, but devoid of character. I had to agree with him. If the lampposts could talk, they probably would have more to say than the girls.

A small charcoal drawing drew my attention. It was a female figure lying on its side. Unlike the Bluebell girls the rendering was softer, more forgiving, almost loving. The face, shown in profile with closed eyes, was expressive. "Now there's an interesting woman," I thought. Obviously Vali thought so too.

I stepped back to view the whole wall. It spoke to me of Vali the eternal exile, searching in vain for a place where he belonged, seeking solace in beauty but rarely finding it. There was solace expressed in the charcoal drawing, and yet that woman wasn't beautiful. Her hips were wide, her form was billowy. Her high forehead was convex, and the artist had accentuated its roundness with the tendrils of some curls. In contrast, her mouth and chin formed straight lines of determination, as if she was struggling with her own nature.

Something about the angles of the woman's profile drew me closer. Where had I seen that nose, that mouth before? Then it hit me. I was looking at a picture of myself. How stupid of me not to recognize my own profile. I wasn't accustomed to seeing myself that way, any more than I would easily recognize the back of my head. It dawned on me that how we see ourselves and how others see us could be completely different. I thought I knew myself, but I never saw myself the way Vali saw me. He must have made that sketch the night I slept at his studio, wrapped up in my indignation and self-absorption. Vali understood, and forgave me.

Was it possible Vali was in New York? It would mean a lot to me to see him again. Maybe I could buy the picture from him. Suddenly I panicked – maybe someone else had already bought it. I asked the woman sitting at a desk near the door. She told me the picture was not for sale, part of the artist's private collection. And was the artist in New York by any chance? No, he'd been there for the opening but now he was back in Paris. On the Rue Fromentin? She looked at me closely before answering. Yes, that was it.

On my way to the airport, I savored the idea of returning to the Rue Fromentin. Vali would know at a glance that I had traveled a road that would allow me to meet him halfway. Wherever we were, wherever we were going, it would be a good place.

As always with Air France, boarding the plane caused immediate displacement. The flight itself was a mere formality – as soon as the hostess said "Bonjour, Madame" and I was handed a copy of Le Monde, I was already teletransported to France. I settled into my seat and looked out the window to say goodbye. The plane sped down the runway and lifted off, separating me from my homeland. I was no longer in America and yet, I knew, I was now able to be many places at once. Physical location was only part of it. Most of it was in my head.

The earth winked at me through openings in the clouds. At this remove, it seemed like a loving, nurturing place. I remembered a song Chloe taught me that contained the words:

> Mother Earth will carry me,
> Her child I will always be.
> Mother Earth will carry me
> Back to the sea.

Suddenly I was back in Algeria, in the Roman ruins of Tipasa, lying in that ancient sarcophagus. The earth had reached out for me then, and hugged me in an ultimate, orgasmic embrace. It was the kind of experience people said they had on acid trips, but I could feel it again without the help of drugs. I would never have to use drugs to feel it. The healing earth would give me the strength I needed. Perhaps I would even find the strength to help my own mother overcome the demons that plagued her. Perhaps I would find ways to make her less unhappy.

Like a loving mother eager to see her child succeed, the earth had gently pushed me up into the air. My temporary release from her gravitational pull brought me closer to where I imagined Daddy and Sparrow to be, somewhere among the stars, out of reach but not really gone. It was a trip we would all make some day, at a time and in a way not known to us. Sparrow had been tricked into her departure. The suddenness, the unfairness of it smarted like an open wound.

With Daddy it was different. He had sailed bravely into death, and then waved to me from over the horizon. Thanks to him, I knew I had nothing to fear.

I was traveling in economy class, and it cost five dollars extra to order champagne but I decided to splurge. I raised my glass with a smile, as if to toast my fellow passengers.

"Bon voyage!"

www.ingramcontent.com/pod-product-compliance
Lightning Source LLC
Chambersburg PA
CBHW070811180626
46818CB00001B/218